*Hope couldn't stop herself
from touching him.*

His muscles were as taut as a bow string. "Jake," she whispered, "it's not your fault."

"I know that." He was tense, and he deliberately moved out of her grasp.

She wanted to wrap her arms around him so badly that it took all her concentration not to.

"What do you want, Hope?" he asked on a deep, shaking breath.

She couldn't find words, and she couldn't stand it any longer. She circled his neck with her arms, pressing her cheek to his.

"Hope," he murmured achingly, resisting for only a moment before pressing his face into the richness of her blond hair, his hand winding around her nape, pulling her down to him until she was forced to straddle his lap.

She was aware how dangerous the situation was. And she didn't care....

Dear Reader,

With all due fanfare, this month Silhouette *Special Edition* is pleased to bring you *Dawn of Valor*, Lindsay McKenna's latest and long-awaited *LOVE AND GLORY* novel. We trust that the unique flavor of this landmark volume—the dramatic saga of cocky fly-boy Chase Trayhern and feisty army nurse Rachel McKenzie surviving love and enemy fire in the Korean War—will prove well worth your wait.

Joining Lindsay McKenna in this exceptional, action-packed month are five more sensational authors: Barbara Faith, with an evocative, emotional adoption story, *Echoes of Summer*; Natalie Bishop, with the delightful, damned-if-you-do, damned-if-you-don't (fall in love, that is) *Downright Dangerous*; Marie Ferrarella, with a fast-talking blonde and a sly, sexy cynic on a goofily glittering treasure hunt in *A Girl's Best Friend*; Lisa Jackson, with a steamy, provocative case of "mistaken" identity in *Mystery Man*; and Kayla Daniels, with a twisty, tantalizing tale of duplicity and desire in *Hot Prospect*.

All six novels are bona fide page-turners, featuring a compelling cast of characters in a marvelous array of adventures of the heart. We hope you'll agree that each and every one of them is a stimulating, sensitive edition worthy of the label *special*.

From all the authors and editors of Silhouette *Special Edition*,

Best wishes.

NATALIE BISHOP
Downright Dangerous

Silhouette Special Edition

Published by Silhouette Books New York

America's Publisher of Contemporary Romance

SILHOUETTE BOOKS
300 East 42nd St., New York, N.Y. 10017

DOWNRIGHT DANGEROUS

ISBN: 0-373-09651-8

First Silhouette Books printing February 1991

Books by Natalie Bishop

Silhouette Special Edition

Saturday's Child #178
Lover or Deceiver #198
Stolen Thunder #231
Trial by Fire #245
String of Pearls #280
Diamond in the Sky #300
Silver Thaw #329
Just a Kiss Away #352
Summertime Blues #401
Imaginary Lover #472
The Princess and the Pauper #545
Dear Diary #596
Downright Dangerous #651

NATALIE BISHOP

lives in Lake Oswego, Oregon, with her husband, Ken, and daughter, Kelly. Natalie began writing in 1981 along with her sister, Lisa Jackson, another Silhouette author. Though they write separate books, Natalie and Lisa work out most of their plots together. They live within shouting distance of each other and between them have published over thirty Silhouette novels. When Natalie isn't writing, she enjoys spending time at her mountain cabin at Black Butte Ranch, where she catches up on her reading.

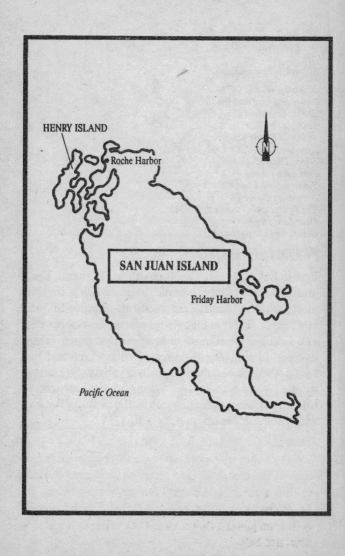

Chapter One

Jake Danziger thrust his crutches across the frozen grass, pulling himself toward the headland. He could feel the crash of the breakers, taste the salty tang of the ocean and hear the cries of the gulls that wheeled high over San Juan Island.

His right leg was hot and pounded like a pulse. The bullet had ripped through the tissue of his thigh with devastating thoroughness. Luckily, his femur had remained intact. The man who'd tried to kill him had been too far away to do the job right.

Jake's fingers tightened around the padded handles of the crutches. One moment he'd been walking toward a meeting with Bill Farrell, a member of the DEA, the Drug Enforcement Administration; the next he'd been gunned down. And they'd been shooting at *him*, not Bill.

He'd spent two days recovering in a Seattle hospital. Two days of reliving the last few moments over and over again. Two days of remembering the last time someone had tried to kill him and the nightmare that had followed.

Jake sucked air through gritted teeth, focusing on the ceaseless waves crashing against the shore, feeling the cold mist against his face. He refused to think about *that* now; tormenting himself with the past wouldn't change anything. Better to think of the present, and why anyone would consider him dangerous enough to kill.

A mirthless smile tightened his lips. As an investigative reporter with the *Seattle Observer*, Jake had done his share of uncovering political corruption, extortion, fraud, and other crimes, but there was nothing about the meeting with Bill Farrell that should have made someone want to kill him. He was currently writing an overview of Seattle's drug problems—more like a five-part editorial—and it wasn't the kind of project that exposed a specific crime or focused on any one person.

It had to be something else. Unless, as the DEA suspected, Bill Farrell had been the real target. Jake had to admit that theory made a lot of sense. But could a hired gunman have been that bad a shot?

Jake was lost in his thoughts for several minutes, his jaw set so hard that his teeth began to ache. Ahead of him lay the same gray sky shrouding a white December sun. The ocean thrashed continuously against the rock-strewn cliffs. A solitary hawk swooped low and disappeared around the curve of the headland, arcing northward toward the Townsends' house.

Almost against his will, Jake's gaze was drawn to the small home tucked beneath a stand of firs. Smoke curled gently from its stone chimney. The paned windows on the southern side reflected light from the afternoon sun. The Townsends' den, Jake thought, his lips twisting briefly. He remembered vividly the last time he'd faced Hope, the youngest Townsend daughter, in that room. His last Christmas in Roche Harbor. Six years ago.

He wondered if she still hated him.

Sighing, he realized his past was too near to him here in Roche Harbor. He couldn't shake it. Not with Hope's family living right next door, and the memory of those awful weeks—weeks when he'd selfishly used Hope and destroyed her innocence—haunting him like the nightmares that still sometimes plagued him from that other long-ago tragedy.

With an effort, Jake dragged his gaze back to the ocean. Only a few feet from where he stood, the path that led to Hope's house dipped downward, skirting the cliff's edge. He'd walked that path often enough as a kid; so had Hope. But the last time he'd seen her, there had only been words of hurt and acrimony; and he'd deserved every terrible name she'd called him.

The pain in his leg was compounded by a corresponding throb in his temples, and he realized he wasn't going to be able to stand here much longer. His weakness annoyed him. When would he recover enough to leave? Staying with his mother on this godforsaken island was going to drive him crazy.

He shook his head and leaned heavily on the crutches. Christmas was still five days away. He hoped when it was over he would be well enough to return to his apartment in downtown Seattle.

Sighing, he aimed the crutches' rubber tips in the direction of his mother's house, heading toward the two-story gray-stone house with its mullioned windows. But a dazzling flash caught the corner of his eye, and he glanced back instinctively toward the Townsend home. A circle of intense light refracted from the windows of the den, as if caught by a mirror. In his mind's eye Jake saw the telescope that had stood in front of the den window for as long as he could remember.

"Oh, hell," he muttered, annoyed to be such a source of speculation. One of the Townsends was watching him.

He furiously thrust forward the crutches. Five more days, he told himself grimly. Then he could get back to Seattle and his life in the city and away from the specters of his past.

Hope Townsend blinked in shock. Jake Danziger was here—*in Roche Harbor*? He hadn't been home in years! Not since that terrible Christmas when everything had gone wrong.

Stupefaction rooted her to the spot. She stood silent, while time ground to a halt. She should at least have suspected he might be here, she supposed. She'd read about the shooting. It was natural he would come home to recover. Nevertheless it was something of a surprise that he was in Roche Harbor—right next door! He hadn't come home for Christmas in six years.

Six years.

Hope clenched her fists and walked from the den to the bottom of the curving stairway. She forced herself not to hurry up the steps to the second floor. But then thoughts of Jake swirled through her head. She heard herself tell him she loved him. And she heard again his cold answer. *I don't love you, Hope. You don't love me, either. This was just an unfortunate mistake....*

"Mom! Mom! Where are you?" Hope yelled to her mother. "Why didn't you tell me!"

Laura Townsend, looking puzzled and bewildered, appeared from one of the bedrooms at the end of the hall. "What?"

"Why didn't you tell me *he*'s home?"

"Who?" Laura asked automatically, but even as the word was spoken her expression altered, and Hope realized that her mother had specifically neglected to tell her Jake was back.

Gritting her teeth, Hope stated flatly, "Ja— Dance," addressing Jake by the nickname given him by his friends. She herself had always called him Jake, but his buddies had shortened Danziger to Dance. Now the nickname seemed more impersonal, somehow, and Hope was determined to keep things as impersonal as possible between her and Jake.

"He—er—injured his leg." Laura swept a straying gray hair back into place.

"I know he injured his leg!" Hope answered in exasperation. "I work for a newspaper and I do read them. He was accidentally shot by a bullet meant for someone else. Somebody named Farrell."

"I guess you do read the papers," Laura commented mildly.

Her mother's fine brows pulled together thoughtfully and something in her expression made Hope look at her closely.

"Do you know something more?"

"No, not really. It's just that Elise thinks Jake's not telling her the complete truth. He could be trying to protect her, I suppose. After all, she's his mother."

A cold feeling enveloped Hope, tightening her chest. "Protect her from what?"

Laura took a deep breath. "According to Elise, it's possible the bullet was meant for Jake, not this Farrell person."

The blood drained from Hope's face so quickly she felt faint. She'd read the papers and called the hospital—anonymously—just to make sure Jake was really all right. She wasn't in love with him anymore; she wasn't sure she even liked him. She'd just needed to hear for herself that he would recover. Now, the thought of someone trying to kill him left her feeling strangely disoriented.

"Why didn't you tell me he was here?" she asked again.

Laura was wiping perspiration from her brow with her elbow, trying to prevent smearing soot from her hands onto her forehead. "I hadn't really found the right moment to tell you," she said simply.

Hope gazed suspiciously at her mother. Laura had been cleaning the fireplace in the master bedroom, getting ready for Hope's sisters, who were due to arrive in just a few days. Now Laura looked tight-lipped and uncomfortable, as if she were sorry the topic of Jake Danziger had ever been introduced. Hope understood why. Jake had ripped Hope's heart apart with devastating ease, and everyone knew it: Hope's mother, Hope's father, her sisters, and even Elise Danziger, Jake's mother. It was humiliating and she felt heat rise to her cheeks in spite of the six years that had passed since. But if she'd learned anything as a journalist, it was to face the truth head-on. Dispassionately. Sparing no feelings.

And those feelings included Jake Danziger.

"Why would anyone want to shoot—Dance?" she demanded. "The DEA said the bullet was meant for Bill Farrell."

Her mother shrugged. "I don't know."

"What kind of assignment was he on? People don't just get shot every day. Even investigative reporters like Dance."

"Elise may be wrong, you know."

Privately Hope thought Elise was, if anything, playing down the seriousness of the situation. If Elise Danziger felt her son was hiding the truth, he probably was. Elise knew and understood Jake better than anyone. Far better than Hope ever had.

"Why would anyone want to hurt him?" Hope asked now, concern creeping into her voice even while she tried to remain aloof. She heard the note of worry and clamped down on her emotions.

"Well, I really don't know. If you want answers, I guess you'll have to ask him yourself."

"Oh, no." Hope turned away and headed downstairs to the living room. Her footsteps echoed against the mellow pinewood floor as she crossed to an overstuffed armchair and sank into the cushions. She might be over Jake, but she'd rather walk across hot coals than see him again. He'd hurt her deeply, and she'd closed off a part of herself ever since. She wouldn't give him a second chance.

Unfortunately, she didn't quite trust herself to be emotionally dead where Jake Danziger was concerned. He was just too attractive. Too masculine. Too *sexy*. She'd developed a crush on him when she was a kid and it had turned into a full-blown case of help-less, hopeless love that fateful Christmas.

The floorboards creaked. Laura stood in the liv-ing-room archway, gazing down thoughtfully at her soot-blackened hands.

Before she could speak, Hope broke in stiffly, "Dance and I have nothing to say to each other. I don't care what he does. I was just worried about his leg."

"You're going to see Jake Christmas Eve," Laura said softly, with a trace of apology.

Hope's jaw dropped. "What do you mean?"

"We've been invited to the Danzigers for Christ-mas Eve dinner."

Hope gazed at her mother in wordless disbelief. Six years ago Jake had told her he wanted her out of his life. *Six years ago after a Christmas Eve dinner at the Danzigers'!*

Drawing a long, calming breath, Hope said simply, "No." She would be forced to meet Jake again soon—very soon, given her new job at the *Observer*, she re-minded herself with an inward cringe—but she couldn't bear it to be in the exact same circumstances as before! "I'm not going to dinner at the Danzigers' Christmas Eve, Mom. Actually, I'm amazed you'd think I would!"

"Elise asked our family to join hers and I said yes. It was a few weeks ago. Before the shooting. I didn't know we would all be together."

"I don't think I could bear it," Hope burst out. "You know how I feel about Jake!"

His name reverberated through the quiet walls of the cabin like a painful, haunting memory. And that's what he was, she thought resentfully: a painful memory of her biggest mistake. She'd been a naive nine-teen when she'd fallen in love with him, but he'd taught her how to grow up in a hurry.

"Why didn't you call and tell me he was here?" she demanded again, turning her anger back on her mother. "You could have at least warned me that he was back in Roche Harbor, and that we would be having Christmas Eve dinner with him! My God, Mom! I might not hate him anymore, but I'm not made of stone!"

Laura dusted her hands together. "Would you have come home if I'd told you Jake was here?"

"Yes." Hope's gaze wavered beneath the direct-ness of her mother's. She'd never been good at lying. Groaning, she closed her eyes. "Oh, I don't know."

"I wanted to see you this Christmas. Having you and Katy and Sharon here at the same time is the best thing that's happened all year to me and your father. The last time we were all together was—"

"Christmas, six years ago. I know," Hope inter-rupted.

"You won't leave, will you?" Laura asked sud-denly. "Just because Jake's home doesn't mean you have to go. You're stronger than that."

"Am I?" Hope's lips curved wryly. But her smile faded almost instantly when she thought of the im-possible situation her mother had inadvertently put her in. "Look, I'm sorry Jake's hurt, and I hope he's better soon, but do I really have to see him Christmas Eve? I mean, come on, Mom," she added with a flash of humor. "Why don't you just pour some more salt into the wound already!"

"Jake didn't do anything so terrible—" Laura began, but Hope cut her off. She'd heard that line too many times.

"I know, I know. But it hurt anyway. I'd rather not relive the past, okay?"

Laura lifted her charcoal-blackened palms in surrender and walked briskly out of the room, muttering under her breath. Hope wrinkled her nose, feeling like an ingrate. But, heaven help her, when she saw Jake again, it was going to be on *her* terms. "Christmas Eve," she muttered, inhaling a deep breath. "Give me a break."

Jumping to her feet, she strode angrily to the fireplace, glaring down at the ashes and kicking viciously at a cold, charred ember. She'd changed a lot in the six years since Jake had left home. Now she possessed a degree in journalism from the University of Washington, lived in an apartment in Seattle, and had just joined the staff of the *Seattle Observer*. Jake's newspaper.

Closing her eyes, she ran her fingers through her blond hair in exasperation, disgusted with the way fate had chosen to treat her. The chance to work for the *Observer* was a dream come true. From the moment she'd graduated from college, she'd sought a position as an investigative reporter at any newspaper that would have her. But she'd been stuck on the general staff of one Podunk paper after another until nine months earlier, when the *Breeze*, a small, fledgling Seattle paper, had hired her for investigative work. She'd worked long and hard and had actually done some fairly extensive in-depth stories. But working at the *Breeze* hadn't exactly thrown her into the hotbed world of crime, nor had it provided much in the way of scintillating reporting. In the interest of furthering her career she'd interviewed with the *Observer*, a paper she'd avoided like the plague simply because Jake was on staff there.

The *Observer* had a position open for a junior investigative reporter. Hope had screwed up her courage and applied. She'd never really expected to be offered the job or she probably wouldn't have bothered to interview. She told herself she would rather dust off old files in the records department of some local yokel paper than work with Jake.

But then, incredibly, John Forrester, managing editor of the *Observer*, had offered her the job. And even more incredibly, for one crazy moment she'd thought of turning it down. Because of Jake Danziger!

Hope's mouth twisted in remembrance. She might not want to work with Jake, but she wasn't such a fool that she would give up a golden opportunity. Last week she'd marched into the *Seattle Observer*'s personnel office and accepted the position. She would be on staff as a junior investigative reporter starting January first. It was too bad the *Observer* was Jake's paper, that Hope had chosen Jake's field of expertise, and that they would probably be working together, at least in some capacity, but it couldn't be helped. She doubted Jake could know of her new job yet, since he hadn't been to work since the accident. But he would find out, come January.

So what did it matter if she faced him Christmas Eve, or later?

Her pride mattered, she answered herself instantly. Meeting him at work, on a professional level, would be a lot different than facing him over the exact same set of circumstances that had led to her hurt and humiliation six years ago. She wanted to see him in the office, not at some intimate holiday affair.

She smiled to herself. Truth to tell, a small part of her couldn't wait for that sweet moment of shock when he would first see her at her desk at the *Observer*, as cool and professional as any hardened newsman, as changed as a person could be from the starry-eyed teenager he'd once known.

What a sweet, sweet revenge!

She picked up the cotton rag she'd forgotten after she'd caught sight of Jake at the headland and began wiping down the pine-paneled walls. Her mother was in a whirlwind of housecleaning, preparing for Christmas guests. Hope, who'd been bursting with excitement over her new job, had happily fled Seattle the day before to enjoy an uninterrupted two weeks with her family. She'd planned to break the news about it at their own Christmas Eve dinner; but now, since they were joining the Danzigers, she didn't know what to do.

In the burnished base of the brass lamp she caught sight of her reflection. Her eyes were clear and green and fringed by gold-tipped lashes; her blond hair was streaked and straight, curving in slightly at her shoulders. She looked younger than twenty-five, but woe to the unsuspecting male who labeled her the kind of young innocent to be molded to his will. Hope could hold her own on the dating battlefield as well as at her job.

Personal thanks extended to Jake Danziger for that lesson in life!

Sighing, she frowned. She wasn't certain the new, tougher Hope could stand up to the old Jake, though. Just thinking about him made her go cold inside.

Hope rubbed down the wood with more fervor than was really necessary. *If seeing him again makes me go all tongue-tied and stupid, I'll... I'll...* She couldn't even complete the thought. Jake had always been supremely male, and that last time she'd seen him in this room he'd looked so good to her—dark, and mysterious, and sensual, and sexy. She'd hated him, yet the attraction had still been there. She recognized it now for what it was. And she knew she might still be susceptible.

Wrinkling her nose at this painful bit of self-awareness, she wiped off the mantel. If only she hadn't made herself believe he was falling in love with her. Those weeks before that past Christmas, Jake had been more somber than usual—almost grim. But there were times when she'd brought a smile to his face, times when the way he'd looked at her had convinced her he was falling in love with her, times when she'd thought they could share a life together. She'd given him everything there was for her to give, and she'd expected the same in return.

But she'd been wrong.

"Hope?" Her mother's voice drifted into the den.

Hope yelled, "I'm just about done in here!"

Laura's footsteps sounded, quick and birdlike. Hope smiled to herself. Her mother hardly seemed to age. Only her graying hair and the soft lines on her face were a reminder of the passage of time.

"I called your father at Maxwell's," she said, stopping at the carved archway that led into the den. "He'll be back later. Would you mind getting the mail? I'd really like to get dinner started."

"No problem."

"Oh, and, I'm sorry for not telling you about Jake. I honestly didn't know how to bring it up. You're so touchy about him that…" She trailed off with a shrug.

"It's all right." Hope folded the rag on the top of her father's desk.

"Does that mean you'll go to the Danzigers' for Christmas dinner?"

"Maybe. I don't know." She smiled sheepishly. "Do I have to?"

Laura smiled. "No. I guess not."

Her mother's fairness made Hope feel like a terrible fraud. She mentally gritted her teeth. So what if it was Christmas? Big deal. It would be infinitely better and braver just to breeze in to the Danzigers' and act as if she'd forgotten the entire incident.

But Jake would know. He always knew everything.

"I'll try," she promised with an effort and was rewarded by the warmth and relief that filled her mother's eyes before Laura headed off to the kitchen. Watching her, Hope sighed. Her mother had always liked Jake. Even Jake's callous rejection hadn't made Laura hate him. It was nearly impossible to hate someone as attractive as Jake, but Hope had certainly tried.

The Townsends' mailbox was at the end of their rambling and twisting driveway, and Hope's lungs hurt from the bitterly cold air by the time she reached the road. The Danzigers' mailbox sat right next to the Townsends', their own driveway winding to the same point on the country road that passed both properties. From here, Hope could see neither house. Her parents' home was nestled inside a grove of firs, and the Danziger house was situated down a slope and behind a line of oaks and firs that all but obscured it from the road.

Today the fog lent its own air of mystery and isolation, and Hope hurriedly pulled open the metal flap of the box. She could see the colored envelopes of Christmas cards and a rolled newspaper. Reaching inside, she grabbed the bundle with one hand, then stuffed the mail inside the front of her jacket, plunging her hands back into the fleece-lined pockets of her parka.

She had taken three paces back down the lane when she heard the approach of an engine from the Danzigers' driveway. Her first impulse was to flee. Good God, what if it was Jake? Then she berated herself for her cowardice. She could deal with him face-to-face. She was going to have to soon, anyway. Besides, there was nowhere to hide even if she wanted to. The fog wasn't that thick and the nearest tree was halfway down the lane.

Belatedly she realized Jake wouldn't be driving anyway. She wasn't completely clear on the extent of his injuries, but he'd been in the hospital for two days and he was still on crutches. She was fairly certain he wouldn't be behind the wheel just yet. So it must be Elise, she decided, stamping her feet and expelling her breath in a frosty cloud. Should she stay and say hello? Maybe she could tell Elise herself that she would be coming Christmas Eve. It would certainly go a long way toward convincing everyone—including Jake—that she'd forgotten about the past.

Hope was still turning over what she would say when the nose of a powerful black Porsche crested the slope of the hill. Her lips parted in dismay. This was definitely not the Danzigers' family car!

Her heart began to beat rapidly. It *was* Jake! It had to be Jake; Elise would never drive something so masculine!

She drew a calming breath. If it *was* Jake behind the wheel, there was no way to avoid the encounter, so she stood perfectly still, frozen, watching the approaching car through wary eyes.

It came to a halt several feet from the mailbox. With mixed feelings Hope saw Elise Danziger behind the wheel—and Jake was sitting next to her in the passenger seat.

Elise thrust open the door. "Hope!" she exclaimed in delight, climbing from the car.

"Hello, Elise." Hope forced a stiff smile of greeting onto her lips. She refused even to glance Jake's way, and since he didn't move, either, she wasn't forced to say hello.

"Can you believe this machine?" Elise laughed, gesturing to the car. "The station wagon won't start. I guess the poor thing's too cold, so Jake and I decided to take the Porsche to pick up the mail and go into town. But I don't think he really trusts me behind the wheel." She glanced back at her son, her brows drawing into a slight frown at his silence. "It's difficult for Jake to get in and out of the car," she added quickly, apologizing for him.

"It's all right." Hope had no wish to draw him into the conversation. "I've got to get back to the house."

"Are you coming Christmas Eve?" Elise asked, her pretty face clouding as she sent her son a reproachful glare.

"I've been meaning to call you, Elise," Hope answered, then risked a glance at Jake's stony expression. He looked as if he were dreading the evening as much as she was! "I'm not sure. I'd love to come, but some friends of mine have invited me to dinner and I might not be on the island Christmas Eve," she lied guiltily.

"Don't let me change your plans," Jake's voice interjected smoothly. "I might not even come down to dinner."

"Jake!" his mother cried, aghast.

He lifted his shoulders dismissively and looked directly at Hope. "The last I heard, your mother said you were going to be here for two weeks. If you're leaving because of me, don't."

Hope was speechless. She'd forgotten how devastatingly frank he could be. "It has nothing to do with you," she declared in a voice that was amazingly strong. "I'm just not sure I can change my plans."

Elise looked from Jake to Hope. "Oh, well. I hope you can make it. We'll miss you if you're not here, but I'm sure you'll have a good time with your friends."

Hope nodded. She'd forgotten other things about Jake, too, she realized with a stirring sense of remembrance. She'd forgotten the hard, masculine shape of his jaw and the intensity of his blue eyes, and the inky blackness of his hair, and the uncompromising way he had of looking right through you. Her heart thumped hard and fast. Did he know she was lying? She had the terrible feeling he did.

Elise, a petite woman in high heels and a fur-lined coat, walked quickly to the mailbox. Unlike Hope's mother, Elise took pains to hide the advance of years, and not a strand of gray showed in her black hair. Though Hope hadn't seen her in years, she felt instantly comfortable with Elise. Jake's mother was nothing like her son, and now Hope felt a pang of regret for cutting Elise out of her life the same way she'd cut out Jake.

"Junk mail," Elise declared, smiling at Hope as she walked back to the car and slid into the driver's seat.

Hope lifted a hand in goodbye and hunched inside her coat. She was trying hard not to look back, but her eyes betrayed her as the Porsche's engine fired. Jake's mocking gaze encountered hers a brief second before the Porsche surged forward, and Hope had to force herself to smile a goodbye.

Back at the house she was furious to find that she was shaking. When she unbuttoned her jacket the mail slid to the floor and skidded across the polished floor. Frustrated, Hope bent to pick it up. Blast it all! Why had she lied to Jake and Elise? It was all so stupid!

Muttering furiously, she yanked off her coat. She *would* go to the Danzigers' Christmas Eve party, by God! She would act like nothing had happened between her and Jake if it killed her! She knew how to be tough around men when she had to be; she could be tough around Jake, too.

While her mother made dinner, Hope spent the next several hours upstairs, airing out the bedding of the two guest rooms. Her sisters would be arriving Christmas Eve day: Katy from Los Angeles, where she was trying her level best to break into the acting business; and Sharon from Vail, where she was a part-time ski instructor. Hope was anxious to see them both. With Katy and Sharon around as buffers, an evening with Jake might be almost bearable.

By the time Hope returned downstairs, her father was seated at the kitchen table and the salty aroma of her mother's Irish stew scented the air. The windows were steamed, creating a family closeness that Hope had missed, she realized as she hugged her father. Because of Jake, Hope had stayed away from Roche Harbor, too. Whenever he'd returned home, she'd been gone, and vice versa. Until now.

"It took you long enough to get home," she teased her father as she scooted into the chair next to him. "What do you and Maxwell do? Play poker?"

Stephen Townsend's green eyes, so like Hope's own, twinkled with mischief. "Actually, he tells outrageous fishing stories and I just listen."

"Hah. Maxwell doesn't fish." Hope snatched a roll as her mother set the basket in the center of the table.

"I didn't say he fished, I said he tells outrageous fishing stories," her father retorted mildly. "Actually, we drank a little Christmas cheer."

"Ah, the secret's out." Hope shared a grin with her mother.

Stephen Townsend had worked as general manager at the Roche Harbor Hotel for over thirty years and had just begun to taste the fruits of retirement.

"Want to take a walk?" he asked her when they were clearing the dishes.

"I'd love it," Hope agreed with a smile.

They chose the path along the headland. By unspoken consent they stopped at a small clearing about halfway between the Townsend and Danziger homes. Hope watched the gulls dip and swoop, and the faint afterglow of the white, fog-shrouded sun as it faded into the horizon.

"So, how's work going?" her father asked, settling himself on a damp, moss-spattered log.

This was the moment to tell him about the *Observer*. "It's going great," Hope admitted. "I just took a new job."

Her father's brows lifted in expectation.

Hope glanced involuntarily over to the Danzigers'. Gold light shone through the mullioned windows like topaz jewels. Smoke curled lazily from the chimney, its sharp, pungent odor spreading easily to where they were seated. Breathing deeply, Hope was struck by a sharp memory of Jake standing in front of a glowing Yule log, his head thrown back in laughter at something one of her sisters had said. He'd had more in common with both Katy and Sharon than with Hope. They were closer to his age.

But they'd never made the mistake of falling in love with him.

"I've been offered a job at the *Seattle Observer* and I accepted," she said lightly.

"The *Observer*?" he repeated in surprise.

"Jake—Dance's—paper. I know." She smiled wryly. "They made me an offer I couldn't refuse," she added in her best Godfather imitation. "And it's kind of silly to avoid the *Observer* just because Jake works there, right?"

"Right." He reached out to hug her.

He sounded happy and relieved. Relieved because she'd gotten over Jake? Well, she could hardly blame him.

"That's great, Hope! Congratulations! What kind of job?"

"As a junior investigative reporter. Can you believe it? Apparently they were looking for a woman to fill the position. Equal-Opportunity Employment and all of that," she added dryly. "I was the most qualified applicant."

"That's great, honey!" he said again. "Just what you wanted."

"Mmm-hmm. It really hasn't hit me yet, y'know?"

His gaze drifted toward the Danzigers' sprawling home. "Does Jake know?"

"'Fraid not."

"You're sure?"

"He's been laid up for over a week now. I just said yes last Friday."

Stephen Townsend carefully examined his daughter's tense, set face. "Is it going to be a problem? I'm glad you got the job. I know it's exactly what you've been wanting, but I know how... betrayed you felt over Jake."

"Dad, relax. I'm over him. It was just an adolescent mistake, okay?" At her father's sober look, she added laughingly, "A terrible, gut-wrenching, I-want-to-die adolescent mistake, but I'm a big girl now. I've had some tough life lessons and I've survived. You've got to be pretty sturdy in this profession. Jake was just a tiny ripple in the river of life."

He raised his brows and Hope had the uncomfortable feeling he saw much more than she wanted him to. But he smiled anyway, tousling her hair fondly.

"This ought to be one interesting Christmas Eve dinner," he commented drolly.

Hope suspected *that* would be the understatement of the decade.

Chapter Two

Jake struggled with his crutches, banging his good shin as he tried to get out of his car. He muttered a string of epithets and then inhaled deeply. A cold blast of ocean air dampened his face, reminding him that it was December. And Christmas. A time for goodwill toward men.

"Just a minute. Let me help you," his mother said as she switched off the ignition.

"I'm fine."

"If you'll just wait, I'll—"

"Goddammit!" he growled in frustration. "I said I'm fine. Just leave me alone!"

There was utter silence except for the soft sigh of the wind as it blew lightly through the open door of the garage and fluttered the edges of the newspapers piled in the corner. Remorse streaked through Jake but he bit back an automatic apology. He was tired of being treated like an invalid. He was tired of *being* an invalid!

"I'll go inside and start dinner," his mother said in a hurt voice as she grabbed two sacks of groceries, nearly staggering under their weight as she headed for the house.

As soon as the door to the kitchen closed Jake groaned and flopped back across the Porsche's front seats, uncaring that the gearshift dug into his lower back. He wanted to scream and rant and rave and throw things. His leg hurt. His head hurt. And he was certain he would lose his mind if he spent one more second in his mother's well-meaning care.

He had a sudden memory of his father being curt and harsh to Elise when he'd been suffering with the heart disease that had finally taken his life. Jake had been furious with him. Furious about the way he wounded his mother time and time again. Yet now he couldn't seem to keep from acting the same way!

He lay quiet, listening to the wind and wondering what was happening in Seattle. He thought back to the shooting that had nearly cost him his life. That, in turn, reminded him of Diana, and a sheen of sweat broke out on his skin. Defeated and shocked that her memory suddenly seemed so fresh, he wondered how he was ever going to survive this Christmas.

Better to think of the here and now, he reminded himself harshly. The Christmas spirit. He was in sad need of a heavy dose of it, or he would ruin his mother's holiday season entirely. If only she wouldn't feel so sorry for him. It made him crazy!

Jake grunted as he struggled to sit upward. That accomplished, he took several deep breaths. Well, at least Hope didn't feel sorry for him, he thought, his mouth twisting wryly. She'd looked horrified that he was still alive and kicking! She did still hate him, apparently. He grimaced. It was probably just as well.

He finally managed to get out of the car and balance his crutches beneath his arms. Guilt swept through him at the sight of one more grocery bag. He couldn't carry it, and his rudeness had apparently stopped his mother from coming back for it.

Swearing, he pushed the crutches across the garage floor, making his ungainly way, until he came to the two steps that led to the kitchen door. Twisting the doorknob, he succeeded in dropping one crutch. In exasperation he threw the other crutch down, then hopped up the stairs and across the kitchen's brick floor to the corner fireplace hearth.

"Jake!" Elise burst out, turning from the sink, her eyes wide.

"What?" he snapped.

She opened her mouth, then swallowed whatever she'd planned to say. He could guess. His stubborn efforts had cost him. He felt the blood drain from his face and now, damn it all to hell, he was fighting powerful waves of exhaustion, the kind that could knock a guy unconscious if he wasn't careful. He couldn't bear passing out in front of his mother.

"What?" he demanded again, clenching his jaw until it ached. Pain. He needed pain to clear his head.

She was staring down at the vegetables she'd laid on the counter and his heart wrenched to see tiny tears form in the corners of her eyes.

"I'm okay, Mom," he said with a sigh. "I'm thirty-three. I've lived on my own for over ten years. I'm incredibly healthy and I'll be better soon. It's nothing for you to worry about."

"You didn't tell me the truth, did you?" she said in a low, serious voice. Jake hadn't heard that voice in years. Not since she'd lectured him about Hope, as a matter of fact.

"I don't know what you're talking about."

"I overheard you with that man from the DEA. The one you talked to at the hospital." She swallowed, and he could see the way her hands trembled. "You think that shot was meant for you."

"No."

"That's what you said. Jake, I heard you!"

"Mother," he said with forced patience, "the bullet was meant for Bill Farrell. I just got in the way. Dumb Danziger bad luck. That's all."

"That's not what you told the DEA man when—"

"I wasn't thinking straight. For God's sake, you wouldn't either, if you felt as lousy as I do!"

She glanced his way. Jake held his breath, hoping he'd allayed her fears. He could suffer some doubts about what had actually happened the night at the warehouse, but he'd rather cut out his tongue than worry his mother.

"You're sure?" she asked uncertainly.

"Positive."

"You're not just saying this to make me feel better."

"No," he lied with ease.

She hesitated, not certain whether to believe him or not. "Can I get you something? Some tea, or a painkiller, or something? You look terrible."

"Thanks," he muttered dryly.

"No, Jake. Really. You should lie down. There's not a bit of color in your face. Please let me get you something. Go upstairs and I'll bring it to your room.''

Jake was too tired to argue. He simply nodded. Elise scurried to bring him his crutches and he smiled crookedly at her. ''Thanks. For everything.''

''You're a beast when you're sick or injured,'' she told him affectionately. ''Just like your father.''

''I know.''

''And you weren't too friendly to Hope when we saw her,'' she added in a rush, as if knowing this moment of truce with her son was about to vanish.

''Mom . . .'' he warned.

''No, Jake. Listen. I know now that you didn't mean to hurt Hope the way you did, but she doesn't know it. And the Townsends don't know it. And they're going to be here Christmas Eve, so please, *please*, be nice.''

''I wasn't lying when I said I wouldn't come downstairs,'' Jake corrected tersely. ''I don't want to see anybody.''

''That'll only make things worse.''

''I don't give a damn what the Townsends think,'' he cut her off. ''And you've got it wrong, anyway. Hope got hurt because she got in the way. I never meant for things to—go so far,'' he explained. ''It just happened. I don't feel like stirring it all up again.''

The look on his mother's face was more than Jake could bear. Digging the crutches beneath his arms he made his way to the stairs. He didn't want to think about Hope, or Bill Farrell, or his mother's feelings, or *anything*. He just hoped to hell he made it upstairs without passing out and losing every bit of ground he'd gained.

* * *

"An investigative reporter?" Katy gushed in wonder, holding Hope at arm's length and eyeing her in disbelief.

"*Junior* investigative reporter," Hope corrected, grinning at her older sister. "It's not much of a promotion from what I was doing at the *Breeze*."

"But at Dance's paper?" Sharon drawled from the bed where she was lying on her back with her hands tucked behind her head. Her plane had just arrived from Colorado that morning, and she was exhausted from both the flight, and the drive and ferry ride from Seattle to Roche Harbor.

Katy, who unlike Sharon seemed to operate on less than four hours sleep a night, shook her head. She was the epitome of the Hollywood starlet, her blond hair long and cut in a wild, layered style, her clothes strictly Melrose Avenue—black boots, electric-blue skirt and fishnet shell over a white tank top. She'd just signed on as a extra on a soap opera and was fighting hard for a real role. "You're really going to be working with him?" she asked in wonder. "What does he think of that?"

"Dance doesn't know it yet," Hope explained dryly. Her sisters were only too aware of her doomed love affair with Jake, though they, like her parents, didn't know all the intimate details. But they knew enough. The way Jake had broken Hope's tender heart had shocked everyone. Nothing had been the same since.

"What happens when he finds out?" Sharon asked, her brow furrowed. She'd been particularly upset over Jake's treatment of Hope, to the point of suggesting creative ways to endanger his manhood. Hope had practically barred the door to keep Sharon from unleashing her anger on him.

"Give him hell, Hope," Katy declared with a smile. "He deserves it. Anybody that handsome deserves it. And Dance especially does!"

"He probably doesn't even remember," Hope said lightly.

"He remembers," Sharon announced in a flat voice. She wasn't as forgiving as Katy.

"He'd damn well better!" Katy agreed. "On Christmas Eve, if he doesn't treat you right I'm going to—"

"No, Katy! Don't even think it!" Hope declared in horror.

"You haven't heard what I was going to say yet."

"I don't want to." Hope shook her head at both of her sisters. "It's over. Dead. A piece of forgotten trivia. I don't want *anybody* saying *anything* that will remind Dance of how stupid and naive I was. If either one of you embarrasses me, I'll never speak to you again. I won't even go to his house, unless you both promise to avoid the topic of him and me."

"Pretty tough," Sharon pointed out, "considering it's déjà vu. Christmas Eve and all."

Hope looked from one sister to the other. She meant what she said. It was going to be hard enough facing Jake under these circumstances; if she didn't have her sisters' promises that they wouldn't make waves, she was taking off for Seattle like she'd threatened to.

"Okay, okay," Katy relented.

Sharon studied her fingernails for several moments. Like Katy and Hope, she was blond, too. But her eyes were darker—hazel—and right now they were filled with suppressed emotion. She always thought

Jake had gotten off too lightly for the way he'd hurt her little sister. "Deal," she said reluctantly.

Relieved, Hope managed a smile. "The whole thing's just so embarrassing."

"Not to mention that it still hurts," Katy put in gently.

"No, I'm long over him. Really. You're all making too big a fuss over a little thing." Hope hugged Katy who was standing right next to her. "I'll see you both later."

She scooted out of the guest room and down the hall to the room she'd used as a girl. Closing the door behind her, she exhaled slowly and softly. She hadn't known it would be this hard to get through Christmas. Katy and Sharon meant well, but they didn't understand what had really happened six years ago. Hope wasn't even certain she did anymore. Jake had seemed so different at first: quiet, withdrawn, aloof; yet somehow vulnerable.

At least that's what the nineteen-year-old Hope had seen.

It had been exciting to have him home again. Ever since he'd moved to Seattle to make his mark on the world, he'd only returned to Roche Harbor occasionally. But that Christmas he'd come back for over three weeks. He was changed. He wasn't a boy any longer. Or an easygoing young man, for that matter. He was a sober, grim-faced stranger with a haunted look about him that had made Hope's heart wrench.

She knew why he'd changed. A bomb had been sent to the *Observer* and blown out an office, resulting in the death of one of his co-workers, a woman. The story had been splashed across the papers and the perpetrator arrested, but the tragedy was bound to have affected even someone as hardened as Jake appeared to be.

In her innocent way, Hope had only wanted to erase his pain, and with that vague plan in mind she'd set about finding ways to accomplish her goal. She had decided to "just happen to run into him" and begun hanging around the footpath, hoping to catch him outdoors. She'd known, via the den telescope, that he spent time alone at the headland, so she started doing the same. It meant several days of frozen fingers and toes as she'd stamped around, hoping he would show up, until one twilight evening, about a week after he'd arrived on the island, she had seen his silhouette and hurried out to meet him. . . .

He was staring out at the breakers, the collar of his jacket pulled up around his neck, his hands in the back pockets of his jeans, his shoulders hunched. He didn't hear her approach and Hope, gazing at his harsh profile, had felt overwhelmed with emotion. Could you fall in love with someone you'd known for years? she wondered. Someone you'd always thought of as a big brother? Could you fall in love that fast? By just *looking at him?*

He turned abruptly, surprised, moving with a lithe grace that made Hope's young heart beat wildly. "What are you doing here?" he asked.

"I just came out to see the ocean, like you." His gaze seemed to strip right through her. Hope held her breath as he spoke again.

"Do you always sneak up on people?" he inquired with the hint of a smile.

"Always," she agreed promptly. That stopped him for a moment, but Jake could recover fast, she subsequently learned.

"So that's what you've been doing this past week? Coming out to look at the ocean, like me?"

"You've—er—seen me?" She hadn't considered that he might be able to see the same stretch of ground from his windows, but now, glancing at his house, she realized that his bedroom windows gave him a terrific view of the whole footpath.

"I've had to change my plans four times because you were here," he stated flatly. "If you wanted to see me, why didn't you just stop by the house?"

Hope's jaw dropped at his devastating frankness. "Who says I wanted to see you?"

"Sharon."

Hope nearly fell over. She hadn't realized her older sister had seen through her plans and then *told* Jake! "Well...she was right," she said weakly.

For a moment Jake stared at her, then he threw back his head and laughed, the same way he laughed when Katy or Sharon teased him. It was one of the rare moments that Christmas when he actually had laughed. Most of the time Hope had been hard-pressed to squeeze even the faintest smile out of him.

"What do you want, Hope?" he asked, and this time he said it more kindly.

"I don't know. I just wanted to talk to you, I guess," she admitted.

"I'm not very good company."

"I don't care."

"Don't you want to know why I'm at such a low ebb?" His blue eyes swept her face, his lips twisting humorlessly.

Of course she wanted to know why. Everything about him fascinated her. She somehow recognized that he wasn't just referring to the bombing. There was something else much darker and more complicated eating away at him. And she knew instinctively that he would never reveal what that was. Tilting her head, she said with certainty, "You wouldn't tell me even if I asked."

"No." His mouth quirked. "I wouldn't."

"Then I won't ask."

She couldn't remember to this day what they talked about next. It hadn't much mattered to Hope, anyway. She'd just been happy they were talking at all!

As soon as she'd made it clear she wouldn't question him too thoroughly about the reasons for his extended vacation, he seemed to relax a little. Until she blurted out, "Would you like to go caroling with me tonight?"

His cold eyes wounded her. "You've got to be kidding."

She shook her head emphatically. "Just a few of us from around the island are going into town. No big deal. I just wanted . . . a date, I guess."

He gazed down into her anxious face for the longest, longest moment. Then he suddenly lifted one hand to her cheek in a gentle caress that robbed her of breath. But she knew what he was thinking. He was trying to find some way to refuse without making her feel bad. But Hope wasn't willing to give up so easily. She pressed his fingers to her cheek and begged softly, "Please."

"I can't go somewhere with you, Hope. I'll ruin your evening. I'm too—too—"

"Miserable?"

"*Old,*" he said through his teeth.

"You're only eight years older than I am," Hope insisted.

"Eight of the longest years of my life," he answered tautly, letting his hand fall from her face despite Hope's efforts to keep hold of his strong fingers. For a moment he seemed to weigh the alternatives, as if he were struggling with himself.

"I've got to get back," he said abruptly, and left her standing on the footpath.

Hope wouldn't let herself be discouraged. At nineteen she hadn't learned the subtle ways one can be rejected. In her heart she believed Jake was suffering from some kind of weary exhaustion and if she just tried a little harder, just tenderly pushed him a little bit more, that he would suddenly transform into the carefree young man she remembered.

She hadn't realized until much later that her memory was faulty. Jake had never been, and would never be, carefree. He was tough, controlled, ruthless, and sensual. The kind of man no sensible woman should pursue. But she'd learned that much too late.

That same evening she showed up at his house at seven o'clock. When Jake opened the door she shoved a sheaf of papers into his hands. "You probably know them already," she said gaily. "'The First Noel,' 'Hark the Herald Angels Sing,' 'God Rest Ye Merry Gentlemen,' et cetera."

He was wearing a black polo shirt and jeans. He looked from the sheet music to Hope, with an expression that made it clear he doubted her sanity.

"Don't say no. Please," she entreated with a smile. "I want you to come with me."

Later, she would wonder what chord she'd inadvertently struck that had made him change his mind, because he had indeed accompanied her with the other carolers. Once or twice she'd even heard his deep baritone, but it had been soft, reluctant, as if he'd been truly a fish out of water and trying to make the best of it.

She managed to scare a smile out of him at her door. He insisted on walking her back home after the friends who'd picked them up deposited them on his doorstep. When Hope primly told him good-night, he smiled lazily, then unexpectedly reached for her and held her close. She felt his heart beating against hers and her pulse soared in excitement and expectation. But he released her almost instantly, as if touching her were taboo; then he headed for the footpath to his house without another word. She called out a goodbye and though he lifted a hand in response, he never looked back.

Hope viewed the evening as an unqualified success, although Jake's feelings were harder to read. Her campaign to lighten his deep mood continued and when she asked him to have coffee with her at a small spot overlooking the sound, he went. Later, when she asked him to go Christmas shopping with her, he went. And later still, when she asked him to accompany her to a local theater production of a family-type Christmas program, he went. Jake seemed content to indulge her, and for those few weeks before Christmas, Hope was walking on air—and falling in love.

Then one night, about a week before Christmas, while Elise was out with friends, Hope joined Jake at the Danzigers' and talked him into stringing lights around the banister. All went well during the first part of the evening. Jake dutifully held the lights and Hope chattered on incessantly about her life at college: what her classes were, who her friends were, what she planned to take the next semester.

And then she inadvertently scraped a very sensitive nerve.

"Someday I'd like to be an investigative reporter like you," she admitted shyly.

Jake had just plugged in the lights to see if they were all working. At her words he turned abruptly, the colored bulbs throwing off flashes of red and green and gold and blue, illuminating the horror and anger on his normally impassive face. "Forget it, Hope! Whatever you do, don't go into investigative journalism!"

She was astounded at this burst of emotion. "Why not? It's what *you* do."

She saw him swallow hard. He looked down at the lights and began systematically to wrap them around the boughs of cedar that were already wound around the banister. She helped, waiting for him to say something more. But Jake could be damnably close-mouthed when he wanted to be, and he didn't say another word.

Fifteen minutes of silence was enough for Hope. When he strode outside without so much as a by-your-leave, she traipsed after him, intending to get to the bottom of this, once and for all. He went straight to the oak stump used for chopping wood, grabbed a chunk of fir, then swung the axe to break it apart.

Hope watched him for several tense moments, supremely aware of the muscles in his forearms. "Why shouldn't I be an investigative journalist?" she'd asked again, when he was panting for breath.

Jake swung the axe a last time, burying the blade deeply into the stump. "It's not for you," he said succinctly and finally.

Hope was both outraged by his arrogance and flattered that he obviously cared. "How do you know it's not for me?" she teased. "Do you know me so well?"

He was silent, and when he glanced her way there was a harshness about his features that frightened her a little. Then she saw how tightly his gloved hands were clenched, witnessed the swift rise and fall of his chest, and the quick puffs of his breath in the frosty air.

"What's wrong?" she asked.

"Nothing."

"No, you're angry. You look upset."

"Hope..."

"What?"

"Just—go away."

He turned back to his task but she foolishly reached out and grabbed his arm, feeling the hard muscles of his forearm freeze beneath her palm.

"Now, wait a minute," she declared angrily. "Every time I ask you anything about yourself you nearly bite my head off. I'm not going away. I'm staying right here. And you're going to tell me what's wrong!"

He whipped around so fast she was taken aback. His blue eyes were filled with some strong emotion. Anger? Despair? Passion? Hope wasn't entirely sure. She stared at him, her own feelings naked on her face.

His eyes narrowed, his gaze focusing on her mouth, lingering there before he took a tortured breath and looked away. Her heart gave a funny little leap at the smoldering desire she thought she saw in the blue depths of his eyes. He muttered something beneath his breath.

"Don't you like me—even a little?" she asked in a small voice.

"Yes, I like you," he said softly.

"Then why are you so..."

"So?" he demanded.

"Unhappy when we're together."

He hesitated, as if pulling his emotions under the control of his iron will. "I'm just not very happy in general, Hope. I warned you I wouldn't be good company."

"But you are good company. I've had a wonderful time these last few weeks."

"You don't understand," he muttered, drawing one hand across his forehead, pushing his hair out of his way with an angry gesture.

"Of course I don't. You won't let me! Whatever's bothering you, Jake, it can't be that bad."

"Oh, really?" He shook his head. "What an incredible optimist you are. Don't you know it's not smart to be that open and trusting? You're bound to get hurt!"

"It's Christmas," she said by way of an answer, and he seemed to understand that she meant this was no time to be cynical and suspicious and careful. This was a time of joy and comfort and celebration.

Then Jake looked down into her eyes and his own were deeply blue and sensual and lit by a flame of passion that made Hope's blood sing through her veins. She knew he was going to kiss her. She could feel the kiss long before his lips actually pressed down on hers. When his mouth did connect with hers the kiss was gentle and light, and she felt his lips curve in a wry smile. Then he squeezed her tightly and buried his face in her lush hair.

"You smell good," he said in a strained voice.

"So do you."

They stood there for a long time. The minutes stretched and Hope heard his breathing and felt the warmth and strength of his arms. When he released her she was certain this time he was as reluctant to let go as she was.

She was in love. She couldn't get enough of just looking at him. She wanted to touch him and for him to touch her. She wanted him.

Three days before Christmas, Jake had dinner with Hope's family. Both Hope's sisters were there, along with her father and mother. Afterward they sat in the living room, drinking eggnog and rum and making plans for Christmas. Hope's feelings for Jake were as clear as the winter evening and her sisters teased her until she wanted to murder them both.

"Dance may not feel quite the way you do," Katy pointed out gently to Hope when they were alone in the kitchen. "Be careful, okay? I mean, he's had his share of women. I just don't want to see you get hurt."

"Why is everyone so sure I'll get hurt?" Hope demanded testily. She didn't like Katy reminding her of Jake's undoubtedly wide experience with the opposite sex.

"Who else said they're worried?"

"Well, Jake, actually," Hope admitted, as Sharon pushed open the kitchen door and joined them.

Katy looked concerned. "Well, I guess that's something. I mean, he is *thinking* about it at least."

"I think I'm in love with him," Hope said soberly, stating her feelings aloud for the first time.

"Oh, God." Sharon grabbed Hope's arm and steered her outside into the biting evening air. Katy followed, closing the back door firmly behind them all.

"What is this?" Hope demanded, jerking her arm free from Sharon's tense fingers.

"Don't fall in love with him," Sharon warned angrily. "You're too young, and you don't know what you're talking about. He'll hurt you. Count on it."

"Hope, listen," Katy broke in, shooting Sharon a silencing look. "Dance is a great guy and all. Sharon and I used to hang out with him all the time. But you're never going to get close to someone like him."

"What do you mean?" Hope demanded.

"He's not made that way," explained Katy. "He's too intense and secretive. And he's got a dangerous job!"

Hope's lips tightened. "It's what I want to do, too!"

"Oh, brother," Sharon groaned.

"You only want to be an investigative reporter because he is!" Katy said helplessly. "Be reasonable, Hope."

Hope was incensed, mainly because she suspected Katy was at least partially right. "Why can't you just be happy for me?"

"Because Sharon and I have suffered our own crushes on him," Katy whispered fiercely, throwing a glance over her shoulder toward the living room as if she expected Jake to be listening. "Dance is dark and handsome and sexy and *unattainable*. The man's got a mystique. All I'm saying is don't get caught up in it."

"He'll hurt you," Sharon persisted.

"You don't know him at all," Hope insisted angrily. "He's unhappy, and I've helped him."

Katy sighed. "I know you have. It's evident. But do you know why he's so unhappy?"

A cold feeling stole over Hope. "Sort of."

Katy hesitated, as if she were unsure how to proceed. Sharon, however, had no such qualms. "Did you read about the bomb sent to a reporter at the *Observer* about a month ago?"

"Yes, of course," Hope said, angry. "A woman reporter died. If you're going to tell me that's the reason you don't want me to become an investigative—"

"That woman was a friend of Dance's," Sharon interrupted. "A close friend. They were unraveling a story together, and she was killed." Drawing a breath, she said, "I don't know the details. The paper's incredibly short on information when it concerns their own," she added sardonically. "But Jake's got to be living in pure hell right now."

Hope blinked. She'd known about the bombing, but nothing she'd read had indicated that Jake was a friend of the woman who'd died. The woman had been married, and her husband had spoken to the press, saying it was all a tragic accident and that he was glad the man responsible was in prison. As awful as her death had been, Hope had never considered that it alone was the reason behind Jake's obvious devastation. His reaction was beyond normal grief for a coworker.

Had he been in love with the dead woman?

Sharon's revelation left Hope feeling both disoriented and strangely encouraged. It was a shock to realize the true reason Jake was so consumed with misery; but she was relieved, as well. The knowledge that Jake might have been in love with another woman in no way diminished how Hope felt. In her uncomplicated way, she determined that the tragedy had, in effect, released Jake from a painful love affair. A love affair with a married woman. His guilt was all that was keeping him from loving Hope.

Later that evening, Hope strolled with Jake along the footpath to his home. At the door she stopped, afraid to speak out but needing to say something. "I heard about what happened," she blurted out. "Katy told me."

"Katy told you what?"

"About your friend—the one who died. I'm sorry, Jake."

There was no moon and she couldn't read his expression. She shivered in the cold damp air, belatedly aware that she'd stepped over the line. Jake was utterly silent, utterly frozen, utterly...out of reach. She realized it the moment before hard hands closed around her upper arms. For a moment Hope's spirits soared as he grabbed her, but then she saw the anger in his eyes and she realized she had indeed made a mistake.

"Don't be sorry." His voice was bitter. "It's all just a part of the job, isn't it?"

"That's a terrible thing to say."

"Is it? Well, when you become an investigative reporter, you can say it, too," he told her icily.

She finally saw how deep his grief was; how much he was trying to cover up. She was embarrassed that, after learning of the woman he'd loved, she'd only thought of herself. She heard her own words again. *I'm sorry, Jake.* How trite they sounded.

She wanted to make up for her selfishness. She wanted to show him she felt more; that she understood and was genuinely remorseful. Without thinking, she slid her arms around his waist and buried her face in his wool jacket.

"Hope," he said in a strangled voice.

She held on tighter, tears threatening to spill from her tightly squeezed eyelids. He pulled her head back with a yank, his hands tangled in her hair. What he saw in her face drained the fury from his expression and then, after a tortured moment, he groaned and melded his mouth to hers.

Relief filled her and she responded with abandon, kissing him back, her mouth opening beneath his like a flower to the sun. But what started as a need to convince him she shared more than cardboard feelings and empty words, quickly turned into something else entirely. It was Jake who tried to pull back first. Jake whose hands reluctantly released her. But Hope hung on firmly, wanting to savor the feel of him pressed against her, the heat and strength of him. It was almost as if she knew even then how badly everything would end, how fleeting these treasured moments would be.

And then his arms slipped around her waist and he molded her small body to his, holding on to her like a drowning man. Hope gloried in the sensation of being wanted and needed. *You're wrong, Sharon, Katy!* she thought with soaring spirits. *He needs me. He loves me!*

The kiss grew deeper, stronger, until she was fighting for air. When his mouth released hers, it followed a path down her neck and Hope gasped at the hot warmth of it, the searing sensation of his tongue exploring her ear. A shiver chased down her spine and she trembled wildly.

"Hope...God, Hope..."

He crushed her so tightly she could scarcely breathe. It was wonderful. Fabulous. Better than she'd ever imagined! She wanted it to go on and on, and had he forced the issue she would have let him make love to her on the spot.

When Jake finally surfaced, he shoved her away and collapsed against the side of the house, his chest heaving, his eyes closed. She saw vulnerability in his face, and anguish, and a naked pain that she wanted to erase with soft kisses. She held his face between her palms and met his mouth again, sliding her trembling lips against his firmly chiseled ones. He responded instantly, but didn't open his eyes.

"We can't stay out here," he said with difficulty, dragging his mouth from hers. "You'd better go home."

"I want to stay with you."

"No."

"Yes."

"*No*, Hope!"

And then he pulled her to him again. The second kiss was even more thrilling than the last. His tongue delved into her mouth. His thighs pressed hard against hers, letting her feel his rigid maleness, leaving her in no doubt that his emotions were as fully involved as her own. She scarcely remembered him pulling her after him to the barn at the edge of the Danziger property, or dragging her inside, or the fact that he seemed to be fighting a fierce inner battle—and losing.

Later, much later, she could recall the scents of hay and dust and the coldness of the air and the warmth of his limbs, but in those heated moments she only remembered Jake; the fact that he wanted her, the fact that he'd apparently made his decision, and she'd made hers.

He forgot whom he was with; he told her later—another crushing revelation on the heels of the discovery he didn't love her at all. They had never quite made it to the hayloft. Jake was kissing her soundly and deeply, melting her, and Hope was willing and the next thing she knew they were on a soft bed of straw in one of the stalls. There was no time for second thoughts. Hope was too fevered and in love to care that Jake's determination to make love to her owed nothing to real emotions and feelings. He was simply a man who needed a woman; and she, Hope, had pushed the issue long enough to break his control.

But she didn't understand that at the time. All she understood was his marauding mouth and hard fingers and tense, taut body making love to hers. Poised on the brink of real experience, Hope did have second thoughts, however. She hesitated, slightly fearful of the unleashed passion in his hard, set face. She tried to voice an objection, but his mouth pushed the words back in her throat and she wound her arms around his neck and gave herself up to him completely.

It wasn't the glorious moment of lovemaking she expected. When Jake took her, it was without consideration for her tender feelings and innocence. With a groan of need, he drove into her full length. Hope gasped, more out of fear than pain, but it froze Jake into a statue as if by unseen magic.

A moment passed. Hope's heartbeat thundered in her ears. Jake braced himself on his arms and stared down at her.

And then she knew. She could see it. She'd been blinded by love, and she could see it in the horror of his own realization of who she was and what he'd done.

"Hope," he said in a strangled voice.

"I love you," she said in a voice suffocated with pain.

He withdrew from her instantly. She could see his shoulders were trembling. "No. No, you don't."

"Yes, I do, Jake. I love you. I want you."

"Hope, for God's sake, don't—"

"No, Jake." She wound her arms around his back. *"I love you."*

"Damn it!" he suddenly yelled, jerking away from her. He yanked on his clothes, throwing hers at her in a way that killed some vital part of Hope. "This shouldn't have happened. It's my fault. I'm sorry, Hope."

Those trite, overused words. They scraped her very soul.

She dressed in silence and he walked her home. Not a word was spoken. She ached for him to say something, *anything*, to make her believe there was more to this one-sided love affair than she'd thought. Finally, he drew a breath between his teeth. "Are you coming to the house Christmas Eve?"

"I was planning to."

He nodded swiftly. "I'll see you then."

Hope was like a sleepwalker the next couple of days. The only things that pierced her self-inflicted numbness were her sisters' meaningful looks and attempts to find out what was wrong. Hope couldn't talk about Jake, no matter how they coaxed her. She was sick. Sick at heart, and sick with love.

Christmas Eve dawned clear and bright. Hope spent most of the day in her room, thinking over what had happened between herself and Jake. Those few moments of lovemaking were foremost in her mind. She wanted a repeat, she realized to her everlasting humiliation. She wanted more. She wanted *him*. She just didn't know how to prove to Jake that she was not merely the youngest Townsend sister, but a woman who loved him.

After hours of reflection she convinced herself that the main problem was that Jake couldn't forget their age difference and consequently felt guilty for using her. Well, he wasn't using her; she loved him. She just needed to get him alone to assure him of that fact.

When she arrived at the Danzigers' she learned there were two other couples there. There was no chance to be alone with Jake. In fact, Jake didn't make an appearance until they were all about to sit down to dinner. His mother had to call him several times, and when he appeared he looked sinfully handsome and somewhat alien in black slacks and a black shirt, open at the neck. He was distracted, however, barely offering a "hello" to Hope's family. He didn't even look at Hope. A visceral fear grew within her. He was shutting her out. Totally.

She watched him surreptitiously throughout Elise's sumptuous meal. He spent most of the time drinking wine, frowning down at his plateful of food, and restlessly turning his fork around in his hand. Only one time did he look at her directly, those gorgeous blue eyes regarding her somberly. Hope's mouth went dry, but he turned back to his plate, then scraped his chair away from the table and excused himself moments later.

Hope's appetite disappeared entirely. She was only half-conscious of the conversation going on around her. Feeling someone's gaze on her, she looked up to see Katy watching her, concern and empathy written across her pretty face.

"Excuse me," Hope murmured, and left the table. She followed in Jake's wake.

He was outside, standing by the back porch of the shed where they'd started kissing just a few days before. Hope opened the door and it squeaked on its hinges. Jake glanced around and saw her, his expression turning glacial.

"You didn't say much at dinner," she remarked, when it became clear he wasn't going to open the conversation. He shook his head, and she asked, "Aren't you going to talk to me?"

"What's there to talk about?"

The cool edge to his voice cut like a knife. "Well, I don't know. Maybe the fact that just a few days ago we were in the barn, making love!"

"That wasn't making love. That was just a reaction to—everything," he snapped in frustration.

Hope wanted to cry, and it took her several moments to find her voice. She'd expected him to care at least a little. "It was making love for me."

"It shouldn't have happened!" he snarled, taking several steps away from her, his hands in his pockets. "I made a mistake, and I'm sorry, but I don't know what to do about it now. I don't love you, Hope. I'm not who you think I am. You're a friend, and I—"

"A friend!" she repeated, miserably.

"Yes, a *friend*." He stressed the last word so there would be no mistake. As if she could mistake how he felt! "It's best if we just forget this and go on. I'm leaving for Seattle the day after tomorrow, and I'm not coming back. You're at college. This was just an unfortunate mistake, and we've—you've—got to forget it. You don't love me, either," he added more kindly.

"You don't know how I feel." Hope was bitter. The hurt was swelling inside her, threatening to suffocate her.

"No, but I know how I feel."

He didn't have to say more. He was sorry they'd made love. Sorry he'd used her. Sorry. Sorry. Sorry. She hated herself for being so stupid. And she hated him for being so cruel as to encourage her, even the slightest little bit.

She was physically sick by the time she left the Danzigers' that evening. Jake didn't even bother reappearing to say goodbye. It was doubly hard when her sisters and family started looking concerned, fussing over her, worrying aloud. And Elise's furrowed brow and especially motherly goodbye hugs didn't help. They knew. They all knew that Jake Danziger didn't love her and that she'd puppy-dogged after him for weeks. What they didn't know was that he'd made love to her and within moments of that passionate union, told her he didn't love her and never intended to see her again.

She saw Jake one more time before he left for Seattle. He stopped by the house and she met him in the den. He'd come to apologize, he said. He was going through a bad period. He hoped she understood. He hadn't meant to hurt her.

She was certain his mother had put him up to it. "I'm tougher than I look, Dance," she said deliberately. "I thought I felt more for you than I did. It was just a fling for me, too."

"You don't hand over your virginity on a fling," he pointed out.

"I do whatever I want to do!"

"Look, I don't want to argue with you, but the girl who went caroling and Christmas shopping with me feels things pretty deeply. I never wanted to do *anything* that would change you or—"

"You give yourself too much credit!" Hope declared bitterly, fighting an uprush of tears. "Just get out of here and leave me alone. Don't act like you've ruined my life! I'm okay! Go away and be miserable by yourself. It's nothing to me."

That stopped him cold. Whatever paltry words of apology and regret he'd been about to utter were never said. He left soon afterward, and the storm of tears that fell in his wake were mostly silent and absorbed by Hope's pillow. Of course, her family figured it out. They tried to talk to her about it, but Hope told them she didn't want to talk about Jake Danziger ever again.

Sharon seemed always on the verge of giving her advice. Luckily, in Hope's opinion, the words never came. Not so luckily, Katy was particularly empathetic, which only made things worse. "You'll get over him," she soothed, ignoring Hope's glare when she brought up Jake's name. "It hurts like hell now, but you will get over it."

And she had gotten over it. She didn't love Jake and she wouldn't dissolve into tears at the mere mention of her foolish infatuation. Six years was a long time.

Glancing at the clock, Hope realized it was time to get ready for another Christmas Eve dinner at the Danzigers'. With grim determination, she pulled out her best outfit from the closet, swiping at the wrinkles left over from packing.

She was going to this Christmas Eve party, and she was going to enjoy herself. Jake Danziger, or no Jake Danziger.

Chapter Three

Elise surveyed her handiwork with a critical eye. The bandage around Jake's thigh was taut without being constricting. "How does it feel?" she asked.

Jake's glance was ironic. "Fine, Mom."

"Not too tight?"

"Nope."

"But tight enough?"

"It's perfect. Florence Nightingale couldn't have done better," Jake said sarcastically.

He was seated on the edge of his bed, wearing only a pair of boxer shorts. Elise stood beside him, looking down at her son through worried blue eyes nearly the same size and shape as his own. She started to say something, then shook her head, touching a hair back in place. "People will be here soon," she said distractedly. "Please finish getting dressed and come downstairs."

The door to his room closed behind her. Jake flopped onto his back, feeling the dull throbbing in his right thigh. He couldn't seem to stop himself from taking out his frustration on his mother. Today had been the worst. Whatever she said or did exasperated him. He snapped at her, and she quietly suffered, and he wanted to drink himself to oblivion and forget that tonight was Christmas Eve and Hope was going to be here.

Sighing, he closed his eyes. He couldn't wait for the day when he could wrap this bandage by himself and get the hell off this island. But his wound was too raw. It still seeped, and until it was better he'd be a fool to think he could take care of it himself without risking infection. He'd toyed with the idea of a private nurse, but that seemed like a waste of money and energy when his mother was so eager and willing. But Lord, he was going to go nuts having to depend on her!

Climbing to his feet, he limped inelegantly to his chest of drawers and yanked out a pair of dark gray trousers, a white shirt and a black pullover sweater. He tried the trousers first, the effort to dress himself causing sweat to bead on his forehead. Clenching his teeth, he quietly and fervently uttered every swear-word in his vocabulary until the deed was done. Feeling marginally better, he rested on the edge of the bed. Below him, he heard the peal of the front doorbell.

The Townsends, he supposed, though he knew the Wallers or the Symonsons, his mother's other dinner guests, might be arriving first. In his mind's eye he watched the Townsends enter the house: Stephen and Laura, Sharon, Katy, and Hope. It was Hope he focused on. Beautiful, lovely, *innocent* Hope. She was a sore spot with him that had never healed. His selfish insensitivity had wounded her deeply, and he'd made a mess of apologizing to her. He'd made a mess of everything. He wished he could just forget it, but it was going to be quite a feat, especially since her emerald eyes would be full of accusations when he finally appeared downstairs.

He forced his thoughts back to his work, to the accident that had brought him to Roche Harbor. Had those shots really been meant for Bill Farrell? He was nearly certain that gun barrel had been sited on *him*, not Bill. And if he were right, it was a miracle he'd survived; by all rights, he should be dead.

Laughter floated upward. Jake listened intently, but the joyous sound came from one of the other Townsend daughters, not Hope. Drawing a breath, he shoved his arms through his shirt and began buttoning it up.

"You look lovely," Elise Danziger said to Hope, her smile sweet and welcoming. "I'm so glad you came."

"I am, too," Hope responded a trifle stiffly. She kept telling herself there was no reason to be nervous, but it didn't seem to do much good. Her stomach was churning and her palms had actually started to sweat. *You need ice in your veins, remember?* she warned herself. *Just think of this as an assignment.*

Katy was laughing at something her father had said. "Oh, Dad," she declared. "You're so out of it!"

"What did he say?" Sharon wanted to know.

"He thinks Milli Vanilli's a chocolate bar."

Sharon smiled. "Isn't it?"

"They're Grammy winners, for God's sake." Katy rolled her eyes.

"What are Grammys?" Stephen Townsend dead-panned.

"Save me," Sharon muttered as Katy broke into peals of laughter. Elise shooed them all inside the living room and took orders for drinks. Hope walked to the window and watched white moonglow illuminate the lawn and grounds all the way to the headland. Did Jake truly intend to spend the entire evening upstairs, as he'd threatened? she wondered.

The doorbell rang twice more. The Symonsons and the Wallers, two families Hope hadn't met, but who also lived on the island, were greeted by Elise. The Wallers were a couple from Elise's generation. Mr. Waller was heavyset with a booming voice and a hearty laugh, and Mrs. Waller was built much the same way. The Symonsons, by contrast, were both petite. Mr. Symonson possessed a shock of white hair that made him look older than he probably was, but his wife's hair was jet black.

Hope's gaze turned to the girl with the Symonsons. Their daughter, she remembered her mother telling her earlier. But Laura hadn't mentioned that the girl was gorgeous, nor that she had thick, lustrous black hair almost the exact color as Jake's, and a pair of the largest, most expressive brown eyes Hope had ever seen.

"This is Maxie," Elise introduced her to the group at large. "She's attending modeling school in Seattle."

You don't say, Hope thought; and then was stunned and annoyed by the little spurt of jealousy and envy that rippled through her. She wasn't envious because of *Jake*, was she? Good Lord. She, better than anyone, knew how disastrous it was to care about Jake. If

Maxie's beauty happened to catch his eye, she should feel sorry for the girl, not envious. She wouldn't want to wish Jake Danziger on anybody.

Hope's father helped Elise fill everyone's drink order, handing Hope a glass of eggnog laced with rum, which she began to sip. The taste, like the Christmas decorations and the soft carols issuing from the stereo, brought back memories of that other Christmas. *Everything* brought back memories of that other Christmas. She was just going to have to be tough enough to ignore the cloying feeling of déjà vu that threatened to overwhelm her.

"You're an actress?" Maxie was saying to Katy, her lips parting in awe. "In *Hollywood*?"

"A struggling actress," Katy answered. "Basically, a waitress, although I did get a small part on a soap opera recently."

"Oh, my God!" Maxie squealed in delight, turning to her parents, her eyes shining at this exciting news.

Hope took another swallow, embarrassed for reasons she couldn't quite explain. She found herself comparing herself to Maxie, whose cloud of black hair was artfully arranged around a delicate, heart-shaped face. The girl wore black harem pants and a tunic that hinted provocatively at her lush curves. Hope glanced down at her own outfit, one of her best, though it seemed old and plain now. She'd changed clothes three times, in fact, before finally settling on her black slacks and oversize Kelly-green sweater that was cinched at the hips by a wide leather belt. She knew it looked good on her, but now she wished she'd chosen something flashier. And her hair! She'd let it hang straight to her shoulders with just the faintest curve in toward her chin. Why hadn't she worked on something more exotic? *What do you care, anyway?* she asked herself harshly, despising herself for regarding Maxie as some kind of competition.

"Where's Jake?" Maxie inquired brightly, interrupting Hope's self-condemnation, her beautiful eyes drawn toward the curving stairway.

"He'll be down soon," Elise responded. As if she couldn't help herself, she shot a glance Hope's way, then covered the awkward moment with a quick smile.

So he's not coming down because of me, Hope thought. Sighing, she glanced at the clock. A couple of more hours and they could all leave.

"I've really been worried about him," Maxie gushed to Elise. "When Mother told me Jake had been shot, I nearly died! I mean, *shot*. That's only something you read about in the newspapers!"

"Or write about," Hope pointed out. "As Dance does."

Maxie blinked, moving up closer to Hope. The young woman positively radiated innocence and youth, and Hope's heart lurched sickeningly. Had she been that transparent when she was Maxie's age? The girl was what? Nineteen? Twenty? Just about the age Hope had been when she'd planned to make Jake fall in love with her and save him from his misery.

She nearly groaned aloud at the memory. How could anyone be so naive?

"He's really got a dangerous job, hasn't he?" Maxie lowered her voice confidingly.

"Dangerous enough," Hope agreed, wishing she'd never spoken up in the first place. She didn't want to talk about Jake to Maxie, or anyone else for that matter.

"Oh, don't say that," Laura said to her youngest daughter. "I don't want to have to worry about you, too!"

"*You're* an investigative reporter?" Maxie was impressed.

"*Junior* investigative reporter." Hope sent her mother a quelling look. She didn't really want to get onto that topic either, especially in front of Elise.

"Wow. I've often thought of doing something different," Maxie confided. "I mean, I don't really think of modeling as a long-term career. I'd like to branch out into something else. Being a reporter sounds so exciting!"

Out of the corner of her eye Hope saw Sharon's head shaking from side to side, as if she couldn't believe her ears. In a taupe sweater and skirt, her blond hair clipped back into a black barrette, Sharon was dressed as conservatively as Hope. Sidling up next to Maxie as the girl chattered on and on about her plans for the future, Sharon pretended to look interested, but more often than not rolled her eyes Hope's way as if to say "Can you believe this?" It almost made Maxie's self-absorbed monologue bearable.

When Mr. Symonson called Maxie over to regale the Wallers with more tales of her plans, Hope turned desperately to Sharon. "Tell me I didn't sound like that at nineteen."

"You didn't sound like that at nineteen."

"No. Say it like you *mean* it."

"I do mean it." Sharon was serious. "You were never like that."

"What about—"

"Oh, Hope, stop worrying." Sharon made a face in memory, then added, "You were good for Dance that

Christmas you followed him around. He was a mess, but you helped him. You really did. And I can still remember some of the looks he sent you. They were hot enough to melt steel.''

''You kept warning me against him and you were right,'' Hope reminded her.

''I remember very clearly,'' Sharon agreed. ''The jerk. But he saw something in you those weeks before Christmas, something good and kind and sweet. You *were* sweet.''

''And I'm not anymore?'' Hope asked dryly.

''No.'' Sharon was blunt. ''You've changed, but for the better in some ways. You've smartened up. You don't wear your heart on your sleeve anymore.'' Sharon eyed her levelly. ''Do you still love him?''

''Good grief, no!''

''I'm glad. I never thought he was right for you. But he did care about you,'' Sharon added, as if sensing her sister needed to hear it.

Hope smiled faintly. Sharon's words were meant to make her feel better, but they didn't. That time with Jake had been Hope's one and only experience; no one else had truly interested her since.

Hope joined Katy and her father, who were standing beside the fireplace. They were involved in a conversation about whether or not Katy should look for a new agent.

''I think I'll go see what's taking Jake so long,'' Elise said as she fluttered past their group in her efforts to keep everyone's drink filled.

''Don't bother,'' a deep masculine voice answered from around the stairway landing. ''I'll be there as soon as I negotiate the steps.''

Hope jumped, her eggnog sloshing in her glass. So much for keeping a cool head, she told herself wryly. Just the sound of his voice sent her nerves screaming.

"Oh, good," his mother said in relief. "We were beginning to wonder about you."

Like everyone else in the room, Hope trained her eyes on the stairway, waiting for his descent. A smile was pinned so forcefully on her lips it felt as if her face would crack. With an effort she relaxed her jaw.

"Need any help?" Elise burst out, as if she couldn't help herself.

"No." Jake was succinct.

"Let me give you a hand, son," Mr. Waller said, heading up the bottom steps.

At that moment Jake appeared on the landing and the look on his face was so severe that Mr. Waller stopped in his tracks, then backed up. Having only seen Jake through the windshield of his car, Hope examined him now through the screen of her lashes and was amazed how little he'd changed in six years. Even with crutches he exuded the same fluid grace and presence that had seduced her when she was nineteen. And though he was lean—leaner than she remembered—he was still supremely masculine, so much so that she felt a pang of remembrance for what they'd once shared. Faintly, from across the room, the deep, woodsy scent of his cologne reached her nostrils.

"Are you sure?" Elise asked anxiously.

"I've never been more positive" was his sardonic answer.

Hope noticed the tension in his right hand as it curved around the banister. This wasn't easy for him, she realized; his fingers were forced to search for support between the Christmas lights that flashed on and off and sent sparkles of color dancing across his somber sweater. And it didn't help that the crowd below had fallen silent, watching his descent.

He must hate this, she thought, knowing how obsessive he was about keeping his personal life private. Now he was the center of attention in a way he would find both mortifying and infuriating.

As she watched him work his way downstairs, she realized something else: he was just as sensually magnetic as ever. Yet, in some ways he didn't seem the same at all. Lines of fatigue were stamped alongside his mouth. His experience showed on his face.

At the last step Jake finally looked up. He glanced Hope's way and held her gaze for a long moment. Her throat closed in on itself, and she sought desperately for something to say. But she couldn't form a proper greeting; she was too distracted by the whole scenario. So she let the moment pass and it was Jake who was compelled to look away first when his mother captured his attention.

"You're a marvel on crutches, Jake," she said, breaking the spell. "I'm sure I'd fall headfirst if I were to try that."

She made a move as if to help him and Jake said quietly and meaningfully, "If I fall you can pick up the pieces, but let me try to get around on my own for a while, okay?"

Maxie Symonson stared at him, hero worship glowing in her dark eyes. "Does it hurt a lot?"

"No, it's painless," he teased her.

Katy sniffed. "I'll bet," she murmured sardonically.

"Hi, Kate," Jake greeted her, smiling with relief. There was wry affection in his voice.

"Looks like you're up to your eyeballs in trouble again," she said, her tone equally wry. "You seem to always be in someone's line of fire."

"Professional hazard, I'm afraid."

Hope saw her mother and father glance her way in alarm. Sharon and Katy looked at her, too. Afraid they would blurt out the facts of her new job situation, Hope quickly stepped toward Jake. "Hello," she said coolly. "Looks like you're on your feet again, so to speak."

He inclined his head. "Hope," he greeted her casually.

It was a fairly ordinary reception, though Hope hadn't expected anything more. During the predinner chitchat, Jake didn't seem compelled to include her in any of his conversations. He spoke to Katy and the Wallers and the Symonsons and Maxie, who hung on his every word, and then turned to Hope's father and mother before engaging Sharon in conversation. Hope stood by, understanding the implied rebuke even if no one else did. Her defense was to ignore him as pointedly as he ignored her.

"It's good to see you, Jake," Laura said in a soft voice somewhere to Hope's right. "I'm sorry it took an accident to bring you home."

"I've been home a time or two recently," he answered.

"Not at Christmas," Hope volunteered, surprised by the sound of her own voice.

"No, not at Christmas," he agreed, his eyes narrowing. "I've been busy the last few months," he added for Laura's benefit. Glancing down at his right thigh, his arms resting lightly on the padded supports of the crutches, he added dryly, "I guess this is one way to get a vacation."

"It's terrible!" Maxie exclaimed from behind his shoulder.

"Yes, it is," Hope agreed.

Jake's disturbing gaze turned fully on Hope for the first time. "I guess I lied, didn't I?" he said in a voice laced with irony.

"Lied?" she repeated, suddenly feeling put on the spot.

"About coming downstairs. I decided to enter the lion's den after all."

This was brushing the subject of their past too closely, Hope determined, aware of how intently he was waiting for her response. Before she could answer, he asked deliberately, "How did you get out of your obligations?"

"Pardon?" Hope blinked.

"You said you might have to go back to Seattle to be with friends."

"Oh." Hope swallowed nervously, mentally kicking herself for letting him get to her. The knowing look in his eyes made her feel a hundred times worse. "I just changed my plans."

"Would you like something to drink?" Elise burst in anxiously. "Stephen's playing bartender, and I'm sure he'd get you whatever you ask for."

Jake's gaze slid from Hope's. "Can you fix me a beer?" he asked her father dryly.

"I'll give it the old college try" was his somewhat overly jovial answer.

The moment passed and Hope moved away, letting Maxie and the others cluster around Jake. She felt both relieved and drained. For so many years she'd worried over meeting him again that, truthfully, it hadn't been as bad as she'd expected. Oh, it was bad, all right; there was no way Jake was going to make it easy for her. But he was, after all, just a man, and it could hardly matter that she still found him attractive—at least on some level—because she was long over him. Long, long over him, she reminded herself sternly.

Elise called them all in to dinner just as Hope was finishing another eggnog. The extra rum made her feel warm and she longed to open the windows and draw fresh air inside the house, hoping to dispel the feeling of unreality that had plagued her all evening. Though tonight was similar to that other Christmas Eve, it was also vastly different, too. Jake was different. And she was different. Time had changed them both, and it was all for the better.

She sat down at the table two seats down from Jake and across the table from Mr. Waller. She'd specifically chosen a seat where she wouldn't have to look at Jake or make polite conversation. Unfortunately, she could still hear him, she realized, as the bowls of cranberries and sweet potatoes and stuffing were passed around. His low-timbred voice filled the room, as soft as a caress, as deep and troublesome as the poignant memories that seemed to drown her in wave after wave of self-recrimination.

She attacked her meal with a vengeance, annoyed with herself for being so affected by him.

"How long have you been with the *Observer*?" Maxie asked him from across the table.

"More years than I want to remember," he answered.

"Have you been assigned to lots of dangerous stories?"

"A few." He was laconic.

"Wow. Have *you*?"

For a moment Hope didn't realize Maxie was talking to her. "Pardon?" she asked blankly.

"Have you had any dangerous assignments?" Maxie repeated.

Jake's gaze was cool but interested. Hope caught it out of the corner of her eye as she answered carefully, "I've been working for the *Breeze*. It's more a community paper. We haven't really investigated a lot of dangerous crimes."

"But you must have run across something! You said you were a junior investigative reporter," Maxie persisted guilelessly.

"Is that the title they give you over at the *Breeze*?" Jake drawled.

"Yes," Hope lied, swallowing a piece of turkey with an effort. She could feel her family's collective stare. Well, they could stare all they liked, she wasn't about to bring up her position in the middle of dinner. Who knew what Jake might do, and Elise didn't deserve to have him ruin the meal because of something Hope said.

Maxie, who seemed oblivious to the undercurrents between Jake and Hope, turned the conversation back to her favorite topic: herself. Hope was at first gratified that she monopolized his attention so thoroughly—it certainly gave her a break!—then was amused to hear the testiness creep into Jake's deep voice as Maxie's chatter ran on and on and on. She was glad someone else was getting under his skin instead of her, and she was equally glad that Jake hadn't fallen head over heels in love with this beautiful little airhead. Why that should matter to her was something Hope didn't care to analyze too closely, however.

"So what happens when you're mended again, son?" Mr. Waller asked Jake.

Jake picked up his wineglass, rolling the stem between lean, tanned fingers. "Back to Seattle. I'll probably leave at the end of the week."

"And back to work at the *Observer*?" Katy questioned.

Jake nodded.

"What are you working on now?" Mrs. Symonson wanted to know. "Or can you tell us?"

"I'm doing a five-part series on Seattle's drug problem. An overview."

"Is that what you were working on when you were shot?" Maxie piped in.

"Maxie!" her mother shushed sternly.

Hope thought it a fair question. She turned expectantly to Jake and caught him staring at her. His gaze was frankly assessing, and she sensed that he found her wanting in some area. She dropped her own gaze to her plate, then was furious with herself. Looking up again, she swept him with frigid green eyes, but he seemed imperturbable as he turned his attention back to Mrs. Symonson.

"I was meeting a man from the DEA," he told her. "Bill Farrell. We met at a warehouse that had been used as an amphetamine lab. The police had staked it out weeks before. It was supposed to be empty, but someone was there—waiting for Bill."

Maxie sighed dramatically. "Wow. Dad said it's the second time you've nearly been killed on the job!"

Mr. Symonson, who was sitting directly across from Hope, jumped in alarm. "Now, Maxie, don't sensationalize everything!"

"Sensationalize!" Maxie was affronted. "When someone sends you a bomb, that's sensational in itself!"

Jake's surprised intake of air was loud enough for Hope to hear.

"A bomb!" Mrs. Waller exclaimed.

Oh, God, Hope thought with concern. Maxie had brought up the one subject Jake never, never discussed.

"That was years ago," Mr. Symonson said a bit desperately. "And it wasn't meant for Jake."

"Who was it meant for?" Maxie asked, puzzled. "I thought..."

She trailed off and Hope said quickly, "As Mr. Symonson said, it was a long time ago. Sometimes it's better not to rake up the past."

"Advice from Hope Townsend, *junior* investigative reporter?" Jake asked insolently.

"If you want to call it that."

"So, you going to finish this series, Dance?" Katy put in, desperately trying to steer the conversation back to their earlier discussion.

"I'm not sure what they'll have for me when I get back," Jake answered flatly, taking a sip of his wine.

Maxie stared at him, wide-eyed. "You mean, they might take you off the story because you got shot?"

"I really won't know until I get there, will I? The shooting's kind of changed things. It shouldn't have happened."

There was silence around the table. "A lot of things shouldn't happen," Hope said aloud, startled by the coldness in her voice. "They just do."

Anger flared in Jake's eyes, and for a moment Hope thought he would blast her with another dose of Jake Danziger's own special brand of humiliation. But then he clamped his jaw tightly shut, as if fighting back whatever he was going to say. Instead, he muttered, "I guess we just have to make sure it doesn't happen again."

"Are we still talking about the shooting?" Maxie asked blankly, looking from Hope to Jake.

"I don't think so," Sharon murmured on a short laugh, and Katy added brightly on the heels of the comment, "Anyone ready for dessert?"

Instantly everyone started talking at once. Stifled, Hope shoved her chair back and walked across the flagstone entryway to the living room once more. She heard footsteps behind her and stiffened, but realized belatedly that it couldn't be Jake since he was on crutches.

"He's kind of a bear, isn't he?" Sharon's voice sounded behind her.

Hope turned around, sighing. "I guess I can't blame him. His leg probably hurts like hell."

"He's really got it in for you."

"You think so?" Hope didn't want to hear that, though she knew it was true.

"Anytime you make a remark he's so-o-o touchy."

She grimaced, knowing Sharon was right. "Wait until he finds out about my job."

"When are you going to tell him? You missed a great opportunity in there."

"Oh, right. He probably would have hurled the turkey at me in a fit of rage. I don't even want to tell him!" she admitted heavily. "Maybe I'll just show up for work next week and make some witty comment like 'Fancy meeting you here,' or 'Isn't this a coincidence?'"

"Jake's not the type one can be flip with."

"Well, he doesn't deserve to be told in a civilized way, at any rate!" Hope said with sudden vehemence. "He's so busy growling at everyone else, he makes me furious. And I, for one, don't feel like putting myself in his line of fire!"

As Elise's guests began filtering into the living room, carrying cups of coffee, Hope readied herself for another confrontation with Jake. But she needn't have bothered; he wasn't with them. In fact, he was nowhere in sight.

For the first time that evening, Hope breathed easily. She hoped he would stay missing until she could make good her escape.

The barn looked even more dilapidated in the bright moonlight than it did in the light of day. Jake leaned on one crutch and pushed on the door until it gave way with a wrenching creak. Stale air and the smell of dust and hay reached his nostrils. He hobbled inside, laid his crutches against the wall, and sank down on a sagging bale.

Hope had changed, he realized with a sense of unwelcome surprise. She was cool and unapproachable now—a real ice princess, in his opinion. Well, what had he expected? He'd treated her abominably, and she was going to make him pay.

He scowled at his crutches. Well, it was nothing to him, he reminded himself harshly. He was sorry things had turned out the way they had, but there was no changing the past.

His thoughts touched on Diana. Damn that vapid-brained Maxie and her nonstop tongue! Having the bombing and Diana's subsequent death brought up over dinner, as if it were a juicy tidbit of news to scavenge over, had jolted him right to the core. He didn't want to think about Diana. Her death had made him crazy for a while. Six years ago he'd been numb. Desolate. Eaten up inside with a sickness of the soul.

He sighed now, his mouth turned down at the corners. And then Hope had been there, demanding he take her caroling, and Christmas shopping, and insisting they decorate the house together. She'd forced him to keep living even though he'd wanted to die. And she'd made him want to bury himself in her innocence, though he hadn't been self-aware enough to realize it at the time.

In hindsight, those lost weeks before Christmas six years ago were painfully clear. He'd selfishly indulged himself with Hope, and then when he'd finally woken up, he'd been cruel and terse and consumed with remorse. The worst of it was that she'd thought she was in love with him. She hadn't been. It was hero worship, nothing more. The same hero worship she'd lavished on him all the while she'd been growing up. But there'd been no convincing Hope.

Then, to make things worse, she'd had some cockamamy idea about following in his footsteps, journalistically speaking. Good Lord. With Diana's death fresh in his mind, he would have juggled hot coals rather than let Hope travel the same path! But she hadn't listened to him when he'd insisted she give up the idea of becoming an investigative journalist. In fact, she'd become more and more dead set on the issue.

Luckily, it hadn't quite turned out for the worst. Oh, sure, she was a reporter at the *Breeze*, but that wasn't in the same league as his job; she herself had said as much over dinner. It meant that she was staying away from the really tough stuff, thank God. He already had Diana on his conscience; he didn't think he could bear to have Hope there, too.

Unwillingly, his thoughts turned to the way she looked tonight. She was heart-stoppingly beautiful, he thought dispassionately. More beautiful than either Katy or Sharon, who were knockouts themselves. At nineteen her beauty had just been developing, but now it had blossomed.

Not that she'd care what he thought of her, he reminded himself quickly. There was no mistaking the disgust in her voice whenever she spoke to him. Or the glacial look in her eyes whenever she stared at him. Hope was a woman scorned; and by God, there was truth in those old sayings....

He glanced involuntarily toward the stall where he'd once made love to her. The memory made him wince. He shouldn't have let it happen. He shouldn't have seduced a virgin. And damn it, if he'd been thinking straight he would have *known* she was a virgin. It wouldn't have taken a genius to realize Hope was as inexperienced as she was young.

You ought to be glad she hates you.

Jake stared at the dusty floor. Was he glad? He wasn't entirely sure. But it hardly mattered after all this time. He'd found solace in Hope's willing arms;

he'd tried to explain his feelings that day in the Townsends' den, but by then Hope was past listening.

Grimacing, Jake raked his fingers through his hair, wishing things were different. But there was no going back now. At least Hope wouldn't suffer the same tragic fate as Diana. He could put that worry to rest and concentrate on getting on with his life.

"Why don't you tell everyone your good news?" Stephen Townsend suggested, squeezing his youngest daughter's arm as he walked by.

Hope gazed at him in frustration and shock. She'd spent the greater part of the evening sidestepping that sensitive issue. Now her father had undermined everything.

"What good news?" Elise asked with interest.

In that swift moment Hope realized there was no turning back. Her father, who obviously felt she should have been honest about her new job from the beginning, hadn't given her any avenue of escape. "I—er—just accepted a job with the *Observer*," she admitted. "They've taken me on as a junior investigative reporter."

Elise was thunderstruck. Luckily, Jake wasn't in the room, Hope thought. She didn't feel up to dealing with him, yet.

"Jake's newspaper?" Elise asked hesitatingly.

"One and the same." Hope's mouth twisted.

"Well, that's—wonderful." Elise's eyes brightened with growing enthusiasm. "That's really wonderful! I'm so pleased for you!" She hugged Hope tightly. "This'll be good for Jake," she added cryptically, and Hope wondered if the woman was thinking clearly.

"He might not share that feeling," Hope said on a short laugh. The skin on her nape tickled and she swung around, dry-mouthed. Jake was standing in the opening between the dining room and the entry hall, leaning heavily on his crutches.

"What'll be good for Jake?" he asked.

"Hope has taken a job with your paper as a junior investigative reporter," his mother told him quietly.

Up to this point the Symonsons, Wallers, and Katy and Sharon hadn't been listening to the conversation, but now everyone turned around. The look of complete stupefaction on Jake's face said it all.

"You're joking!" he snapped.

"No. I start next week," Hope admitted. "Right after New Year's."

"You'll never cut it," he predicted coldly. "You're not tough enough. Go back to the *Breeze* and stay where you belong!"

Hope hadn't expected him to be overjoyed, but neither had she believed he would be so totally arrogant, unfair—and *mean*! She was shocked, and angered. Her eyes flashed with fury. His very certainty that she wasn't good enough made her determined to succeed, come hell or high water!

"Who gave you the job?" he demanded.

"Jake, you look pale." Elise burst into the fray.

"Your managing editor, John Forrester," Hope replied evenly, never taking her eyes from his.

"John and I are pretty close friends. He listens to what I have to say and tries to keep me happy. I wouldn't count on that job just yet."

"Oh, Jake," Elise murmured unhappily, her cheeks pink.

Hope stared at him in furious disbelief. The others in the room started making noises about it being time to leave. Hope's mother brushed past her, patting her arm and saying, "It's time to go, honey," but Hope refused to look away from the superiority and condescension evident in Jake's unfairly beautiful blue eyes.

"I don't know what your problem is," she said in a voice throbbing with fury, "but John Forrester hired me because I was best for the job."

"Is that right?"

"That's right!" she answered evenly. "And just because you're God's gift to journalism doesn't mean someone else can't 'cut it'! You don't know me or what I'm all about anymore *Dance*, so I'd be careful if I were you. I'm going to be treading on your heels. Just waiting for a chance to slide into first place ahead of you!"

The room became utterly silent. Someone was tugging on her arm, but Hope shook herself free, too incensed to think clearly.

"Come on, Hope," Katy warned in her ear.

"You really think you're ready to play ball in the major leagues, *Miss Townsend*?" Jake was scathing.

"Just watch me," she declared, turning on her heel and sailing through the front door, imperious as a queen, determined to put as much space as possible between herself and Jake Danziger before self-recriminations caused her to stammer out an apology she didn't really mean.

Chapter Four

Hope gazed out at the breakers, wrinkling her nose at the scent of decay and brine that seemed especially strong today. She saw a boat motoring just beyond the crashing surf and longed to be down on the beach. The footpath followed the headland but the descent to its face was so sharp and covered with loose pebbles that a body risked life and limb. She'd scrambled down easily enough when she was a child, but now she had visions of herself tumbling down that rocky cliff to her death or, at the very least, a long stay in the hospital.

She was freezing inside her wool-lined parka and her breath misted in front of her face. The breeze off the ocean whipped her hair into her face, stinging her eyes to tears, but Hope merely brushed the silken blond strands aside and continued to gaze broodingly at the gray ocean far below.

It had been two days since this latest Christmas Eve disaster at the Danzigers'. She was leaving for Seattle in another five, on New Year's Eve. Goodbye Roche Harbor and hello *Seattle Observer*. Goodbye Jake Danziger, and hello Jake Danziger.

Sighing, Hope stamped her feet against the cold that was seeping through her boots. She'd seen Jake only once since. She and her mother had been in Roche Harbor proper. Hope had crossed the street to the card shop and had nearly run over Jake who was struggling to climb out of Elise's station wagon. They'd stared at each other for several seconds, then Hope, realizing Jake had no interest in either apologizing or explaining himself, walked away without a word. What was there to say, anyway? Jake had made his stand and she'd made hers.

Her father had made the only comment about her fight with Jake. "Another Christmas Eve to remember," he'd said to her late Christmas Day, his voice threaded with irony. "I'm afraid you and Jake are going to have to learn to get along, or this new job is going to be a tough one."

Hope had come to the same conclusion on her own. She didn't believe Jake could get her fired just at his own request, but she was fully aware that he carried a major amount of clout at the *Observer*. At the very least, he could make her life so miserable that she would want to quit. Though she'd ridiculed his being "God's gift to journalism" there was no denying that Jake Danziger was a star reporter.

Elise had stopped by once. She'd seemed so anxious to convince Hope that Jake just wasn't himself these days, that he hadn't meant half of what he said, and that deep down he was a sensitive and caring and all-around great guy, that Hope could scarcely keep from staring at her as if she'd lost her mind. As far as Hope was concerned, Jake didn't possess any feelings at all. He was so wrapped up in himself and his career that he'd forgotten how to act like a human being!

She must have deluded herself completely that other Christmas six years ago when she'd fallen in love with him. How could she have been so lovestruck by someone as arrogant, self-centered and unworthy as Jake? Unbelievable! The way he made love to her then pushed her away hardly qualified him for Sensitive Male of the Year! How could she have been so blind?

Youth, she told herself now. Naive, unsuspecting, ignorant youth. Well, she was older now, and smarter. And Jake's assumption that she couldn't cut it in investigative journalism made her see red. What a classic, chauvinistic attitude! She suspected he just didn't want her around. She was a living memory of one of his most selfish, destructive moments. If there was even a kernel of feeling left in his cold heart—which she sincerely doubted—then he would know he was being unfair. But Jake Danziger was as damnably arrogant and blind as he was handsome. He was the worst kind of male: self-serving, superior, stubborn, impatient, autocratic, condescending—

"Hope?"

She nearly fell over at the sound of his voice so close to her left ear. Whipping around, she saw him leaning on his crutches about twenty feet away, looking almost as surprised to see her as she was to see him.

"Hello," she managed stiffly. An apology rose in her throat for her actions the other night and she had to bite back the words. He'd been the one to challenge her professionalism first. If anyone owed an apology here, it was Jake.

He wore mostly black today. A black shirt and jacket above a pair of disreputable blue jeans, the knee of one leg threatening to break through at any moment. The other pant-leg was stretched taut around his thigh. Hope could see the outline of his bandage.

"I didn't expect you to still be around," he said, impatiently swiping at his wind-tossed hair. His hair was long for Jake, Hope realized inconsequentially. Or at least, longer than he used to wear it.

"I'm here till New Year's Eve."

"And then you're starting at the *Observer*."

He carefully kept the censure out of his voice, but Hope heard it nevertheless. "I've already moved apartments," she said. "I just need to transfer a few last things, and then I'll start work the day after New Year's."

Jake eyed her thoughtfully and remarked, "John must be out of his mind."

Hope sighed impatiently. "I don't need to hear all this again. If you've got a problem with me, then it's just your problem. I can handle myself."

"Have you ever considered what investigative journalism entails?" he asked. "Look at me." He swept a hand to encompass his crutches and injured leg. "It's not about being clever and smart and figuring out the clues. It's dangerous. And it's hard work."

"Fine." Hope shrugged.

"You don't know what you're getting into."

"I know exactly what I'm getting into."

"People get hurt in this profession. Sometimes killed," he added tightly, glancing toward the ocean.

"Thanks for the warning, but I don't need it. You're not the only one who can 'cut it.' "

"Oh, for God's sake," he muttered impatiently.

"Just leave me alone, Jake. I've made my own decisions for a long while and they don't revolve around you."

Immediately she regretted those last words. They sounded childish, and she despised being childish.

He shot her a look. "That why you chose my paper?"

"I 'chose' the *Observer* because it offered the best job. It just happens to be your paper."

"You chose journalism because it was my field."

She fought back a scream of frustration. "I can't believe you. Your ego is unreal."

Shrugging, he said, "I just don't want to see you get hurt."

"Oh, please," she murmured in disgust. "I've heard that so many times I want to get sick every time someone says it." Hope glanced away. For all his faults he'd never big-brothered her before; she wasn't going to put up with it now. And she was incensed that he thought her so inept that he had to protect her!

"Hope, wait," he said, reaching for her arm when she would have turned away. His left crutch fell as his fingers wrapped around her upper arm. Heart lurching, Hope carefully extricated herself from his hard grip and bent to retrieve the crutch for him.

"What?" she asked suspiciously, holding out the crutch to him.

He ignored her and instead, with a sound of annoyance, flung the other crutch to the ground, too, balancing gingerly on both legs. "God, I hate being an invalid! Look, I didn't mean to come down so hard on you the other night.''

"Didn't you?"

"Stop answering questions with questions," he snapped.

The wind whipped her hair in front of Hope's face again, and she nearly jumped out of her skin when he brushed it aside for her. But the tender gesture was only so he could read her eyes. His mouth was tight and he was intent on some purpose of his own.

"What do you want, Jake?" she demanded, glancing back toward the house.

His lips thinned. "Never mind," he said tautly, and before Hope realized what he was planning to do, he'd snatched up his crutches and headed back down the footpath to his own house.

She tried to sustain her anger, but something in his manner had reached her, tugging at her heart. He wasn't half as tough as he thought he was. It bothered her that it took so little on Jake's part to make her ire cool and that stupid, forgiving part of herself unfurl, but, nevertheless, her gaze clung unwillingly to his retreating back as he headed toward the Danziger house.

Lifting her eyes, she saw lights glowing in the windows though it was scarcely three o'clock. She could almost make out Elise's figure through the kitchen window. Watching Jake stump to the back door, Hope felt a pang of loneliness. There was no one home at her house. This afternoon her parents had taken Katy and Sharon to Sea-Tac Airport, so her sisters could head back to Los Angeles and Vail respectively. The ferry schedule being what it was, the whole family planned to spend the night in Seattle. Katy and Sharon were flying out in the morning; her parents were boarding the first ferry back to San Juan Island. Hope had been asked to join them, but she'd opted to stay home, wanting to be alone. Now, however, with time on her hands and this last encounter with Jake fresh in her mind, she wished she'd agreed to the trip.

Walking back to the house, she tried in vain to push Jake from her thoughts. The scene Christmas Eve and his sudden, abortive attempt to apologize chased each other through her mind as if on a circular track. Frustrated, she called herself names under her breath as she pushed open the kitchen door.

He could have been a little nicer, she thought to herself as she searched through the cupboards for something to eat. A little more supportive. She didn't care if they were never friends again, but he didn't have to be such an autocratic bastard. She wasn't going to let herself be swayed by his halfhearted attempt at an apology. After all, he still didn't think she could make it in the "major leagues."

She snorted in irritation as she reached for a can of soup. She, Hope Townsend, was bound and determined to prove him wrong, even if it killed her, which she thought with a wry smile, he seemed certain it would! Jake apparently saw her as the weaker sex, and that was as far as it went. It didn't matter that she was capable, and fairly intelligent, and systematic and *good* at what she did. He'd already labeled her. It was too bad he worked for the *Observer*, but no one said life was perfect, and besides, she'd taken the job with her eyes open. If he could "cut it," so could she.

She was just congratulating herself on how grown-up and reasonable she was being when there was a knock on the door. No car had driven up, so Hope knew whoever it was had arrived on foot. Jake? Her heart fluttered nervously. Steeling herself, she set the can of soup on the counter and walked down the hall to the front door.

"Who is it?" she asked, twisting the knob.

Elise stood on the threshold, clutching her coat to her throat to ward off the cold. An apologetic smile was pinned to her lips. "It's just me," she said. "I probably should have called first, but I decided it would be best if I just popped over and caught you unawares."

"Caught me unawares?" Hope waited expectantly.

"Well, I know Stephen and Laura took the girls back to Seattle and that you're staying alone."

"Oh, don't worry about me, Elise," Hope answered with a smile. "I'm used to being by myself. It's having a crowd around now, that's hard."

"That's not really why I came over," Elise answered with difficulty, flushing a little. "It's just that I'm going to Seattle myself, tonight, and I won't be back until late tomorrow. A friend of mind is in town just for the day, so I really can't miss seeing her."

"Sounds like you have to go," Hope agreed easily.

"Yes. So, I was wondering…" Elise gazed at Hope anxiously, as if she weren't certain how to continue. She looked tired, Hope thought and wondered if Jake were somehow to blame.

"Would you like a cup of tea, or something?" Hope asked, holding the door wide. "Unless you're late for the ferry."

"Hope, I stopped by to ask you a favor," she blurted out. "It's—Jake. He needs someone to look in on him while I'm gone."

Hope blinked several times, certain she'd heard wrong. "You want *me* to look in on him?"

"He'd die if he knew I was asking you, but the truth is, he's not taking good care of himself. He's continually worn-out and he won't rest. If you were to stop by and just make sure he's got everything he needs...?" She hesitated, but when Hope made no attempt to hide her horror, she added, "I know that you and Jake don't get along very well anymore. But in his own way, I know he feels badly about how things ended. This could be a chance for you two to patch up your differences."

"Elise—"

"He has a short temper these days. A really short temper. But I know he doesn't mean to come down on you so hard. It's that job he has. It's too demanding, and frankly, I wish he'd quit."

"Elise—" Hope stressed.

"He doesn't want anything to happen to you. That's why he's so adamant about you not working on the paper. He's afraid for you. And I don't blame him. It's terrible worrying about the people you care for. Do you know how I felt when I heard he'd been shot?" She stared at Hope and for a moment her blue eyes were filled with naked torment. "I thought I'd die. I thought, 'First George and now Jake. Why not me instead?'"

"Elise, please." Hope's heart twisted painfully. Though her assumptions were all wrong, Hope understood her worry over Jake. "I'll do it," she added, feeling even worse as she realized Elise was fighting back tears.

"You know Jake," she said, fussing through her purse for a tissue. "His bark is worse than his bite. He likes you, Hope. He doesn't mean to hurt you."

Wanna bet?

"If you'll just stop in later tonight, and maybe tomorrow morning. He won't ask for anything, but if you could kind of try to anticipate what he might need? I know it's a lot to ask, but truthfully, I think he wants me out of the house." She tried to smile and failed. "He's so independent. He hates his mother waiting on him. So if you could just, drop by later...?"

"I'll be happy to. Now stop worrying. I'll take care of everything."

"Thank you, Hope," Elise said with heartfelt gratitude. "I'll be back tomorrow afternoon."

It wasn't until after she'd left that Hope considered the possibilities. At first she was filled with dread at encroaching on Jake's territory and having to listen to him rant and rave about not needing any help. But then she saw a chance to exact a small revenge, and Hope wasn't above putting that plan into action.

She made a tray of sandwiches, covered it with plastic wrap. Then, after pulling on her parka, carried the tray along with several cans of pop down the footpath to the Danzigers'. She should have called first, probably, but she was certain Jake would never have agreed to see her anyway, so what was the point?

Hope knocked on the door, shivering. When Jake didn't immediately answer, she knocked again, more loudly. Finally, she turned the knob.

To her amazement he was seated at the kitchen table, reading the paper. "You're right here!" she declared, affronted.

"Isn't this where you expected me to be?" He turned the page lazily.

"Why didn't you answer the knock?"

"Because it's too much trouble to get up. Anyway, I figured it had to be you since the rest of your family's gone."

She was going to kill him. Right now. There must be some way to wipe out his smug complacency. Lord, how she hated it when he thought he *understood* her! "For your information, I brought this tray of sandwiches over because your mother seems to think you need someone to look after you."

"My mother doesn't know what she's talking about."

"*Your mother* is a really great lady, and I like her!"

He glanced up from the newsprint, a puzzled look on his face she was certain was largely faked. "I like her, too," he said, as if he couldn't understand Hope's irrational feminine mind.

"Stop it," Hope said suddenly. "I hate it when you act glib and flip and pretend nothing affects you."

Jake closed the paper, his tone freezing. "All right, I'll give it to you straight. My mother treats me like I can't take care of myself and it's driving me nuts. I don't need you butting in and bothering me. I can feed myself," he added, eyeing the sandwiches. "Thanks anyway."

"I don't believe you," Hope muttered, shaking her head.

"It's the truth. I mastered the fork and spoon years ago. Although," he added with a faint twist of his lip, "the knife still gives me some trouble."

It was the first sign that he actually still possessed a sense of humor, but Hope was too annoyed to appreciate it much. She pulled back a chair and sank down into it. Beyond Jake a fire roared in the huge kitchen/family-room fireplace. Heat poured outward and Hope pulled off her parka, deliberately avoiding Jake's narrowed-eyed gaze.

"What are you doing?" he demanded.

"Taking off my coat."

Beneath her parka she wore a white sweater tucked into a pair of black jeans. Her boots were fuzzy sheepskin. It wasn't exactly the most stylish attire, she supposed, but it kept her warm on cold December days.

Jake's gaze moved downward, hovered somewhere around her breasts, then jerked away, focusing on the pile of wood stacked against the wall. "How long were you planning on staying?" he drawled insolently.

"How about till New Year's?" Hope answered brightly. "Wouldn't that be nice?"

His lashes lowered briefly and she wondered if he were deliberately hiding some emotion. Could it be that he didn't know how to deal with her when she dished back his own type of remark? Laughter danced in her eyes and when he glanced up for a moment he held her gaze.

It maddened Jake that this fresh, beautiful woman had the ability to tease him even when he was acting his worst. Her eyes sparkled like sunlight on green water, and her mouth was a soft cherry pink curving gently over white teeth, one of which flared gently over another in a thoroughly entrancing way. He'd thought her cute when she was younger. And sweet. And naive. She was none of those things now. She was grown-up, cool and sophisticated, with a tart sense of humor. She was drop-dead gorgeous, too; and when she smiled, like now, she was potently irresistible. Looking at her made something shift inside him, as if the ashes of his lost hopes and dreams and innocent beliefs were stirring to life.

Memories danced inside his head like fireflies—bright spots of pain inside the empty spaces of his soul. He saw Diana again, her body limp across his outstretched arms. She'd died without a whimper. Her last breath had ended on a long sigh; and she'd ceased to exist.

Jake swallowed. The room was suffocatingly close. His stomach dropped and he suddenly wanted Hope *out*. Out of the room, out of his sight, *and out of his life!* "Go home and leave me alone," he growled, focusing intently on the swimming newsprint in front of his eyes.

He couldn't have crushed her more if he'd tried. Hope's brief flare of warmth for him burned out. But she was tired of being ordered around. She'd leave when she was damn well good and ready. "I don't know about you, but I'm hungry." She reached for a sandwich and a soda, popping the can and taking a drink without looking at him. Let him bluster all he wanted, the grouch. She could take it.

His hand suddenly shot across the table; she was so surprised that a little gasp escaped her lips. "What is it with you?" he snarled through his teeth. "I don't need a baby-sitter, and I don't need you!"

She twisted her arm, trying to release his fingers. "I'm here at your mother's request."

"To hell with my mother and to hell with you!"

"Let go of me, Dance," Hope gritted.

For an answer his fingers squeezed even tighter. An angry blue flame burned brightly in his eyes.

"It's been six years, Hope," he said slowly.

Alarm skittered along her nerves at his sudden change of tack. The low timbre of his voice didn't help, either. She eyed him warily.

"I wasn't in love with you then," he continued deliberately. "I just used you. You told me you hated me and I believed you. Let's leave things like that."

She knew instantly that he was purposely trying to wound her. And he'd succeeded, she marveled. Even after all this time, his cold tone could tear away a piece of her heart. Swallowing, she opted for basic honesty, knowing he was brutally and systematically battling all her painfully erected defenses. "I don't hate you anymore. And you don't have to be so mean to me."

"Don't I?"

She shook her head, and silence settled between them. He was trying to hurt her and he'd done it with consummate ease. Her shell of indifference wasn't as hard as she'd hoped. In fact, right now she felt downright weak and miserable. Why had she thought she could play the game on his terms? He was right. She couldn't cut it. Not when her emotions were flayed bare.

She stared at the quarter of tuna-fish sandwich she'd bitten into, feeling his gaze drilling into her. He expected her to leave. She *should* leave. She'd seen he was all right, and there was no reason to stay and suffer more.

But somehow this meeting had become a contest of wills, of proving who was the toughest, the most capable, the *best*. Jake thought she wasn't tough enough to make it in a largely male profession, and she had to prove him wrong. Yet, she was so susceptible to Jake Danziger, the man, that it was going to be an uphill battle. She could never let him see how much he affected her; how even the slightest criticism made her wince, how cruel words made her shake inside.

She reached deep, deep within herself to a core of strength—a core forged by Jake's special brand of rejection and humiliation. Taking a deep breath, she yanked her arm free and declared coldly, "When you want to be a bastard, you're first-rate at it. The best. Better than anyone else."

"I warned you about me, but you wouldn't listen."

"I'm listening now. And this time, I believe you." Calmly, Hope picked up her soda, and though she had to fight back a gag, she took another bite of her sandwich. She risked a cool glance his way. His attention was on the newspaper. Or at least his gaze was. In fact that hot glare looked as if it could burn a hole right through the paper.

And then he looked up. Hope was ready for him. *Take your best shot, Jake,* her eyes warned him.

The faintest glimmer of admiration appeared in his eyes, extinguished almost before she really saw it. He seemed disconcerted. Seconds passed and then he heaved a sigh and reached for one of the sandwiches. They ate in wary silence. Hope wasn't certain if she'd won this round or not.

The clock on the mantel suddenly purred, clicked and chimed sweetly nine times. It was past time for her to leave, but a ridiculous part of herself stubbornly refused to go. She didn't question what she hoped to accomplish. She was bound to lose, anyway. But she wasn't ready to give up this opportunity with Jake.

"What happened when you were shot?" she asked, breaking the silence.

Jake didn't respond for several seconds, as if he were debating which way to answer. He chose sarcasm. "I fell down and lay on the concrete and bled."

Hope went on, blithely ignoring his nastiness. "I meant the circumstances that led up to it, like—"

"I know what you meant."

Hope gazed into his guarded eyes. "But you're not going to tell me what really happened."

"No."

"Will you be investigating this case when you get back to the paper?"

"There is no case," he said testily. "Bill Farrell was shot at by someone he was trying to set up. I'm sure Farrell knows who, and I'm also sure it's an ongoing DEA case. Whoever it was may have found out Bill was DEA. I don't know, and I don't care. That's not what I was doing there."

"Oh, come on. You're not the type to walk away from a hot story."

"I'm not about to screw around with the DEA," Jake argued flatly. "They trust me to tell a story when it can do the least amount of damage to their men. I'm not going to risk someone's life by jumping the gun, so to speak. That's not responsible journalism."

"That's not what I said. I said you wouldn't walk away from a hot story."

"And I said there's no story."

He was lying. Right down to his socks he was lying. "Are you afraid I'll try to take this one from you?" she guessed softly.

He swore beneath his breath and looked at her with loathing. "Since you're not going to leave, I will." Grabbing his crutches, he struggled to rise from the chair. Hope didn't make any move to help him, knowing it would only increase his wrath. He stumped away but stopped at the archway to the entry hall. "I'm going upstairs. Lock up when you leave."

"You're hiding something, Jake," she said matter-of-factly. "I think your mother's right. That bullet was meant for you. You know something more than you're telling."

"Get this straight!" he snarled. "My job is none of your concern. You're no detective, Hope. You're just a frustrated woman trying to prove you're a man!"

"If I wanted to be a man," she answered calmly though fury licked through her veins, "I sure as hell wouldn't be here taking lessons from you. I'd find someone with a heart instead of a poor facsimile thereof."

That did it. He looked ready to chew her up and spit her out. Hope marveled at her own serenity. Let him be the one to fret and rave and carry on, for once. He twisted around and jabbed his crutches in the direction of the stairs, disappearing around the corner.

Hope slowly strolled to the entry hall and watched him negotiate the steps for several moments until he's struggled halfway up. The effort was costing him dearly, and remembering Elise's warning that he wasn't taking care of himself, she swallowed her misgivings and asked, "Can I help you upstairs?"

"Get lost."

"Don't be a hardheaded fool. This isn't easy for you. You may hate it, but you need some help."

"I can get upstairs on my own!"

His fury and frustration blasted at her. Hope was suddenly equally furious herself. She swept up the stairs behind him. As Jake tried to sidle upward, one crutch under his arm, the other laid flat on the banister as he pulled himself up, hopping inelegantly, Hope reached for the crutch he wasn't using for support.

He saw her hand out of his peripheral vision and jerked sharply away to the right, stumbling in the process. Hope reached out for him automatically. Jake growled, tried to catch himself and overbalanced. His torso collided into her chest, swift and hard, and it knocked the breath from her lungs.

"Jake!" Hope cried in fear as he yanked himself away from her as if she'd burned him. She lunged for his arm as he inadvertently put his weight on his bad leg. The leg offered no support. In a slow motion whirl she saw him fall backward, tumbling down the stairway to the oak floor below.

"Oh, God!" She rushed downstairs. Jake lay on his left side, his teeth gritted in pain, his hand pressed tightly to his right side. His eyes were closed, his face white. Hope was sick with remorse as she knelt down beside him, her heart racing. "Are you all right? Oh, Jake, I'm so sorry."

"I'm okay," he managed to get out.

"Your leg..."

"It's okay."

"I'll—call a doctor," she murmured shakily, staggering to her feet.

"No!"

"Jake, please..." Hope's teeth started to chatter.

"If you—so much as touch—that phone—I'll wring your lovely neck." He sucked air between his teeth. "As soon as I'm able."

"Let me call Dr. Morrow," she suggested urgently, referring to the doctor who'd attended both of them practically since they were born.

"No. I'm fine."

"You're *not* fine. Stop being so ridiculously tough!" Hope's voice rose nearly to a scream. "I'm sick of it. I'm calling Dr. Morrow and there's nothing you can do about it."

The string of epithets that followed her were enough to make a sailor blush, but Hope was determined. After all, besides the fact that she didn't trust Jake to be truthful about the pain and injury, she was partly responsible. She had to make certain he was all right for her own peace of mind—*and* that he wouldn't blame her later, should something go wrong.

"Dr. Morrow's office." An answering-service voice picked up on the second ring. "The office is closed, but if you would like the doctor to call you back—"

"This is an emergency," Hope cut her off.

"Then call number 757-3324. Someone there will help you."

Hope tamped down her impatience and called the emergency number. A nurse answered. When Hope explained her problem, the nurse explained that Dr. Morrow was unavailable until after the holidays and that Hope should take Jake to the hospital emergency room.

Hope was frustrated practically beyond bearing. "I can't get him to the hospital," she cried. "He won't let me."

"I'll tell you what," the nurse spoke soothingly. "Why don't you check the wound yourself? See what you think. Since he doesn't want to go, he might not be as seriously injured as you believe. If, after checking the wound, you still think he needs to go to the hospital, call an ambulance."

Sound advice, but not what Hope wanted to hear. "Thanks," she replied tersely.

Check Jake's wound? *That* would go over like the proverbial lead balloon. Hurrying back to his side, she was relieved to see spots of color returning to his cheeks. His eyes were still closed and his breathing was labored, but he looked marginally better. She could tell he was fighting back pain.

"The nurse told me to check your wound."

"For God's sake, Hope!" he exploded. "Play nursemaid to someone else!"

"You must be all right or you wouldn't have enough energy to scream at me," she said briskly.

"I *am* all right." But he didn't attempt to get up.

It was then she noticed the dark stain seeping through his pant leg. Blood. The fall had reopened his wound. "You're bleeding," she stated tonelessly, deliberately hiding the sick worry that jolted through her.

His answer was to grit his teeth, open his eyes and glare at her with supreme fury. He moved slowly, pulling his legs under him. Hope reached to help him and he froze.

"Let me at least give you a hand," she pleaded. "Don't make things worse just to prove a point."

He let her put her arm around his waist. His back muscles were taut, straining with effort. He tried to get to his feet without using her support, but it was no use. Panting, he leaned against her, his arm slung heavily over her shoulders, his hard hip bumping against hers. He aimed for the couch in the living room and Hope walked slowly with him, feeling the shudder that ripped through him whenever his injured leg supported his weight.

Sweat had beaded on his forehead when he sank gingerly onto the cushions. "Get a towel," he ordered between his teeth. "My mother will lose a year of her life if I get blood on this couch."

"She'll understand."

"Just do it. Please," he added when she turned away without a word.

Hope ran downstairs and searched the laundry room, finding several towels folded in a narrow cupboard. By the time she returned, Jake's hips were perched on the edge of the couch, his head resting against the back cushions. "Here're some towels," she said.

"Thanks." He lifted his hips and Hope laid the cloths beneath him. The stain on his right thigh had spread.

Catching her look, he said sardonically, "All I need to do is change this dressing."

"Where's another bandage?" Hope asked.

"In my room."

"I'll get it."

"You don't have to," he snapped, then shoved his hands through his hair. His gaze softening slightly, he muttered, "But I don't suppose I can stop you, can I?"

Hope was already heading for the stairs. "Not unless you want to bleed to death," she pointed out.

She heard his half laugh. "God, you're stubborn."

"So are you."

Jake's room was at the top of the stairs and straight to the back. As a kid, Hope had been inside it on several occasions. Then, she'd seen trophies from basketball and soccer, pennants of his favorite teams tacked on the wall, shelves of books he'd read, and pictures of girlfriends stuck in the frame of his mirror. But those remnants of boyhood were gone now.

The walls were unadorned and painted white. The double bed was covered with a peach-colored comforter that reflected Elise's tastes, not Jake's. The furniture was white and modern, the kind imported from Scandinavia. Gone was the dark oak. Gone were memories of Jake. The room was a guest room.

Hope saw all this in a glance. She moved to the bureau where medical supplies were stacked neatly in a pile—some kind of prescription ointment and a roll of gauze and a bottle of pills. Hope swept everything into her arms and returned downstairs, a sense of bitter poignancy lingering with her. It was a reminder that she didn't know the Jake Danziger downstairs at all.

Color had fully returned to his cheeks by the time she rejoined him. "You look better," she observed.

"I'm not ready to meet my Maker yet," he said dryly.

"First, you need to get those jeans off."

"Stop trying to be so goddamned efficient," he muttered. "I can get the jeans off myself *and* change the bandage. And I'd rather do it in private."

"The nurse said I should look at your wound."

He was very explicit about what the nurse could do with her advice. Hope prudently decided that if he were well enough to come up with such a colorful image, he was probably capable of rebinding his bandage. At least she wasn't going to have to race him off to the hospital. "I'll be in the kitchen if—" She stopped herself short from saying *If you need me.* Jake's swift, derisive look told her she'd been wise to keep mum.

She stood in the center of the kitchen, rubbing her arms with her palms, feeling chilled. From the other room grunts of disgust and fury and muttered obscenities drifted to her ears. Hope smiled to herself. How he hated being helpless. She didn't much like it, either, she realized.

"Need any assistance?" she yelled to him.

"No." His answer was a tad long in coming. Hope could hear him panting from effort.

Steeling herself, she walked back to the living room. Jake looked up in surprise. "What are you doing?" he demanded tautly.

"You look like you could use some help. No, don't say it," she cut him off. "The sooner you're back together, the sooner I leave."

His jaws clamped together. Hope, whose courage surprised even her, surveyed him, careful to keep her expression detached and neutral. He'd managed to pull off his jeans and he sat in a pair of Jockey shorts, the bandage on his right thigh half-unwrapped. Blood oozed and Hope had to swallow once and push the thought of his pain to a deep corner of her mind. "Looks terrible," she observed in a light tone.

Jake snorted. He unwrapped another thin layer of gauze. Hope bore down on her feelings and, risking another string of verbal abuse, took the gauze from his fingers and finished unveiling his wound.

The stitches had been taken out to prevent scarring and the tissue surrounding the jagged wound was still red and tender. The cut was open now, raw and purple. Hope's heart started pounding in her temples. Unsettled, she nevertheless fought her own body's reactions and said in a calm voice. "Do you want more of this on it?" and lifted the tube of ointment.

For an answer he took the tube, squeezed about a teaspoonful of the clear paste into his palm, and carefully applied it around the area. Hope unwound the fresh roll of gauze and began rewrapping his wound.

Jake sat utterly motionless. The throbbing in his thigh was nothing to the feather-light touch of her fingers against his hot skin. He was afraid to even breathe. The brush of her fingertips was a sensual rub and it made him feel weak in a way the fall down the stairs hadn't been able to. God. He had to make her stop. But he couldn't force his throat into speech. He was a victim of her touch. There was nothing left but to grin and bear it. Oh, God, what was she doing *now*?

"Did that hurt?" Hope asked swiftly, her blond brows knitted in concern, her eyes darkening with embarrassment.

"No." That, at least, was the truth.

"I didn't mean to—" She couldn't bring herself to go on.

She'd accidentally brushed against his crotch as she'd wound the tape around. Jake stared over her bent head, to the window beyond and the cold, crystalline snow that was drifting lightly outside. His jaw was tense. He'd be lucky not to react. Damn lucky. If he did, and she noticed—and hell, she noticed everything!—he'd be sunk. His only defense was to pretend an indifference to her, an animosity toward her, when in truth those feelings no longer existed. Inside him was something new, and far more dangerous—a real desire to gather her close and bury his face in her hair. It wasn't exactly sexual; yet it was a need that welled up inside him and made him want to cry out with pain.

It scared him.

"You might have to have it restitched." Hope worried aloud, gazing down at her handiwork.

"It'll be fine." His voice was tight and clipped. Controlled—thank God. He fervently wished she would remove her fingers from his thigh.

"You look like you're in pain," she said, biting her lip.

"I am." Jake was ironic.

"Maybe I should—"

"No. Whatever it is, don't do it." When she didn't move immediately, her hand still touching his thigh, he added warningly, "I think you've done enough, Hope."

She stepped away, inhaling sharply. She looked flustered. Well, good. He was damn well flustered himself. It didn't help that the scent of her perfume— light, airy, with just a hint of something deeper—tantalized his nostrils. Jake clamped down on his emotions and said tightly, "At the risk of sounding like a broken record, when are you leaving?"

Her green eyes flicked to his. "I don't think I will leave," she said slowly, as if thinking through every syllable.

"What does that mean?"

"It means I don't think you should be here by yourself. You might end up needing to go to the hospital, after all, if this reinjury is worse than it looks."

"You can't be serious."

"I don't think you should attempt the stairs again. I'll make up the couch for you."

He was already fighting wave upon wave of unwelcome awareness. He couldn't conceive of having her spend the night in his house! "There is a telephone," he said calmly, coldly. "If I need anything, or *anyone*, I'll call."

To his astonishment and consternation, she sat down on the couch beside him. "I'll sleep in one of the guest rooms upstairs. I can't leave you tonight, Jake. My conscience won't allow it. You don't have to like it, or be nice about it, or even try to understand it. But I'm not leaving, so let's make the best of it."

With a satisfied, "I mean business" smile hovering on her lips, she left him sitting on the couch, a trail of evocative perfume in her wake.

Chapter Five

Hope lay on the twin bed in the small room at the head of the stairs. It was the room closest to the steps, and, since she'd left the door open, the easiest room from which to hear noises from downstairs.

Jake, naturally, had nearly come unglued when she'd made her announcement about spending the night. She'd struck him speechless first, but that hadn't lasted long. He'd told her not to come back when she went to her house to pack an overnight bag, and when she did return he did his damnedest to let her know she was an unwanted guest.

She was a bit surprised how little his blustering, insults and carrying on had bothered her. She'd known she'd developed a hard shell, but it had still been something of a shock to find she'd grown tough enough to deflect the worst of his cruel verbal missiles with very little damage sustained. Something of a shock, but satisfying, too. Let him rant and rave. He was helpless to do anything about her company.

Grinning to herself in the dark, Hope wasn't bothered at how childish she was being. Jake wasn't exactly acting like an adult, either. In fact, he was behaving like an obstinate child. Tit for tat, Hope figured as she punched her pillow into a comfortable mound and lay on her back, gazing at the shadowed outlines of the exposed fir beams above her head.

She did feel terrible about his fall, however. If she hadn't interfered, it might not have happened, and then none of these precautions would have been necessary. She could be home now, in her own bed, setting her sites on her return to Seattle instead of baby-sitting Jake. She wished she'd let him struggle up the stairs on his own.

She sighed heavily. Amazingly enough, even though Jake had been very clear that he wanted her to leave him alone, he hadn't out-and-out blamed her for what had happened.

Which was neither here nor there, since she certainly blamed herself.

Outside the window she could see thick white flakes of snow drifting silently down from the sky. She doubted it was sticking; it rarely did at Roche Harbor. She strained her ears to listen for any wind and became aware of the comfortable ticking of the dresser clock. Glancing toward it she read the time: 2:15 a.m. She must have fallen asleep for a while, she realized, though it felt as if her mind had been racing since she'd turned out the light.

She thought about her job, but as soon as she felt buoyed by being part of the *Observer*'s staff, she remembered Jake and the obstacle he represented, and her enthusiasm faded into uneasiness. She wished she could just tell him to forget the past; she certainly was trying to. She just wanted to get on with her life.

A low moan echoed from downstairs. Hope stiffened, a chill sliding down her spine as she strained her ears. Was that Jake, or was it her imagination? Listening hard, she heard the sound repeated seconds later, followed by a string of unintelligible words. It *was* Jake!

Gathering her thin robe from the end of the bed, Hope tossed it over her nightgown and fled the room. She fervently hoped Jake was sound asleep and her worries were all for nought, but hearing the cry wrung from his throat she knew something was desperately wrong.

He hadn't had the nightmare in years....

Jake struggled upward from the depths of sleep, knowing he was dreaming, unable to completely pull himself from the powerful grip of his own guilt.

The package sat on his desk. He was running for it, but his feet were leaden. Diana sat at his desk, waiting for him, the last seconds of her life ticking silently away. He was ten feet from the door when the blast exploded, the glass wall surrounding his office shattering into a million shards of glittering shrapnel. He heard her scream, then remembered she hadn't made a sound. It was too late. Too late. Too late....

"Jake," Hope whispered, aware he was in the grip of some terrible dream. He thrashed out with one arm, moaning incoherently, his hand brushing her breast, sending shock waves through her system. His hair was damp with sweat as if he'd been running a marathon. "Jake."

"Don't . . . don't . . ." he murmured. "Please don't . . . please don't . . ."

She touched his bare shoulder, which was hot and sticky. His arm swung wildly her way again and she caught his hand. "Jake," she said a bit louder. "It's me, Hope. You're dreaming."

His body was shuddering with violent emotion. That emotion telegraphed to her, and she felt frightened.

"You're having a nightmare," she told him calmly. Placing her palms on either side of his face, she gasped when he tried to fight her off. "Jake! Wake up!"

He jerked to sudden and complete awareness, his eyes opening wide, his hands grabbing her wrists. Hope was half leaning over him, her expression full of anxiety. For Jake, it was a moment caught between two worlds: the hellish nightmare world where Diana lay bloody and silent in his arms, and the real world, where Hope stared down at him, her robe gaping to allow a view of some kind of silken nightgown, her blond hair tumbling around her shoulders and tickling his left cheek.

He realized with a painful kick of his heart that it hadn't been Diana who'd been dying in his dreams. It had been Hope. Hope's face, cold and white. Hope's limbs dangling over his arms in the terrible abandonment of death.

"Jake . . . ?" Hope asked uncertainly.

Impulse won over common sense. Drawing a deep breath, he gathered her into his arms, wanting the feel of her warm, live body to calm his racing heart and convince his wounded subconscious that she was real and safe and *right here*!

Hope choked on a gasp when Jake's arms closed around her—closed around her so tightly she couldn't breathe. His heart pounded beneath hers, hard and fast. Her own pulse started picking up speed, thundering in her ears, racing with sudden, inexplicable desire. She wanted to jerk back but didn't dare. Whatever demons haunted him were very real right now. Real enough to make him want to press his flesh against someone else's, to ensure that he was alive.

He buried his face in her hair, his mouth so close to her ear that Hope's throat went dry. Her robe gaped, her breasts pushing against the sheer fabric of her nightgown, pressing against his bare chest. A jolt of awareness passed through her—electric, embarrassingly intense.

He released her just as suddenly, drawing his arms down and away from her. Hope wanted to cry out in anguish. She was furious with herself for feeling anything! *Why did it have to be Jake?*

"Hope," he murmured unsteadily, obviously at a loss for words.

"You were having a nightmare, I guess. I was worried you were in pain," she explained, trying to regain her calm.

"I am in pain," he said, and though his voice was its normal dry tone, she heard something beneath it. Something unsure. Something vulnerable. Something he was desperately trying to hide.

She looked at him and wondered if she'd been wrong about him. Could he feel hurt and emotion as much as she did?

"Do you—need anything?" she asked.

"Need anything?" he repeated blankly.

"For the pain."

He drew a breath and collected himself. She could almost feel the shift inside him, the shoring up of his defenses. "Nothing you can give me."

"What *is* it, Jake?" she asked suddenly. "Is it this investigation? Is that what brought on this nightmare?"

He gazed at her, his eyes hooded. "So now it's 'Jake,' huh? When I'm down and helpless?"

She ignored that. "What's going on? It *is* this investigation, isn't it?"

"No." He was terse. "I'm not going to tell you anything about it, so you might as well give up now."

Hope gazed down at him, sensitive to the fact that he wasn't quite under control yet. "I can see you're hurting," she went on softly. "And it's not just your thigh, though God knows that must be killing you. This is something else. Just like six years ago. You're carrying some kind of awful burden—"

"Shut up, Hope." His tone was so cold that it brought her up short. "Leave it."

"What are you afraid of? Letting people see you're human? Letting *me* see you're human?"

His mouth tightened with fury. "You think this is what it takes to carry on an investigation? Badger your interviewee with psychopop comments like 'letting people see you're human'? Jesus, Hope. I thought you'd grown up. You sure put on a great act. But you're just as naive as ever."

Had she thought his cruel barbs didn't hurt anymore? She'd been wrong! "All I want to do is help," she said in a voice fraught with emotion.

"If you want to help, then leave me alone," he answered tiredly. "That's what *I* want."

"I guess that's clear enough."

She tugged on the ends of her robe, her face flushed even though she doubted he could see it. Behind her, outside the window, the snow kept falling, only to melt upon hitting the damp ground. She felt as pointless as that beautiful snow. It didn't pay to keep trying. She was doomed to failure where Jake was concerned. She'd been right to stay out of his path, remembering only the bad things.

Feeling the weight of his gaze, she glanced sharply his way. His eyes were centered on the lace-edged neckline of her gown, which still peeked out above her robe. For once his expression was open and honest— and full of raw need. Hope's breasts tingled in response, a response she was helpless to deny. Bearing down on her rampant emotions, she mentally castigated herself for being so susceptible.

But she wasn't the only one whose emotions were rapidly racing out of control, she realized. Jake was sensitive to her, as well. She could read it in his eyes and hear it in his shallow breathing. The knowledge rushed to her head like too much wine. He'd played havoc with her senses for so long, it felt good to wield some power in return. She hoped he desired her as fruitlessly and with as much frustration as she'd desired him. It would go a long way to making up for the hurt he'd caused.

"What are you thinking about?" she couldn't stop herself from asking.

She heard the smugness in her voice at precisely the same moment he did. Too late! She'd given herself away.

And Jake, being Jake, refused to let her enjoy her fleeting moment of power. "You already know," he said sardonically, the same moment his hand swooped around the back of her neck and drew her mouth down to his. He kissed her hard and long and with absolutely no degree of tenderness. Hope squeaked out a protest. She automatically braced herself, her arms on either side of his chest, her hands flattened against the couch's cushions.

She knew he was teaching her a lesson, and though it infuriated her she was distracted and bemused by the feel of his lips against hers. She hadn't been kissed this passionately by anyone else. She hadn't *let* anyone kiss her this passionately! Though she wanted desperately to pull away from him, some lingering, masochistic part of herself let the kiss continue, stroking a flame of long-dormant desire to blazing life.

The kiss ended abruptly, and at that same moment he released his hold on her nape. Her lips throbbed. Her breath was light and shallow. She was glad for the shadows, not certain her face was as closed and inscrutable as his.

"Now, this is playing with fire," he said softly.

Something inside Hope rebelled. "Are you through making your point?" she demanded, determined to bluff her way out of this intolerable situation if necessary.

"I'm not sure." He studied the shape of her mouth for a long moment. Then his thumb followed the same path his gaze had traveled and Hope's blood surged wildly through her veins. It was all she could do to maintain her cool, but maintain it she did, meeting his speculative gaze with frigid green eyes.

"I'm not about to fall at your feet again," she told him. "I'm not nineteen anymore."

"So you're completely—detached—from this?" he questioned.

"You mean your kiss?" Her tone was scornful. "I hate to be the one to break it to you, Dance, but you aren't completely irresistible!"

"Maybe not. But *you* want me."

His arrogance left her incredulous. "You're the most conceited, self-involved man I know! What did I ever see in you?" She tried to get to her feet, but his hand grabbed her wrist. "Let go of me, or I'll do something drastic!"

"Wait," he commanded.

"Not on your life! I came down here to make sure you were all right. I can see now that you're more than fine, so I'm going back to bed."

"Don't be so indignant. If you can't admit your feelings, fine. But they're sure as hell plain to me."

Hope wanted to wring his neck. "Lord save me from men who think they *understand* me," she muttered. She yanked on her wrist and he yanked right back until she nearly tumbled across his chest. She reared backward and her foot tangled with his right leg, which was half off the couch. Visions of another scene like the one on the stairs raced through her mind and she caught herself. Jake, however, wasn't finished; he jerked her arm hard until her face was within inches of his.

"Kiss me again and I'll bite your lip," she warned.

"Go ahead," he answered and pulled her mouth to his.

Her lips were parted to denounce him and it was her worst mistake yet. She was vulnerable, and trembling with emotion, and when his mouth possessed hers, she couldn't bring herself to do as she'd threatened. Even when his tongue invaded the moist sweetness of her mouth, she didn't fight him. But the feel of his palm caressing her breast through the filmy material of her nightgown brought her back to the present with a bang.

She desperately grabbed his wrist, stopping his marauding hand. "Don't."

"Let me," he said, an underlying note of urgency in his voice. It was the sweetest irony, she thought bitterly. It wasn't all a game. He wanted her now. All the cold self-possession he'd shown her was blatantly missing. His mouth was hungry on hers, his hand trembling as it brushed lightly over her erect nipple, his other hand digging into her hair, his body shifting to accommodate hers so that she could lie more fully atop him.

Hope's overloaded senses registered everything simultaneously, and she twisted away from him with an effort, breathing hard. She could see the evidence of his arousal through the cotton Jockey shorts, and the desire that smoldered in his gaze was impossible to miss.

"Good night, Jake," she said determinedly, cinching her robe tightly around her, the effect only spoiled by her hectic breathing. And then she turned and half ran for the stairs.

"Good night, Hope," he answered when she was halfway to the landing, then added ironically, "Sleep well...."

The cold light of day.

Hope pondered those words with new insight as she dressed. She was angry with herself for letting him get to her. She'd been trying to be a good Samaritan, and what had it gotten her? A night full of fractured dreams where she tossed and turned and longed for Jake's total possession of her body.

Groaning aloud, she covered her face in her hands. There was no real harm done, she soothed herself. She'd walked away—well, run away, she reminded herself harshly—before the evening could continue to its logical end. Thank God for the eleventh-hour return of sanity. How on earth could you dislike someone as much as she disliked Jake, yet want him physically?

You don't dislike him.

Pulling on her jeans and an oversize black sweater, Hope brushed her hair with furious strokes until it crackled with life. Okay, she didn't dislike him completely. But she certainly disliked a lot of his traits.

And it really was depressing to think she would have to see him again this morning and be at least marginally polite before she could make good her escape.

Fifteen minutes later she pulled on her suede boots, stopped by Jake's room to collect a change of clothes for him, and resolutely headed downstairs, her overnight bag in hand. It was only a little after seven, so she half expected Jake still to be on the couch.

At the bottom of the stairs she turned left, toward the kitchen, glancing back at the living room and the sofa where Jake had lain.

He wasn't there.

Belatedly, and with a great deal of guilt, she remembered his injury. Jake was a master at both hiding his feelings and turning attention away from his own problems. While she'd been worried about her reaction to his sexual magnetism, he'd managed to make her forget how serious his fall had been.

She ran into the kitchen and nearly collided with him. He was standing by the table, his arms resting loosely on his crutches, his attention focused on the window and beyond. Hope came to a skidding halt.

"Good morning," he said, not even looking her way. "The snow stuck."

He was wearing yesterday's shirt and bloodstained jeans. Just as Hope suspected, Jake was still a bit weak to take on the stairs; she was glad she'd brought him fresh clothes. He looked tired, a bit haggard. Her sleepless night had painted dark rings under her eyes, as well, so she didn't comment. Instead, her gaze followed his through the misted windowpane.

The snow had indeed stuck. A white, sparkling blanket covered the grounds, with only a tuft or two of leggy beach grass showing through. Somewhere during the night the ground had dried, enough to let snowflakes build up and create this dazzling wintry scene.

"I'd better get home and make sure none of the pipes have frozen," Hope said.

"Do that."

His ready agreement irked her. "I don't really feel like spending another moment than I have to with you, either," she informed him, placing the clothes she brought him on the table.

He shrugged. "Thanks for all your—care."

Ignoring his insinuation, Hope asked, "How's your leg feel this morning?"

"Godawful, as a matter of fact. But I checked under the bandage and everything looks okay."

She was thankful he'd deigned to give her an honest account. "I'm really sorry about what happened."

Jake, who'd been studying the blindingly white landscape outside the window, slid her a look from beneath his lashes. "You mean on the stairs, or on the couch?"

"Both," Hope answered frankly. "I don't want to fight with you. We're going to be working together soon, and I want everything to go smoothly. I don't need the stress."

"We're going to be working at the same paper," he corrected flatly. "We won't be working together."

"Fine." Hope's nostrils flared. "We won't be working *together*! But I would hope that when we see each other, we can at least be civil."

"Civility is my middle name," he drawled.

"I know what your middle name is," she spat back through her teeth. "And it's not civility, nor is it amiability, nor is it 'let bygones be bygones.' Goodbye, Jake. See you next week in Seattle."

The door slammed behind her and through the window he watched her break a path through the snow toward her house. Her breath puffed ahead of her in soft white clouds. He couldn't tell if it was exertion, or anger, making those puffs look like the steam from an engine charging down the tracks.

He'd sure made a mess of things last night. He blamed everything on the nightmare. It had unbalanced him. That first embrace had cost him, and then, when she'd looked at him so smugly because she *knew* he was fighting a losing battle with desire, he'd lost all reason. He'd set out to teach her a lesson and the whole thing had backfired; and now he felt like an idiot. An idiot with an uncontrollable sex drive, he berated himself, remembering how much he'd wanted Hope last night.

The night of frustration he'd suffered after she'd gone back to bed had been a thorough-enough punishment, however. Even now he could still feel a stirring lust, he thought in disgust, shoving his hands in the pockets of his jeans.

Well, it was something he was just going to have to get over, he told himself harshly. Thrusting his crutches toward the stairs, he pushed thoughts of Hope Townsend to a far corner of his mind.

Chapter Six

The offices for the *Seattle Observer* sprawled over the second and third floors of the Tarkette Building in downtown Seattle. John Forrester, the *Observer*'s managing editor, was the funnel for the newsroom's information to the editor-in-chief and "the people upstairs." Forrester, a personal friend of Jake Danziger's, was said to be an extremely fair man with a reputation for excellence and accuracy. He couldn't abide sensationalist reporting, and several people had been quietly asked to leave when John felt the scruples of the *Observer* had been compromised.

As Hope entered Forrester's office on her first day of work, he was standing behind a functional metal desk, frowning at the sheaf of papers he held in his hands. Hope, who'd only spoken to him over the phone and briefly in person, faced Forrester with a certain amount of trepidation. Working for the *Breeze* had sensitized her to the existence of a political system within each paper; she'd quickly learned how to fit in and accomplish her goals with a minimum amount of angst. She was worried that Jake had already assassinated her character to the point of ruining whatever chances she had to prove him wrong.

Now, however, gazing at her new boss, she breathed a sigh of relief. From his expression and countenance, her second impression of him was completely positive: he looked as if he'd be fair, tough when he had to be, a bit impatient at times, and wore a beleaguered expression etched into his face from fifteen years as a newspaperman.

But he *was* Jake Danziger's close, personal friend.

"Hello, Townsend," he greeted her with the barest of smiles. "I've told Marshall you're starting today, and she'll show you to your workstation. She's been at the *Observer* a couple of years and will fill you in. You'll find her straight back—" he gestured past the glassed-in walls of his office to the densely packed cubicles of the newsroom "—corner of the north wall right next to the coffee machine. Let her take you around. I've got something I might have you work on, but it'll keep till next week. Okay?"

Hope nodded, slightly surprised that she'd been dismissed so summarily, "Does Marshall have a first name?" she asked. One aspect of the *Breeze* that Hope had liked was its job informality.

"Probably. But nobody calls her by it."

"I see," Hope said slowly. "Thank you," she added as he returned his attention to the sheaf of papers.

"Marshall" turned out to be a petite brown-haired woman who seemed to exist on coffee and chewed-up pencils, since she kept the former in a paper-cup trail across her desk, and one of the latter clenched firmly between her teeth. As Hope approached her work space she was hunting and pecking her way across her computer keyboard.

"Hi," she greeted Hope, yanking the pencil out of her mouth and taking swig of coffee. She replaced the pencil automatically, her gaze never leaving the glowing amber words on the screen in front of her.

Hating to interrupt such studied concentration, Hope said diffidently, "John Forrester sent me to you. I hope you don't mind showing the new kid on the block around."

"You Townsend?" she mumbled around the pencil, still not looking up.

"I believe so," Hope answered dryly.

"Just a minute. I've just got to finish this thought...."

It took her nearly twenty minutes before she really looked up at Hope, her serious eyes still faraway, her head obviously still filled with her story. Hope had been there too many times not to recognize the symptoms. But then she focused sharply on Hope, slowly pulling the pencil from her mouth, her brows drawn into a line of surprise.

"I'm Tammy Marshall," she said, reaching out her right hand. Hope extended hers and they shook hands. "You don't look like an investigative reporter."

"What do investigative reporters look like?" Hope countered with a smile.

"Well, I suppose, like Dance—that is, Jake Danziger—who's kind of dangerous-looking himself. Ever seen his picture?"

"Um, yes, as a matter of fact." Hope was reluctant to bring up her own association with Jake so soon. She wanted to settle into the job and meet her co-workers before—and if ever—she had to explain.

"You look a bit fragile, if you ask me," Tammy went on, her tone entirely matter-of-fact. "Has Forrester given you an assignment yet?"

"No, he wants me to follow you around, I'm afraid. He said he might give me something next week. Actually, I'm kind of hoping something will crop up in-between, so I can get started."

Tammy's eyes crinkled at the corners. "If that's a polite way of apologizing for getting stuck being my shadow, don't worry about it. I don't mind. Did Forrester tell you I'm on metro? Every once in a while I get a great story, but a lot of it's fluff. Today I'm going down to the Ribtickler Restaurant. They're in a major lawsuit over their name and they're going to court tomorrow. It's really not much of a story, but they've got great food. We'll enjoy lunch."

Hope laughed. "Sounds great."

"Come on, I'll show you your workstation."

Tammy led Hope down the aisle that ran in a fairly straight line along the cubbyholes next to the west-side windows. "I feel a little like a fish out of water," Hope admitted as she kept up with Tammy's rapid foot-steps. "The paper where I worked before was pretty rudimentary compared to this. And I didn't have to...compete with a name like Jake Danziger," she added casually. "I understand he and John Forrester are good friends."

"They're pals." Tammy shrugged and grinned. "But don't worry about Dance. He'll probably be handling the really tough stuff, and Forrester'll divvy the rest to you and Hughes."

"Hughes?"

"Martin Hughes. No competition. He's just plain lazy, but he's a good writer. Too bad he's such a wasteland for ambition. Forrester hired you to kind of fill the gap between Hughes and Dance, I think. Work hard and you're in. That's all it takes. Oh," she added, wrinkling her nose as if encountering a bad smell. "And don't get on Dance's bad side. The last reporter Forrester hired screwed up one of Dance's stories so badly it cost him his job."

"Cost him his job?" Hope repeated, her heart sinking. "How did he screw up one of Dance's stories?"

"He was trying to get his own name in lights, so to speak," Tammy said with a certain amount of disgust. "Took over one of Dance's stories that was just simmering, turned it into a half-baked fiasco, then tried to add Dance's name to the byline. Dance told Forrester to fire him, and that was that."

"Danziger has that kind of power? To get someone fired?" Hope's confidence suffered a beating.

"The jerk deserved it," Tammy said bluntly. "Would you want someone messing with your story, then blaming *you*?"

"No."

Tammy went on to tell Hope a little bit about some of the other reporters and editors at the *Observer*, but Hope listened with only half an ear. She was too worried. Whether the reporter deserved it or not, she couldn't quite forget Jake's part in getting the man fired. If Jake wanted Hope off the paper, for whatever reason, she had a feeling he would get his wish.

Gritting her teeth, Hope determined that if Jake talked John Forrester into firing her, it would *not* be over the quality of her work! She was going to make certain everything she turned in was top-notch stuff, glowing, *stellar*. John Forrester might listen to Jake, might even go so far as to fire her. But, by God, Forrester would feel rotten because deep down he would know that he'd fired her only for political reasons.

"Here's your cubby," Tammy announced as she showed Hope the small modular space with its light gray, softly carpeted five-foot walls, its crammed desk and computer terminal, and its matching gray office chair. The carpet was a deeper charcoal and was nearly obliterated by the thick plastic protector laid over it so she would be able to roll her chair back and forth with ease. A tensor light hung suspended over the computer monitor like some poised bird of prey. Hope was gratified to find she had a window, and as she looked through the thick pane she could see a patch of gray Seattle sky high overhead. Straight across her line of vision was a row of commercial buildings sitting cheek by jowl, and three stories below, the snarl of bumper-to-bumper vehicles reflecting Seattle's growing traffic problem.

"This is *your* space," Tammy stressed. "Do with it what you like. Forrester doesn't really impose restrictions as long as you deliver the best piece you can and make it *on time*. That's the cardinal rule."

"It was the same at the *Breeze*," said Hope.

"Forrester's human," Tammy added. "I can't say the same for Berger. He's the city editor and an absolute grouch. You can't scare a smile out of him. The only reporter he can stand is Dance."

Hope's expression was ironic. "How come I'm not surprised," she murmured.

"Oh, it's not Dance's fault," Tammy quickly came to Jake's defense, misunderstanding Hope's reaction. "It's to his credit, actually. Berger's mean, but he's fair. Just don't let him get to you. You want an introduction now?"

"How about a little later," Hope suggested. "I think I'd like to arrange a few things here first."

"Sure. Dance is supposed to be here later today, too, so you'll get your chance to meet him."

The reverence in Tammy's tone sent a warning prickle down Hope's spine. Just how much did Tammy like Jake? And in what way? Not that it was any of her business, Hope reminded herself darkly; but it would be nice to know just in case she fell unwittingly into an emotional pitfall. She liked Tammy already, and didn't want to blow their friendship before it truly began.

"I'll look forward to it," Hope said dryly.

Tammy shot her a look. "You don't sound all that keen. Has someone told you something about Dance to color your judgment? Whatever it is, don't believe it. The guy's extremely well-liked around here, and not just by Forrester. He's kind of intense, but he's totally professional. He's great-looking, too," she added, lifting her brows meaningfully. "It's hard *not* to like him, if you know what I mean!"

"I know," Hope said feelingly.

"Not that I'm one of them fighting for his attention," she added quickly. "Who needs the aggravation? I mean, sure, if Jake showed any interest I'd probably jump at the chance to go out with him, but I'm not interested in stepping over writhing feminine bodies just to talk to him."

Tammy's imagery was a little more graphic than Hope was ready for. "He's that popular?" she asked in spite of herself.

"Oh, yeah." Tammy rolled her eyes. "It's an embarrassment to our sex the way they fall at his feet. Not that he notices much. That's why Penbrook left. She made a fool out of herself over him and became the office joke. Since then, the general moaning and sighing over Dance has been kept to a low roar. Nobody wants to be the next Penbrook."

Hope didn't comment. She felt slightly sick thinking of the "moaning and sighing" she'd done over him. Unbidden, the memory of his hard body lying beneath hers suddenly filled her senses; her heart lurched as she recalled the way his hand had felt on her breast, his mouth hot on hers. Heaven help her, she had to inure herself to his sexual magnetism or she'd suffer even worse humiliation!

"Between my boyfriend and my husband, I've got enough man troubles anyway," Tammy added on a heartfelt sigh. "Although I suppose if Dance looked my way I'd find room."

Hope wasn't certain she'd heard correctly. She surfaced from her worries over Jake to gaze blankly at Tammy. There was a twinkle in the pert reporter's eye, so Hope said, "All right, I'll bite. You have a boyfriend *and* a husband?"

"Yep."

"How interesting for you."

Tammy laughed. "They're one and the same. He used to be my husband, then we got divorced. Now we're just dating."

"That's... unique," Hope answered for lack of anything better to say.

"He wants to get married again, but since it didn't work the first time, I'm not all that eager to go for seconds." She shrugged. "I've dated a few other guys from time to time, just to kind of remember what it's all about."

"How's that going?"

"The pits," she admitted. "Sutton's the only one around here who enjoys that scene. *She* actually wangled a date with Dance, as a matter of fact, but it never came off because of his accident. You know about that, don't you?"

Hope nodded, sitting down at her desk. "I read something about it,"

"Forrester hasn't given anyone else Dance's story yet, so I guess that means he's been saving it for him. But I understand Dance is on crutches. That might kind of slow him down."

Don't count on it. His injury certainly hadn't seemed to affect him much so far.

Hope, who was rapidly growing tired of this discussion on Jake, saw an unexpected opportunity to learn more about the story he was working on. Maybe Tammy could enlighten her. Jake had been obsessively closemouthed, but that didn't mean the rest of the *Observer*'s staff felt the same. "Didn't someone tell me he's working on a series of some kind? Or was he really involved in an investigation?"

"It was a six-part series that was more like an editorial, but you can bet it's an investigation now," Tammy admitted candidly. "The powers that be haven't made any formal announcements yet."

"'Powers that be' meaning John Forrester and Jake Danziger?"

"Mmm-hmm. Dance plays it pretty close to the vest; he doesn't give anything away. And that's just the way Forrester likes it, too."

"So, you think there's something else afoot?" Hope mused.

"There's always something else afoot. Come on, let's get some coffee. I'll give you the grand tour and introduce you to Berger the Bear...."

If there was one thing Jake couldn't stand, it was sympathy. That was the main reason he'd thrown the damn crutches away and moved to a cane. Still, the sight of any kind of handicap seemed to bring out the good Samaritan in everybody. A lady overloaded with a bulging briefcase had gone out of her way to hold the elevator door for him, even though she looked in danger of toppling over herself. A stooped, reed-thin elderly man had wanted to help Jake off with his coat when he saw Jake prop his shoulder against the wall to do the deed himself.

Lord, it was embarrassing! Now, working his way from the elevator to the *Observer*'s doors, the back of his neck burned from imagined stares and pitying glances.

Sighing, he thrust his way inside the newsroom. Forrester's office was to the right and Jake limped slowly toward it, wearily hoping he could make it through the door without being seen by his co-workers. The hope was a vain one, at best, since he knew, from Forrester's own lips, that the staff was literally holding its breath and waiting for him to return. He didn't flatter himself by believing they'd actually missed Jake Danziger, but he was completely aware how much gossip and speculation his getting shot had created.

Surprisingly, he made it to Forrester's door without being accosted. The glass walls brought a wry smile to his lips. Anyone walking by would see him, framed, as it were, inside the spacious confines of the managing editor's office. But he doubted anyone would approach him until he was done talking to Forrester.

Sinking into one of the squashy chairs in front of Forrester's ugly metal desk, Jake sighed deeply. There was no sign of Forrester. The room was empty. Feeling drained, he was glad of the respite, but after ten minutes of undiluted quiet, he began to wonder where everyone was.

Was that laughter he heard from the center of the newsroom, from the inner maze of cubicles that made up Kevin Berger's editorial workstation? And was that *Berger*'s laughter? Impossible!

His brows drawing into a frown, Jake looked toward the lighthearted music of a woman's answering laughter. Who...? he asked himself, even while his subconscious dredged up her name.

Hope.

Her laughter was filled with vibrancy, and for several moments Jake sat utterly silent, absorbing the intoxicating sound of it. A moment later Hope appeared, surrounded by Berger, Tammy Marshall, and several other doting idiots who seemed to hang on her every word. What in God's name was she telling them?

With a supreme effort of will, Jake pulled his eyes from the lovely young woman in the black skirt and short blue-and-black jacket and concentrated on the rather garish piece of contemporary art sitting on Forrester's credenza. A gift from his nieces, Jake remembered. But though his gaze was fixed ahead, his inner vision was full of Hope Townsend and his ears were tuned to her musical voice. For the first time in years, Jake suffered the disconcerting and somewhat amusing feeling of being completely invisible at his place of work.

"You have any questions, let me know," Kevin Berger told Hope, lifting a hand as he wound his way back through the cubicles to his desk. Had she known him better, she would have been amazed at the spring in his step. Instead, she marveled that Tammy thought him a bear at all when Berger had turned out to be a pussycat dying for some honest, personal attention. All it had taken from Hope was to show an interest in the picture of his daughter, which was sitting in an elegant little frame on his desk.

"She looks confident," Hope had observed, smiling, as she picked up the photo of a brown-haired girl astride a black pony. "How old is she? Ten?"

"Eleven," Berger had grunted.

"Is she as poised as she looks? When I was that age I was a mass of insecurities. Your daughter looks like she could take on the world."

While Tammy looked on in wonder, Kevin Berger changed his usually monosyllabic answers to long, informative sentences about his daughter, who lived in California with her mother. They chatted for nearly ten minutes and then he actually posed a question.

"How long have you been an investigative reporter?" Berger asked Hope, his normally stern features pulled into what could only be termed a smile.

Tammy sucked in her breath, signaling wildly behind Berger's head for Hope to tread carefully. Ignoring her, Hope answered blithely, "Officially? I suppose about forty-five minutes. An hour, if you count the time I stood outside the *Observer*'s front doors waiting for my stomach to settle. I'm too green to know enough to lie to you."

Then Berger laughed, and Tammy's eyes grew round with incredulity.

"I've never seen that before," Tammy said now, staring after Berger's retreating back as if she'd witnessed a miracle. *"Never!"*

Hope grinned in relief. "You had me shaking in my boots about him. I had to do something!"

"You frighten me, Townsend. You really do."

Tammy showed her to the conference room, and they ran into John Forrester, who was heading toward Berger's desk. He flashed a Hope a small smile as he walked by.

"How are you getting on?"

"Infamously," Tammy drawled.

"This is a little more grandiose than I'm used to," Hope admitted, looking around herself. "But I'm settling in."

"Good, good." He seemed distracted. "I'll hand out assignments next week," he added again.

It bothered her a little that he'd reiterated his intention to wait before giving her some work. Was that professional courtesy? Or was he regretting hiring her already?

You paranoid idiot, she berated herself as she and Tammy parted ways and Hope headed back to her desk. Jake hadn't even arrived at work yet. He hadn't had time to work on Forrester. Her boss was simply giving her a chance to find her niche.

Sitting down at her chair, Hope drew a deep breath, a sense of personal satisfaction and triumph stirring within her. She'd handled Berger the Bear, hadn't she? And Tammy was fast becoming a friend. Several of the other reporters seemed happy to make her acquaintance. So far, this first day wasn't as awful as she'd anticipated. In fact, so far it was wonderful. She was here! She'd made it! She'd proved herself tough enough, capable enough, and intelligent enough to become a full-fledged reporter at a major city newspaper.

Smiling to herself, she touched the keyboard, bringing the monitor to sudden life. It only took one button to call up the local wire, and Hope did so, reading the news and enjoying an expanding feeling of well-being.

It lasted about fifteen minutes before there was a stir by John Forrester's office. Excited voices rose above the soft roar of the newsroom. Hope glanced over her shoulder automatically, even though all she really could see were gray room dividers. Rapid footsteps approached from behind her and she swiveled around to see Tammy heading her way.

"Ready?" Tammy asked, eyes bright.

"For lunch?" Hope glanced at her watch. It was only eleven.

"Lunch later," she said. "Right now you get to meet the *Observer*'s star reporter. Dance just came out of Forrester's office. Sutton spotted him and she's got him pinned by the front doors. Normally he's pretty elusive, but it looks like he doesn't get around so fast now."

Hope had been too distracted earlier by the amount of names Tammy tossed about to focus in on "Sutton." But now she realized why that name had seemed familiar. Sutton, the woman who'd somehow captured Jake's attention and wangled a date out of him, was Regina Sutton of the society page. "Oh," she murmured. "Regina Sutton?"

Tammy laughed sympathetically. "She's not as bad as her copy. Really. I mean Regina Sutton is 'The Society Page,'" Tammy said in a voice that mocked the pretentiousness of Regina's title. "But she has her moments. Anyway, we can say hello to both Sutton and Dance, and then head downtown to the Ribtickler."

Hope's sense of well-being fled in a rush. She didn't want to have to face Jake yet. Searching desperately for some way to put off the inevitable, she sat in silence for several moments—enough time for Tammy to frown at her in bewilderment.

"Something wrong?"

"Um, no. Just let me get my purse," she said when she could think of no way out.

Hope followed after Tammy, self-consciously tugging on the hem of her bolero-length black and royal-blue jacket. Was she too dressed up? Tammy was in a pair of soft gray cords and cotton tank complemented by a knee-length red cardigan. Facing her first day on the job, Hope had dressed for success, but now she wished she'd worn more comfortable clothes.

It bothered her that these thoughts surfaced only after she learned she was about to face Jake.

"There's our Regina," Tammy said as they rounded the corner.

Regina Sutton did appear to have Jake pressed against the wall. He was listening to Regina with the appearance of hanging on her every word; but, as Hope well knew, appearances, where Jake was concerned, could be deceiving.

Feeling unequal to the task of meeting Jake straight on, Hope turned her attention to Regina Sutton. She was a brunette with a winning smile, an amazingly deep tan that must have cost her hours in a tanning salon, and a compact, dynamite body. Though fairly new to the *Observer*, Regina was already making a name for herself. Hope had read her column a few times. It wasn't all just fluff; in fact, sometimes it was downright interesting.

"A helluva way to take a vacation," Regina was observing with a grin as she looked Jake over from head to foot. "Couldn't you have just asked for the time off?"

"Nah. That'd be too easy," Martin Hughes observed. Hughes was as large as he was lazy, and he seemed to puff out the words from his massive chest and belly. "Dance has always had a flair for the dramatic."

"That's me, all right," Jake drawled, but Hope recognized the signs of tension beneath his easy manner. She knew him well, she thought with a start.

He looked up and met her gaze at that moment. She could see him stiffen, but he relaxed almost instantly, quirking one dark brow at her as if he found the situation mildly amusing. A neat trick, Hope thought, and determined to perfect it herself.

"Hello, Hope," he greeted her, his low, sexy voice penetrating her forced calm.

"Hello, Dance."

"How's your first day?"

As if he really cared, she thought as she studied his cool countenance. "About as I expected."

"You two know each other?" Tammy's brows lifted and the look she sent Hope was of someone who'd just discovered a traitor in her midst.

Hope opened her mouth to deny it, but Jake gave her no chance.

"Didn't she tell you?" he asked in mock innocence, never taking his gaze from Hope's flushed face.

"No," Tammy admitted, her own eyes full of accusations. She'd been honest with Hope and had not received honesty in return. Hope didn't blame her for feeling betrayed.

"We—er—both grew up in Roche Harbor," Hope explained uncomfortably.

"Well..." Tammy's brows lifted.

"So, you went to school together?" Regina Sutton asked casually.

"Actually, we lived right next to each other," Jake put in helpfully. "In fact, we saw each other just last week over Christmas." The smile he sent Hope was beatific. She wanted to kill him! "Hope spent the night at my house taking care of me. She's quite the little Florence Nightingale."

"Really?" A chilly smile touched the corners of Regina's lips.

Hope met Jake's mocking blue eyes. So he was determined to make things difficult for her. Well, fine. She could give as good as she got. "That's right," she said, smiling indulgently at Jake. "His mother asked me to look in on him. Poor Dance. He really is a terrible patient, and then when he fell down the stairs and reopened his wound, I thought I was going to have to drive him back to the hospital. Luckily, all we had to do was put on a new dressing."

"Luckily," Tammy murmured, gazing with fascination at Jake. She had never heard anyone talk about the *Observer*'s number-one reporter in such a fashion.

Jake had gone ultraquiet, but his eyes glittered dangerously. "Let's hope you're a better reporter than you are a nursemaid."

Hope flushed. Drawing on her flagging professionalism, she said quietly, "I am."

Tammy, Regina and Martin Hughes all looked at one another, then at Hope and Jake. Before anyone could comment, Forrester's voice boomed across the newsroom.

"Dance!" he bellowed, motioning toward his open office door. "Get on in here!"

Jake left without another word, leaning heavily on his cane. Hope turned blindly toward the outer doors. At her elbow, Tammy said in a voice so quiet it was nearly inaudible, "You're going to have to tell me the real story between you and Dance, or I won't like you anymore."

"It's not that interesting a story."

"Let me be the judge." Tammy punched the button for the elevator, her eyes alive with curiosity. She waved a finger in front of Hope's nose. "You held out on me. Now you pay the price."

"Buy me lunch at the Ribtickler and I'll hit the highlights." Hope sighed.

"Hah! Nothing doing unless this is an in-depth interview."

Hope smiled wanly. "It's a messy story."

"Oh, good."

"And it's boring, and trite, and without any meaning whatsoever. And I'll only tell you the highlights, no matter what you say or do," she warned.

Tammy grinned. "Okay, okay. Just the highlights. Every juicy, dirty, low-down gossipy highlight you can think of!"

Jake scrunched down into the leather chair in front of John Forrester's desk. He was coldly angry—at Forrester, at the office staff, at himself, but mostly at Hope. When had she become such an unbending bitch? It infuriated and horrified him to see she'd turned out just like Regina Sutton—unflappable, superior, brittle, and with blood cold enough to create ice floes.

Jake was so immersed in his anger, he completely ignored the fact that he'd been the one to attack first. Innocent, naive Hope had looked down her pert little nose, measured him with those frigid green eyes and, with just the right tone of mockery to rub his nerves raw, had delivered a speech calculated to embarrass and humiliate him. If he'd cared about losing face, as he once had, he'd have been burning for revenge right now. Instead, he was seething with fury. She was so hell-bent on being tough that the Hope he'd once known was gone. Dead and buried.

Except she'd looked frightened to death when he'd fallen down the steps and reopened his wound, and the taste of her had been warm and inviting and full of promise, the feel of her in his arms so intense it could have been pain.

"Have you heard a word I've said?" Forrester demanded. "Dance, you worthless bag of feed. Pay attention!"

With an effort, Jake dragged his mind away from Hope. Forrester was looking peeved. "Worthless bag of feed?" he repeated.

"Where on God's green earth have you been? Didn't you hear what I said about Farrell?"

Jake sighed. "You said Farrell's been calling for me."

"That's right. Every day for the past week. The man's got something to say and he only wants to say it to you."

"Probably wants to thank me for getting in the way of his bullet."

"He thanked you at the hospital." Forrester's gaze bored into Jake's. "Maybe he's coming around to your way of thinking."

Jake shifted in the chair, damning his own big mouth. He'd told Forrester his suspicions right after the shooting. Now, however, he wished he'd kept his theories to himself. Everyone had believed the bullet was meant for Farrell, and why not? Farrell was the Drug Enforcement Administration man; the only real threat. Jake Danziger, investigative reporter, hadn't even been on the case at the time of the shooting. There was absolutely *no reason* anyone would want to see him dead.

And yet . . .

"I don't know anything that would get me killed," he said. "I was meeting Farrell for an overview story— the kind of thing we could discuss in generalities. I wasn't asking him to name names."

Forrester nodded.

"Farrell's been DEA for years," Jake continued. "He knows tons of incidents and specifics that could make some people very, very nervous, but that wasn't why we were meeting.''

"Maybe your would-be assassin didn't know that."

"Maybe." Jake grimaced. "But it still doesn't make sense. Coming after me, a reporter, is really stirring up the hornet's nest, wouldn't you say? The hue and cry just from this bullet wound is enough to make any self-respecting drug lord shake in his boots."

"Well, maybe this particular drug lord considered you a potential threat. You don't happen to know who it is, do you?" Forrester asked hopefully.

"Sorry. I didn't get that far with Farrell."

Forrester's chair squeaked as he got to his feet and paced to the window, staring out at the rain-drenched Seattle streets. "I trust your instincts, Dance. Whatever you decide generally tends to be the way it is. You convinced me at the hospital that that bullet was meant for you." He shot Jake a look from beneath bushy gray brows. "You're very convincing. But if you really believe you were wrong, then okay."

Jake didn't answer. He wanted to handle this investigation his way, and he knew damn well that if he confided in Forrester, someone else would be assigned to help him—either Hughes or—God forbid!—Hope.

"I'll call Farrell this afternoon," he told Forrester.

"Good." Forrester held open the office door. "How's the leg doing?"

"It'll be okay."

"I know you're not going to like it, but..." Forrester began.

Jake had been aiming his cane out the door, but Forrester's tone stopped him. He waited.

"I've hired a new junior investigative reporter—"

"Hope Townsend," Jake interrupted. "I know."

"She's pretty good at what she does. Has a nice, crisp writing style and unusual empathy. Plus she's factual without being boring. And—"

"Is there some reason you're telling me this?" Jake again interrupted impatiently.

John Forrester was rarely surprised by anything, but Jake's sharp question caused his lips to part in amazement. "I was going to ask you to take her under your wing and help her out."

"I'm nobody's baby-sitter," he said coolly.

"I know that, Dance. But I want to keep this girl. She's good. And because she came from that know-nothing paper, the *Breeze*, she's dirt cheap. Right now she's happy to be here because she thinks I gave her her big break. As soon as she starts work, that myth'll go the way of the dinosaur. Then I'm going to have to *convince* her to stay. That's where you come in."

"Keep me out of it," Jake snapped.

"You've got a terrific reputation, some of it earned, some of it fostered by your godawful attitude. I'm betting Hope Townsend will want to stay because of you, because she hopes some of your glory will rub off on her."

Jake stared in open astonishment at John Forrester. Rarely did the man miss the beat so completely. "You don't know a damn thing about Hope Townsend!"

"And you do?"

"Damn right!" Jake growled. "And if you want her so badly, you'd better make a choice between her and me."

"*What!*"

"Because we don't get along. I have no intention of letting her be a tagalong. You want to keep her? Give her a column, just like Regina's. She'll eat it up. But whatever you do, don't try to sweeten the pot by bringing up my name. She'll chew you up and spit you out. That's how much she thinks of Jake Danziger's professional reputation."

Forrester suddenly threw back his head and laughed heartily. It was so out of character that Jake's eyes narrowed suspiciously.

"By God, Dance," he said, wiping the tears from the corners of his eyes. "I didn't believe it when I heard the two of you going at it tooth and nail in the newsroom. Finally, some woman has gotten to you. I was afraid it would never happen again!"

Forrester's oblique reference to Diana made Jake's voice more somber than usual. "I've known Hope a long time. Since she was a kid, in fact. I don't like what she's become."

Forrester smiled an "Oh, really?" smile. It irked Jake, but there was nothing he could do about it. Then Forrester's smile faded and he continued in a soft, serious voice, "Diana's been gone a long time. It's time you slowed down and took less chances. It won't help bring her back, y'know."

"Diana and I were friends, that's all. In case you've forgotten, she was married."

"But in love with you," Forrester said, admitting something that neither of them had ever discussed before.

Jake felt his breath trapped in his lungs. Unwillingly, he recalled Diana in perfect detail: tall, tan, fearless, and grimly determined. She'd been as eager as he to expose the world of crime to an unforgiving public. She'd doggedly tracked members of organized crime, unscrupulous political figures, flamboyant rip-off artists, and even the occasional penny-ante crook. He and Diana had been an unbeatable team.

He felt Forrester's hand on his shoulder, and he dimly recognized the expression of friendship and regret; Forrester felt terrible about raking up the whole thing. For his part, Jake could hardly think of that time without breaking out in goose bumps. To make matters worse, he'd gotten an award for excellence the following week for a story he and Diana had worked on together. He'd even received a special commendation from the mayor.

Those awards were now buried in a cardboard box shoved to the back of his closet. He'd buried thoughts of Diana even more deeply.

"I don't want any woman fouling up my investigation," he said flatly, referring to Hope.

"Now, Dance. You never were a chauvinist before."

"I'm thinking of becoming one. It'll keep my life simple and clean."

"No, it won't. Life is messy. And Hope Townsend is a good reporter. Stop thinking of her like Diana and you'll be a lot happier." He smiled again, the cagey old fox. "She's single, and if you haven't scared her off completely, one really nice-looking lady."

Jake turned abruptly, banging his shin with his cane for his efforts. Forrester thought he knew everything about Jake's feelings, but he didn't. He didn't understand about Hope at all. And Jake intended to keep it that way.

Chapter Seven

It was no surprise that the Ribtickler specialized in ribs. Beef ribs, pork ribs, and baby backs were teamed with corn bread and beans. Hope scanned the menu and breathed a sigh of relief when she discovered they also served salads. Her stomach was in knots—courtesy, once again, of Jake Danziger—and she didn't want anything heavy. Tammy, however, had no such compunction. She ordered pork baby backs with the works.

"Okay, Townsend. Tell me about Dance."

"Don't you have to do your interview first?" Hope asked, glancing meaningfully in the direction of the barrel-chested restaurateur, Brian Barron, to whom Tammy had already introduced her.

"Nope. Brian's lawyer is in a meeting with Tickle My Ribs's owner's lawyer as we speak. I'll have to wait and hear the outcome later. It's all a big mess, but a great comic story.''

''Who's suing whom?'' asked Hope.

''Tickle My Ribs was here in Washington first, but the Ribtickler's a chain, started years ago, and they feel they should be able to open in Seattle with their name.''

''Mmm. A ticklish situation,'' Hope murmured.

''Hah, hah. Very funny. Tickle My Ribs doesn't see things the same way the Ribtickler does. I've got this great tongue-in-cheek story going. This'll be my third and final installment. I'm betting on Tickle My Ribs. They're local, family owned, and they've really got better food. But I like Brian, so I'm kind of hoping for him. So, now, on to Dance...''

Hope had a moment of reprieve when the waiter appeared, but Tammy refused to be derailed. Shaking her head, Hope said, ''Okay, what do you want to know?''

''You grew up together in Roche Harbor?''

''Right next to each other. Jake was really closer to my older sisters.''

''You call him Jake?'' That surprised her.

''I used to,'' she amended. ''He's Dance now, but I haven't quite got the knack of it yet.'' She took a sip of water. ''I will, though,'' she added—more for her own benefit than Tammy's.

''How close were you?''

Now here was dangerous territory. ''Not all that close growing up.''

''There seems to be some animosity between you two.''

''Purely professional,'' Hope managed to make the lie sound like truth. ''He doesn't like me treading in his field," she added more honestly. "He doesn't think I can cut it."

"Are we talking about the same guy here? Dance isn't judgmental. He's a great one for believing in 'Live and let live.'"

"News to me." Hope attacked her salad with vigor.

"He's been very supportive of me."

"Maybe he likes you," she muttered, then winced at the hard edge in her voice. She hoped Tammy didn't misconstrue that as jealousy.

Tammy was silent for a while, negotiating the tricky hazards of eating pork ribs without ruining her clothes. Toward the end of the meal, she said thoughtfully, "He really came unglued when you made that comment about his mother asking you to take care of him."

"I didn't notice anything."

Tammy's laugh was full of reproach. "Oh, come on. The look he sent you could have cut through steel. He hates it when anyone starts talking about his personal life. No one dares."

"Really?" Hope was scornful. "Maybe it's time someone took him down a peg or two. He's just one man and he's not as perfect as you all seem to think."

"Really?" Tammy matched Hope's tone, her lips twitching with amusement. "That sounds suspiciously like someone who's had firsthand experience in a most intimate way. But I won't ask," she went on, smiling hugely when Hope flung her a dark look. "No one can accuse Tammy Marshall of not having tact. Someday, when you're feeling—" she searched around for the right word "—*stronger* about Dance, then you'll tell me."

"Don't count on it," was Hope's grumbling reply.

* * *

Jake sat at his computer monitor, trying to find a way in which he could bend his leg without major discomfort. His work space was in the corner behind one of the partitions. No longer did he have his own office—a personal choice—and though sometimes he resented the intrusiveness of his fellow workers, the idea of working in a closed space with a glass wall dividing him from everyone else was more than he could bear. He'd done it once. That was enough.

Picking up the receiver, he called the number John Forrester had given him for Bill Farrell. It was Farrell's home number, as it turned out, and after Jake left a message on the man's answering machine, he called the DEA office where Farrell worked.

To Jake's amazement, Farrell was in, and within seconds Bill's booming voice came on the line.

"Bill, Jake Danziger here."

"Dance!" Bill burst out, as if he were intensely relieved to hear from him. "My God, son. How are you?"

"Alive and nearly kicking," Jake replied sardonically.

"The last time I saw you, you looked bad. White as those hospital sheets and sure the whole damned underworld was after you."

Jake winced at his loose tongue. Yet, if he wanted information from Bill, he was going to have to trust the man a little. "I'm still wondering what happened that night," he said.

"So you think that sniper wanted you, hmm?"

"Yes." Jake was blunt.

There was a momentary pause, as if Farrell were weighing his words. Jake's attention sharpened, even before he heard the underlying nervousness in Farrell's next request.

"I want to talk to you—alone. Just like we planned before."

"About the series?"

"Among other things."

"When?" Jake stared unseeingly out the window. His mind flew back to the night of the shooting and he could almost smell the dust and diesel of the warehouse.

"Tonight. And let's meet somewhere open, son," Farrell added, his thoughts obviously running along the same lines as Jake's. "Meet me at Key Largo around four."

Key Largo was a tiny bar about halfway between the Tarkette Building and the DEA office. It wasn't nearly as idyllic as its name implied, and was more a hole-in-the-wall than a hot night spot.

"I'll be there," Jake said.

As he hung up he felt a prickling at the back of his neck. A vaguely familiar feminine perfume reached his nostrils and he swung around. Hope was standing there, watching him, her blond hair swinging softly against her shoulders, her expression closed and cautious.

"Well?" he demanded, irritated.

"I know you didn't want me to work for your paper, but since I am, I'd like to make the situation easier for both of us."

He quirked a brow. "And how do you propose to do that?"

She wrinkled her nose in a truly enticing way. "If we overreact every time we see each other, people are going to ask questions. I've already suffered through the third degree from Tammy over lunch.''

He searched her face, so pale and set. "What did you tell her?" he asked in spite of himself.

"Not a lot," Hope admitted. "She knows I'm holding out on her, but she was too polite to delve deeper."

Jake snorted. "Marshall's not polite. You must have somehow convinced her you weren't going to talk. Otherwise she'd be after you like a barracuda." A reluctant note of admiration crept into his voice and Jake frowned when he heard it.

"I hardly know what to say," she admitted with refreshing candor.

"You could tell her I seduced you and you've hated me for it ever since."

Her fine blond brows snapped together. "I could tell her a lot of half lies if I felt like it," she agreed coolly. "But since my job is reporting the truth, I'd like to start at home, so to speak."

"Is that what you think your job is? Reporting the truth? Listen, Hope," Jake said, becoming serious, "we've both chosen a profession that requires us to make choices. Sometimes, sitting on the truth is safer than telling it. Sometimes it's *smarter* than telling it. If you haven't learned that yet, you're in trouble."

"I'm rather practiced in the art of subtlety, when I have to be," she answered in a voice that dripped ice. "You don't need to lecture me. And as far as our past is concerned, you were the one who blurted out that tantalizing bit of gossip."

Since that was patently true, Jake couldn't argue. He was, in fact, still wondering what had possessed him to make an issue out of his association with Hope.

Irritated, he changed to another topic, deliberately introducing one that was equally sensitive and therefore guaranteed to change the direction of her thoughts. "I've been thinking about the night you spent at my house," he said slowly.

She was instantly tense. "What about it?"

"I was thinking about how you felt in my arms." He slid her a look from veiled eyes. "How you felt lying atop me..."

Her only reaction was a deepening of those brilliant eyes, a flash of panic in their emerald depths. Good, he thought triumphantly. He'd been racking his brain, trying to work out a way to deal with her, and had just about exhausted his entire arsenal. Maybe he could send her running with a bit of sexual pressure. As long as it didn't backfire, he reminded himself quickly.

"Is there a point to this?" she asked crisply.

"I wondered if there was a chance for a repeat performance."

Embarrassment painted her cheeks a becoming pink. "What do you really want, Jake?"

"Jake?" he repeated, annoyed with himself for loving the sound of his name on her lips.

"Dance," she snapped. "If you think sexual harassment will get me to quit, think again. Try anything you like, but I'm staying!"

Her lips tightened, but even so they were lusciously soft and wide. Jake stared at her mouth and felt the rigid wall he'd erected around his feelings crumble just a tiny bit more. He wanted her, he realized with a jolt. And it was going to be hell keeping his hands off her, despite the fact that she couldn't seem to stand him. After all, she hadn't really resisted that last kiss.

" . . . All I wanted to know was if you cared to present some kind of image to our co-workers," Hope continued tersely. "I should have known Jake Danziger doesn't give a damn what people think. I've wasted my time talking to you."

She turned sharply and headed down the hall, the black jersey of her skirt clinging seductively to her derriere. Jake dragged his gaze back to his computer monitor, haunted by the scent of that soft, airy perfume.

"The hell with her," he muttered, grabbing for his cane. It was hours until he had to meet Farrell, but he was in sudden and dire need of a drink.

One week later Hope, who was rapidly growing accustomed to her new job, picked up a cup of coffee and strolled to Tammy's workstation. She'd been Tammy's shadow, and although she was happy that she'd gotten to know Tammy and it was fun helping on her stories, writing that Tickle My Ribs had been allowed to keep their name was hardly high-risk reporting. She longed for something more—something like what Jake worked on—but so far, Forrester seemed to have forgotten she existed.

Jake, too, looked right through her whenever he chanced to run into her—a far cry from his rather loaded comments her first day of work. Of course, Jake was hardly around anyway, so there hadn't been time for him to work up any new methods to disconcert her, she supposed.

And disconcert her he had. That comment about lying atop him, delivered in his sexy, deep baritone, had made her stomach twist and her pulse jump. He'd done it deliberately, she was certain, but it hadn't minimized its effect. On the contrary, his words had run across her mind over and over again in the past week until she was furious with herself. And she was alarmed that what she'd convinced herself was a mild and controllable attraction might be something far worse.

Could you really *want* someone as she apparently wanted Jake, without being in love with him? Other people seemed to have no problem with this particular dilemma, but Hope had always felt she was immune to basic physical attraction—even knowing the way she reacted to Jake. She'd been amused by other women who'd confessed to panting after some gorgeous, well-developed hunk. She, Hope Townsend, had too much self-control for that; Jake had taught her well.

So how in heaven's name could she actually entertain thoughts of *the man who'd taught her that painful lesson*? She was just plain lucky he wasn't around the office much, or God knew what innovative trick he could play on her and whether she could withstand it and still hold on to the tattered remains of her pride.

"Townsend?" John Forrester's voice questioned.

Hope, who'd stopped just before reaching Tammy's workstation, her brow furrowed in concentration, jumped at the sound of his voice. "Yes?"

"Come into my office. There's something I'd like to talk over with you."

Her stomach plummeted. His tone wasn't encouraging. Had Jake followed through with his threat to get her fired, after all? She'd almost forgotten about that during her busy week. She'd actually believed Jake had changed tactics and was bent on removing her through more subtle means. But now, following

Forrester into his sparsely decorated office, she felt her confidence sag, sure that Jake was behind the managing editor's somber tone.

"Sit down," Forrester invited, indicating a chair. As Hope sank into the leather cushions, he strolled to the window, gazing out at the traffic pensively. "I told you I'd start handing out assignments this week. I'm sure you know that since Dance has been back I've let him take all the urgent stories."

Hope nodded. On the computer terminal, when anything of importance had happened around the city, a beep sounded and you could press a button and pull the information onto your screen. If it sounded like a story worth covering, the reporter charged for the door. Hope had been forced to tamp down her desire to follow up on several stories because Jake, and Martin Hughes—when he was motivated to actually *move*—were the only ones Forrester wanted going after those leads.

But now, watching Forrester, Hope's heart lifted a little. He was going to move her into the ranks of Jake and Hughes; she could sense it.

"Dance is involved in a rather detailed assignment right now," he went on. "So I'm moving you up. You and Hughes can pick up anything that comes over the wire."

"Thank you," Hope said, then colored a bit as she realized how breathless and eager she sounded.

He glanced her way and smiled for the first time, though his forehead was lined with worry. "I've also got something else for you."

"Oh?" Hope gazed at him expectantly.

"Before he was shot, Dance was working on a six-part series concerning Seattle's drug scene. It's an overview, actually. Mainly interviews with police, DEA men, a couple of known dealers who're serving prison terms, and one or two people whose lives have been completely ruined from years of substance abuse. Dance has got most of the stuff in notes already. All you have to do is pick up where he left off and finish it. The second installment should be in next Sunday's edition, if you can make it.''

"You want me to take over Dance's assignment?'' Hope questioned carefully, certain she'd heard wrong. She was both awestruck by Forrester's faith in her and coldly nervous about Jake's reaction. He would *never* want her to finish what he'd started, no matter what it was.

"Like I said, he's working on something else. He just needs someone to tidy up after him on this, if you don't mind being Dance's backup, so to speak,'' he added politely, giving her an avenue of escape as he sat down behind his desk.

Hope wasn't about to turn down her first assignment just because Jake had been the primary investigator. She might be foolish where Jake was concerned, but she wasn't *that* foolish. Wondering what Jake's current assignment was, she let her gaze rove over Forrester's careworn face, sensing instinctively that if the managing editor had wanted her to know, he would have told her already. "I don't mind,'' she said.

"Good. Then you can start today.'' The decision made, he handed her several files from his desk and told her to search out Jake if, and when, she had further questions.

Slightly bemused, Hope tucked the files under her arm and turned to the door, then stopped short as if her feet had been nailed to the floor. Jake was standing on the opposite side of the door. Pushing against the panel, he ducked his head inside and said tersely to Forrester, "Call me at home if you need me. I'm out of here until further notice."

Hope offered an inward prayer of thanks that he hadn't overheard.

"Dance..." Forrester stalled him, glancing at Hope with a thoughtful look. "Hope'll be taking over the series you were working on."

The silence was total and full of tense expectation. Hope forced herself to meet Jake's eyes, then was puzzled and alarmed at his sudden loss of color.

Jake recovered himself quickly. *"The story on the drug scene?"*

Forrester nodded. "It's more a cleanup now. She can finish for you."

Jake's dark head swiveled around so he could stare at Hope. He assessed her so thoroughly that she felt her knees quiver a bit in spite of herself. Then, as if he'd dropped the matter from his mind, he said in a casual tone to her, "Don't do a half-baked job."

"I have no intention of it," she answered through her teeth.

"You got a minute?" Jake asked Forrester, ignoring her rising temper completely.

Forrester motioned him inside and only when he was completely out of the doorway did Hope get her legs in motion enough to stalk out of the room, eyes flashing with indignation, chin held high.

Forrester's gaze followed her and he shook his head dolefully from side to side. "For a man who usually treats women with respect, you sure know how to fall off the wagon."

"What the hell do you mean by putting her on that story?" Jake raged. "That's my story and I want her off it."

"Didn't you just tell me you're working on a new angle with Bill Farrell?" Forrester's brows lifted. "If memory serves, you *asked* to have time for this, and only this one investigation."

"I've changed my mind," Jake said shortly. "I'll finish the series."

Forrester steepled his fingers under his chin. "Tell me about Farrell."

Jake—who'd limped from one end of Forrester's office to the other, feeling the older man's thoughtful gaze upon him the entire time—now stopped short, forcing himself to a cold calm. "I don't know more than I told you last week. When I met him at Key Largo, he told me his suspicions about Jarvis, and that's where we stand."

Raleigh Jarvis was a known crime boss who'd recently relocated to Seattle. Though the DEA and other law-enforcement agencies were certain he was connected to a powerful Colombian drug cartel, and that he was systematically shipping raw cocaine to the Seattle area, nothing had been proven. Farrell, who'd been on Jarvis's trail for months, had apparently gotten too close and been marked for murder. The night Jake had been shot, the target had been Farrell. Now Farrell was certain his days were numbered unless Jake, and the *Observer*, intervened. Since his cover was blown anyway, he wanted the story public enough to ensnare Jarvis and make it impossible for him to kill Farrell without a huge public outcry and a tremendously in-depth investigation.

At least, that's what Farrell had told Jake. There was no reason for Jake to disbelieve the man, either, except that Raleigh Jarvis was not the type of man to send such an inept sniper as the one who'd mistaken Jake for Farrell, and Jake had said as much to Farrell the night they'd met at Key Largo.

"Well, now, I know you think differently, but it was dark and they just thought you were me," Farrell had said. "Besides, does it really matter? If the department hadn't shown up when it did, we'd both be dead, because Jarvis doesn't leave witnesses, son. You know that."

"He wasn't far enough away to mistake me," Jake insisted. "And they'd try to kill you first in any case, because you'd be more likely to be armed."

"Well, now, that's right, but you were in the line of fire first, not me. I think it was a matter of expediency."

Jake hadn't argued after that. What was the point? Instead, he made the only decision he was capable of, considering what he wanted. "How close are you to catching Jarvis?" he asked.

"Not close enough," Farrell answered on a sigh. "But getting closer."

"Let me help you get him."

"No. No, son." Farrell shook his head gravely, but Jake persisted, and he wasn't above using a subtle form of extortion.

"You owe me," Jake told the older man with a wry smile, leaning heavily on his cane. "I've got a scar forming on my leg the size of Alaska, and it's all because of you."

"Now, Dance..."

"You've helped me before, and I've helped you. Give me a chance. I won't let this thing blow up in your face. It'll be on the front page *after* Jarvis is in custody."

He'd had to argue with the bullheaded Farrell for over an hour, but finally the DEA man had reluctantly consented. Now Farrell was Jake's direct pipeline from the DEA, especially as it concerned Raleigh Jarvis.

Jake had then sketchily outlined the whole plan to John Forrester who'd long ago given the nod to anything Jake wanted to do. They were more partners than boss and employee; Jake in fact, had been asked by the "powers that be" to take over Forrester's position when the older man retired, which was rumored by everyone to be imminent. But on the issue of Raleigh Jarvis, Forrester had been less enthusiastic than Jake.

"You've got a bum leg," the managing editor had pointed out with perfect logic. "And Farrell'll make you hit the ground running on this one."

"I can handle myself," Jake had answered determinedly.

Now Forrester stared at him, concern deepening his voice as he asked, "When are you meeting Farrell again?"

"Tonight. Maybe later on in the week. That's why I want the flexibility."

"But you don't want Hope on the series?"

"Hell, no! That's how I got shot in the first place!"

Forrester barked out a hearty laugh, his eyes filling with sheer amusement. "You're not her keeper, Dance, as I'm sure she'd tell you if she were in the room. I just asked her to type up your notes. She's not going head-to-head with Raleigh Jarvis.''

Jake was being irrational and he knew it, yet it took a supreme effort of willpower not to argue his point home. Forrester was right. Hope would be safe from harm finishing this story. It was thinking of the next assignment, or maybe the one after that, or the one after that, that caused his heart to constrict. It was the assignment he would be powerless to stop her from taking, the one that might seem innocent on the surface and then turn out to be as lethal as a bomb in a brown paper box.

''Go ahead and let her finish it,'' he ground out angrily, then strode purposefully out of the managing editor's office. Unfortunately, his escape wasn't quite quick enough. Forrester's amused chuckle floated to his ears and seemed to linger long after Jake was back at his desk and immersed in his work.

Chapter Eight

Hope's apartment was small and overlooked a minuscule courtyard that boasted one maple tree and a rather ragged row of junipers. It was far from grand, but it was utilitarian; and when she'd taken the job at the *Observer*, she had only wanted to move closer to her place of work. She could always move again.

Shifting still-unpacked boxes from the small round table that served as both her dining-room table and desk, she belatedly wished she had just a tad more space. Though the apartment had one bedroom, it wasn't much larger than a studio. Hope had refused to break into the money her parents had given her upon graduation—the same gift they'd given both Katy and Sharon upon their respective graduations—just to rent a more luxurious apartment. It was for the future, for a time when something special was needed: a down payment on a house, a new car, or maybe a wedding....

Grimacing, Hope swallowed the last of her coffee and opened the folder of Jake's notes. The file was thin and she suspected there was a lot more information, either still in Jake's possession or simply left unwritten. If she were a truly dedicated reporter, she would interview Jake, but the thought was so daunting she set it aside for the moment.

His first article, the one that had run the week before the shooting, lay atop the pile of papers. Hope read it and was reluctantly impressed with his sharp, concise style. It was an introductory piece that set the stage for subsequent articles. It also began the tale of one Barbara Thomas, whose spiraling nosedive from middle-class housewife and mother to drug addict was nothing short of horrific.

The second article was to be a continuation of the first. Glancing through pages of notes scrawled in Jake's nearly illegible handwriting, Hope read interviews with friends of Barbara's and other people she'd contacted in the course of her decline. Through them, she'd learned what she'd already guessed: Barbara had eventually died from an overdose. Jake had written the time and place at the end of a page along with a cryptic note: "Check Plegman story."

Hope worked for three hours, outlining the five stories to be written from Jake's notes. One area distinctly incomplete, though touched upon in Jake's first article, was how law-enforcement agencies were handling the problem.

"Bill Farrell," Hope mused aloud, the DEA man who'd escaped a gunshot wound because Jake had been with him that night. Tomorrow she would go through the *Observer*'s three-week-old stories on Jake's accident, gather the facts on Farrell, then ask John Forrester a little about the man before she approached Jake.

Thursday morning, Jake woke up with a headache and a mouth so dry it felt as if someone had cleaned it out with a cotton swab and left the damn thing inside. Wincing, he remembered his meeting with Farrell last night, his subsequent phone call to Forrester, and the amount of liquor he'd consumed afterward. The argument with Forrester had really steamed him. Slamming down the receiver, he'd sat at his desk in a kind of controlled fury and written some of the worst journalism of his life while he drank himself into near oblivion.

Glancing at his bedside clock, he groaned. It was five-thirty and he didn't want to get up. But Hope, curse her industrious little hide, had forced him into this miserable state and course of action. With an effort he hauled himself out of bed, limping only slightly now as he made his way to the shower.

The wound on his thigh was purple, but the swelling had gone down considerably, Jake thought with no real interest as he glanced down at the jagged scar. Needles of water pounded into his back, then he stuck his head under the shower head, gritting his teeth. What time had he called Forrester last night? One o'clock? No wonder the guy had been such a grouch. Jake had been forced to exert undue pressure to get what he wanted, and now Forrester was furious and Jake was irritated and even more determined on his course of action.

Hope had called Bill Farrell. Called him for an interview! She'd taken on this series as if she were bent on winning a Pulitzer, and she'd made Bill Farrell so nervous that Jake had spent the better part of two days calming the man down.

Jake wanted to wring her pretty little neck, and he'd said so, rather violently, to Forrester last night on the telephone. Forrester, however, seemed more interested in making certain Jake knew what time it was rather than acting on his suggestion to fire Hope immediately. In the end they'd compromised: Forrester was taking Hope off the series temporarily, but he wanted Jake and Hope to work *together* instead of against each other.

Jake's colorful answer had only further angered Forrester, who'd then promptly hung up on him. It had taken a supreme effort of will on Jake's part not to rip the phone out of the wall and throw it across the room.

Instead, he'd reached for the Scotch and spent the better part of the evening making certain he would suffer a hangover this morning.

Twenty minutes later, Jake felt marginally better as he drove to work, his mind on traffic, not Hope. But as soon as he'd parked in his designated spot beneath the Tarkette Building, his black mood returned. He would wait for her to breeze in this morning and then he was going to set her down, hard.

To his utter disbelief and renewed fury, Hope was the first person he saw when he entered the city room. She was straight ahead, near the west windows, pouring herself a cup of coffee from the coffee machine. She looked fresh and alive, and a thoughtful frown was creasing her brow as if she were deep into a story and had been for hours.

"What the hell are you doing here so early?" he demanded, striding toward her.

Hope straightened abruptly, glancing at him in surprise. "You're not limping," she observed.

His thigh throbbed from the effort but Jake wasn't about to tell her that. "Don't tell me. Let me guess. You're writing up your interview with Bill Farrell."

"I didn't get an interview with Farrell," Hope answered slowly, staring at him. "He wouldn't give me one. He told me to talk to you."

"Which you didn't do," Jake pointed out, speaking through his teeth.

"Not yet. I haven't had time yet."

"Why didn't you ask me about him first, hmm? Why didn't you just *ask*—instead of calling him up?"

Hope's eyes searched his as if she thought he'd lost his mind. "I don't see that it mattered who talked to him first."

"Don't you? Well, then, let me open your eyes."

To Hope's amazement, Jake grabbed her arm and propelled her toward his workstation so quickly that she had to juggle her coffee cup to keep it from spilling. She was so infuriated by the time he let her go, she was sputtering.

"Who the hell do you think you are?" she asked in total outrage. "For God's sake, Jake, you really *are* the worst kind of male!"

"Now, listen to me," he said flatly, ignoring her flushed, angry face. "I'm working on a story with Farrell. I'm having to drag information out of him. When you called him up and started asking questions he got nervous. Nervous enough to phone me last night and accuse me of shooting off my mouth about some rather sensitive issues.''

Hope's rage calmed to a simmer as she realized her blunder. "What kind of story are you working on?"

"It's about the shooting," he answered tersely.

"Does he think the bullet was meant for him, or you?"

"He thinks it was meant for him." Jake's tone was flat, discouraging more questions, but Hope hadn't learned to be an investigative reporter by being timid.

"So, who was behind it?" she asked.

"This isn't your story," Jake pointed out with unerring logic. "So stay out of it. Completely out of it."

"All right," she conceded. "But in that case I have a few questions for you. Bill Farrell's with the DEA, and that must mean he's been treading on some toes if someone's trying to gun him down, right?"

"Now there's intelligent reasoning for you." Jake was sarcastic. "Don't you hear, Hope? I said, *stay out of it!*"

"I have a story to finish, too, in case you've forgotten," she shot back.

"Not anymore."

Hope hesitated. "What do you mean?"

Jake's blue eyes were hooded. "I mean, you're off the assignment. I'm going to finish it while I'm doing this other story. Forrester's got something else for you."

Speechless, Hope stared at him. "Did you have me removed from that story?" she demanded in a shaking voice.

"Talk to Forrester."

Too hurt and humiliated to speak further, Hope turned on her heel. She half expected Jake to try to stop her, but he didn't. All the way back to her work space she stoked her own fury, knowing she would need it for artillery when she faced Forrester herself, but all she could work up was a sense of defeat and desolation. Jake had her boxed in on every side; and the sooner she faced that, the better off she'd be.

Forrester didn't make an appearance until after ten o'clock. As soon as his office door closed behind him, Hope beelined across the newsroom. He'd barely had time to pick up his coffee cup when she burst into his office. Something in his gaze flickered and she knew then, she *knew*, that Jake had definitely called her off the case and that Forrester had agreed.

"Dance tells me I have a new assignment," she said woodenly, seating herself on the edge of the chair, her expression tight and controlled.

"I hope he told you why," Forrester answered on a sigh after several moments of thoughtful silence.

"He implied that he wanted the assignment himself."

Forrester frowned at his cup, running his thumb over the rim. Hope had the impression he was stalling. "I got a call from a Seattle school-board member who suspects there's been a misappropriation of school funds. I called Tom Wilkes, the superintendent of schools, and he assures me there's nothing wrong. He's got all the necessary proof. I want you to interview him and see if you believe him."

"Are you saying the reason I've been reassigned has nothing to do with Dance?"

Forrester was noncommittal. "I'm aware that you and Dance have some—er—personality conflicts. I also want you on this story."

Hope lifted her brows. Though he didn't say it, she could hear the added thought: *I don't want you working together on the same story.* She felt a flush creep up her neck. The entire newsroom knew she and Jake shared some kind of history that had created this animosity between them. It was embarrassing and totally unprofessional and she knew she had to put an end to all the speculation.

With as much grace as she could muster, she announced, "I'd be happy to work on the school-board story."

Forrester almost smiled. "Good. I'll tell Dance."

"No. I'll tell him. Our communication isn't the greatest, and I want to get past all that and get to work."

She was gratified by the pleased expression on Forrester's face as she left his office. It would make the upcoming interview with Jake almost bearable.

"I've been taking things too personally," Hope said in a cool, flat tone, "but from now on I'll be professional. If I have a question about something you've worked on, I'll come to you first. After that, I can do research wherever necessary. The rest of the six-part series is yours again," she added, in case there was any question. "I'm interviewing the superintendent of schools on a suspected misappropriation of school funds."

Jake was lounging in his chair, eyeing her suspiciously, his arms folded over his chest. He waited patiently while Hope talked—so patiently, in fact, that she wondered if he was even listening. In the end she simply trailed off lamely, out of explanations and a little bewildered by his attitude. The more she made allowances, the more he seemed to draw into himself.

"What I'm trying to say," she finally admitted in exasperation, "is that I don't want things to continue the way they have been."

"How's that?" he asked, breaking his silence.

"Like we're on opposite sides," she answered on a deep sigh.

She was standing at the edge of his workstation, one shoulder propped against the partition, gazing down at him. It should have been a position of power, but she felt like fidgeting and shifting her weight from one foot to the other. Jake was supremely unaffected. He seemed hardly to notice her while *she* noticed everything about him: the soft gray denim trousers molded to his thighs, the open neck of his dark shirt and the brown column of his throat rising above it, the soft scent of his cologne, the way the black hair at his nape brushed his collar, the strength evident in his bared forearms where his shirt sleeves were rolled back to his elbows, and the angular dimensions of his serious face.

"It's no secret I didn't want you working here," he said bluntly, startling her. "But I'm as ready as you are to forget the past and make the best of today. I'm sorry you got yanked from my story, but personally, I think you're better suited for the one Forrester gave you. You're new," he pointed out, scrutinizing her to see how she was taking his rather harsh opinion of her abilities, "and no matter how good you are, you're inexperienced. We were all inexperienced once."

That was as close to an acceptance of her as a newswoman as she was apparently going to get. She nodded, then couldn't help adding, "I suppose it's best to make certain all my bases are covered before I join the major leagues."

The faintest smile touched his lips. "Some players never make it out of the minors."

"I'll bear that in mind."

"Townsend?"

A man's voice caught her attention and Hope swiveled around expectantly. Kevin "the Bear" Berger was striding her way, a strange expression on his face. He glanced once at Jake and nodded, then said gruffly to Hope, "Got a minute?"

"Sure."

He inclined his head in the direction of his desk, bidding her to join him. Feeling Jake's gaze boring into her back, Hope nodded to Berger as she fell in step beside him.

"I was wondering if you'd have dinner with me," he asked in what was an extremely long sentence for Kevin.

"Dinner?" Hope repeated blankly.

"Sometime soon."

Seeing how nervous he was, Hope realized how difficult it must have been for him to work up the nerve to ask her out. Touched, Hope said kindly, "I'm free Friday."

"Good." Relief washed over his face. "Write down your address and I'll pick you up at seven."

Hope wrote her address and phone number on the small notepad he produced. Her skin prickled as she handed him back the pad, and she glanced around, seeing Jake's somber face as he walked past them. If he'd overheard anything, he gave no sign of it, and Hope didn't kid herself that it would matter to him if he had.

Pamela Durn, the school-board member who'd cried foul, gazed at Hope with resentment, as if it were Hope's fault that the alleged misappropriation of funds turned out to be completely unsubstantiated. Pamela wanted a fellow school-board member, a man she'd apparently been involved with, to be indicted for theft and embezzlement.

"I'm afraid there's less here than meets the eye," Hope told Pamela, then turned to a relieved Tom Wilkes. "I'll send you a copy of the story before it runs," she assured the superintendent.

"Thank you," he said gratefully.

Pamela marched out of the conference room without another word.

Hope left the offices where she'd spent the last two days poring over information from all the schools that had been supposedly cheated of their funds. She'd gone over reams of figures, only to discover that the thousands of dollars that had been suspected of being stolen or misused had simply been rerouted. The money had been placed in another account, one used for special projects. No one had checked the special-project fund, as the person in charge was on vacation. Zealous Pamela had discovered the error and gone shrieking to the press, hoping to blame the man with whom she'd had her differences.

End of story.

As Hope drove back to the Tarkette Building, she decided she wouldn't play up the bumbling school-board angle. Instead, she would write about how nice people made mistakes, too. Less sensationalism; more truth.

It was late Friday night by the time she finished typing up her story. Glancing at her watch, Hope let out a squeak of dismay. "Oh, God!" Tonight was her night to go out with Kevin Berger and she was two hours late.

There was only a skeleton crew in the newsroom, but Hope raced to Berger's desk anyway, on the off chance she'd find him still working. When he wasn't there she sank down in a chair and dropped her head in her hands. What was the matter with her? She *never* forgot appointments!

Immersed in her self-castigation and misery, Hope didn't realize she had company until Jake's voice drifted from the other side of the partition.

"What's the matter?"

She jerked in surprise, then leaned forward to peek around the gray half-wall to where Jake was leaning against a vacant desk. He was holding a stack of papers, papers he'd apparently been looking over before he left them on Kevin's desk. It was possible for an editor to read a reporter's story on his screen, but Jake, Hope had already heard, preferred to deliver a hard copy.

"I inadvertently stood up my editor. Do you suppose it'll mean my job?"

"Probably," Jake answered, looking thoughtful. "I hear they're hiring at the *Daily Report*."

Hope fought a smile. The *Daily Report* was the shoddiest paper around. The *Breeze* might have been small, but at least it had a well-deserved reputation for fairness and accuracy. "Do you think they'll take me?"

"If you're breathing and you don't mind bending your ethics a bit, they'll step over dead bodies to hire you."

"Seriously, will Berger understand that I got lost in my work? I just—forgot."

"Did you get the school-board story finished?"

She nodded. "No scandal, just a string of mistakes. One of the members wanted to pin the blame on another member. A case of unrequited love, it seems."

Silence fell between them. Hope's last few words seemed to echo with recrimination. She suddenly felt very uncomfortable.

Jake glanced at his watch. "You must have missed dinner, then."

Hope nodded absently, her thoughts returning to Kevin Berger.

"Why don't you join me?" Jake asked casually. "As I recall, your culinary skills involve tuna sandwiches, and since I've got the makings for them at my place maybe you'd consent to helping me put some together."

Hope was so astounded she could scarcely speak. "You're asking me to—join you for dinner?"

"Actually, I'm asking you to *make* me dinner."

"Why, Jake?"

The teasing light in his eyes faded. "Maybe I like the way you say my name. If you don't want to come, just say so. I was just joking about the tuna. I'm sure there's something else to eat."

"I'll come," Hope answered before either of them could change their mind.

Chapter Nine

This stunt must have stemmed from some remote and pathetic juvenile side of his personality, Jake derided himself as he pulled into the underground parking lot of his apartment complex. He glanced in his rearview mirror and saw Hope's headlights appear on the ramp that led downward. Muttering to himself, he switched off the engine, then climbed out of his car and waited for her to join him.

Just knowing she was going out—going out with *his* editor, for Chrissake!—had twisted something inside him into a hard knot. He'd barely done more than grunt at Berger since he'd overheard him ask Hope to dinner. But learning Hope had stood the man up had caused Jake to smile to himself with a certain degree of satisfaction.

Then he'd followed that ignoble reaction with another: he'd asked her to his place.

Now, watching her cross the cement floor, her footsteps echoing throughout the cavernous, half-empty garage, he felt a tightening inside himself that both exasperated and defeated him. No matter how much he tried to convince himself otherwise, Hope Townsend had a strong effect on him. His gaze traveled appreciatively over her slim legs to her narrow waist. She wore a long black coat, opened, and the two halves of it fluttered out as she walked. Her hair hung in lustrous burnished waves of honey gold around her neck, tumbling in glorious abandon over her shoulders and back. Thick, curly, gold-tipped lashes framed her bright emerald eyes. His eyes were drawn to her mouth, and he couldn't help the stab of awareness he felt when he remembered those soft pink lips pressed to his.

"What are you staring at?" she asked, bringing Jake back to earth with a bang.

"You." His voice was clipped. "Come on upstairs."

The elevator was smooth and sleek, a silver cubicle with gray carpet. Jake watched the numbers to the tenth floor. He lived in an expensive high-rise; he'd lived here since Diana had first picked out the apartment for him. It wasn't really his style, but he'd never cared. Seeing the way Hope was looking around, however, made him wish he'd never embarked on this fool's journey. He suddenly, fervently, didn't want her to enter his personal life.

"What is it?" she asked perceptively, as he hesitated by the door to his apartment.

He didn't answer her as he turned the key. The first thing that hit him when he stepped inside was the feeling of emptiness, as if he'd been on an extended trip and the apartment had been vacant long enough to pick up an atmosphere of neglect. He wondered if Hope felt it, too.

"This is—gorgeous," she said after a stunned moment.

Jake glanced around. A sumptuously thick cream carpet stretched across the room, highlighting the satiny finish of the rosewood table in the dining area. A glass coffee table on a pewter-colored base sat in front of a black leather couch. On a rosewood stand in front of the panoramic view of Seattle's glittering skyline was an elegant arrangement of silk flowers.

"My decorator," he said in an amused voice when he saw her spy the flowers.

"Your *decorator*?" Hope repeated in disbelief.

"Actually, a friend of mine coordinated it all," he answered carefully. "I don't notice it much anymore. In fact, I don't notice it at all."

Hope heard more in what was left out of that statement than the message itself. "It's fabulous," she affirmed, walking across those acres of carpet to the windows.

"Is it?" He strode in the direction of the kitchen, snapping on a light so Hope, from her angle, could see him from behind a rack of long-stemmed wineglasses, hung upside down. The apartment itself was beautiful; whoever had ordered and arranged the furnishings had done quite a job.

"Thanks for inviting me over," Hope said, walking to the counter and leaning a hip on it, slightly bemused to see Jake staring into his refrigerator, a frown on his face, as if he were the picture of domesticity.

"I was wrong about the tuna fish. Nothing in the cupboards, and nothing in the refrigerator that isn't in danger of poisoning us.'' He pulled out a bowl covered by plastic wrap and dumped a dubious mixture of *something* down the disposal. ''We probably should go out,'' he added, glancing at her.

The look of consternation on his face made her laugh, the sound of her voice ringing through the quiet rooms. She didn't know why he was making such an effort to please her, but she wanted so badly for them to have some kind of normal relationship that she didn't want to spoil the moment. ''How about grilled cheese?'' she suggested with a grin.

''How about I order a pizza to be delivered?'' he countered, reaching for the phone even while he spoke. ''Pepperoni okay?''

''Fine. Um, do you happen to know Berger's home number? Maybe I could reach him there.''

''It's on the list by the phone in my bedroom.''

While Jake placed the order, Hope went in search of the other phone. She hesitated at the door to his room, then chided herself for always overreacting. This was no different than entering his bedroom at his mother's place.

But it was. The scent of him was strong and seductive. He hadn't made the bed this morning, just tossed the covers aside, and the tangled evidence of the blankets and the indent of the pillow where his head had lain reminded her of the feel of his limbs against hers.

She walked to the bedside phone and flipped through the card file beside it. She dialed Berger's number and was both relieved and disappointed to get his answering machine.

''Did you get hold of him?'' Jake asked when she returned to the kitchen. He was holding a bottle of beer in one hand and a glass of wine in the other. He handed her the wine, his fingers grazing hers briefly.

"I got his answering machine and I apologized profusely."

"He'll forgive you," Jake predicted.

"Oh yeah? Less than an hour ago you said I'd be looking for another job."

"I lied." He smiled slightly. "It's one of my most endearing traits."

Hope ignored the pull on her senses. She didn't want to think of Jake this way. "Actually, you're obsessively frank. I almost prefer the lying."

"Now *that* is an even worse lie than I tell."

Hope just smiled. But it was true that Jake's devastating frankness had made her uncomfortable on more than one occasion.

The sadness in her smile touched Jake, and he frowned down at his beer. He'd known how poorly he'd treated her but hadn't realized until now just how deeply that hurt might have gone.

The doorbell rang, announcing the arrival of the pizza. Jake paid the delivery boy and set the cardboard box directly on the beautiful rosewood table.

"Oh, stop!" Hope cried in dismay. "You'll ruin it." Quickly she grabbed several dish towels that were tossed over the oven-door handle and laid them on the table, setting the box atop them. "It's a wonder this table has remained so lovely, the way you treat it," she accused.

"You sound like my cleaning lady" was Jake's amused response.

While they ate, Jake directed the conversation to Hope's just-completed story. With the kind of uninhibited manner and sardonic delivery she usually reserved for her close friends, she told him all about Pamela and her malicious need for revenge. Enthralled by this new side of Hope, Jake listened in comparative silence.

Flushing, Hope suddenly realized she'd been talking nonstop. "I didn't mean to jabber on like that," she said, embarrassed, surprised that she'd felt so at ease. Even when she'd thought herself in love with him she'd never been so relaxed and comfortable. This new feeling was disconcerting.

"You didn't jabber on. You were . . . entertaining." He got up to get himself another beer and replenish her wineglass.

"Entertaining!" Hope groaned.

"Did I insult you somehow?" he asked in surprise, tipping the bottle of white zinfandel and filling her glass three-quarters full. The color of the wine was nearly the exact shade of the blouse she was wearing, Jake noted, a luscious peach color that looked as soft and sweet as a confection.

"I don't want to be entertaining, Jake," she admitted with a rueful twist of her lips. Sliding back her chair, she got up and walked to the other side of the table. Jake was sitting at the table's head, his eyes following her careful retreat. "I want to be . . . I don't know . . . *respected*, I guess."

"You don't think I respect you?"

Now, here was dangerous territory, Hope thought with a painful little jerk of her heart. "You haven't exactly complimented my journalistic skills," she pointed out lightly.

He lifted one dark brow. "You seem to have tackled the school-board story with discretion and insight."

"Why are you being so nice to me?" Hope asked suddenly.

Jake didn't answer immediately, and in those tense moments while she waited, she counted the beats of her heart. "Now who's being frank?" he countered softly.

"A couple of days ago, you were biting my head off. What made you decide to treat me like a human being instead of an empty-headed 'wanna-be'? In all the time I've known you, Jake, even when—even when I thought I really *cared* about you—" she admitted painfully, "you were never really nice to me. You've indulged me, and been attracted to me—" his gaze, which had been lazily sweeping her face, focused sharply on her eyes at that, but Hope forged on, undeterred "—and treated me like poison, but you've never been honestly *nice* to me. Why now?"

His lashes lowered and she saw the tightening of his lips. She added tautly, "And this time, *don't lie!*"

"I'm nice to you because you're safe," he answered mildly, after a thoughtful moment.

"Safe?" Hope repeated blankly. At his nod, her mind latched on to the only possible explanation she could come up with for such a comment. "I'm safe, as in *nonthreatening*? Oh, God! And I thought *entertaining* was bad. Well, for your information, you may think I'm safe, and young, and naive, but I think you're downright dangerous! And I think I'd better leave before you make me mad enough to kick you!"

She swept toward the living room, then gasped when Jake's hand shot out and grabbed her wrist, stopping her short. "I meant you're safe from harm," he corrected softly. "I didn't like it when you called Farrell.

It scared me. I don't want you to get—'' He cut himself off abruptly.

Hope, whose heart had sped into overdrive at his low, attractive and intense tone, managed to pull herself under control. "Hurt?"

"*Physically* hurt," he explained, still holding her arm.

"You don't have to protect me. In fact," she added with a trace of bitterness, "your pal Forrester's doing a bang-up job of that all on his own. He took me off the Farrell case before I even had a chance to work on it. I'm safer than safe. You can stop worrying."

"I took you off the Farrell case," Jake admitted flatly. "Forrester wanted you to stay on it."

Hope gazed at him, wounded.

"I doubt that comes as such a big surprise. You knew how I'd react when I found out."

Hope jerked her arm free. "You aren't paid to be my protector, Jake Danziger!"

"I know," he answered.

She glared at him, furious and frustrated and hopelessly intrigued all at once. She wanted to scream at him for his bullheadedness, but she understood that he wouldn't react this way if he didn't care for her on some level. And though she told herself not to put too much weight on that fact, she was completely aware that Jake, though he proclaimed long and loudly that he didn't want anything to do with her, was as enmeshed in her life as she was in his.

He saw the play of emotions across her face. Her skin was as soft and glowing as satin, and suddenly he didn't give a damn anymore about proving a point, or protecting his emotions, or keeping things in perspective. Just like six years before, he was overwhelmed by the need to lose himself in her sweetness, because like it or not, Hope *was* sweet. She wasn't like Regina, and she wasn't even like Diana. She was Hope Townsend. The girl next door who'd grown into a beautiful, desirable, exciting woman.

"Don't look at me like that," she warned in a breathless voice, her lips quivering slightly.

"I want to make love to you."

She gulped on a laugh. "Oh, God! I told you I'd rather have you lie. You never, never listen!"

Jake threw back his head and laughed. It was more seductive, more detrimental to her carefully erected defenses, than any words of desire could ever be.

When he looked at her again his eyes were warm, his mouth twitching with amusement. "What do *you* want?" he asked meaningfully.

"I want to hold on to my sanity and go home," she said, watching him slowly rise from his chair. "I want to be able to face myself in the morning."

He stopped several feet away from her, his expression somber. "Are you sure that's what you want?"

"Absolutely, totally positive."

He nodded thoughtfully. "There's something I haven't told you. To get him to take you off the series, I had to promise Forrester you and I would work together."

"That's an illogical statement. You promised to *work with me*, then had me taken off *your* story?" she questioned him.

"If you stay away from Farrell, I think we can work together on this thing," he said carefully. "I'm willing to try."

There had been a major change in Jake, Hope realized. From pushing her away, he'd come full circle.

He was beginning to pull her toward him. He wanted to make love to her, and to that end, he was going to let her work with him. Inwardly, she winced. Was it really just a trade-off? "I'll stay away from Farrell," she said softly.

"Good."

In the unspoken silence that followed Jake covered the distance between them, tipping up her chin to search her eyes. Hope swallowed, dying to feel his arms surround her. Could she have an affair with Jake without all the ripping emotional pain? Could she treat him casually? As casually as he apparently wanted to treat her?

He gathered her close and she fought the desire to rub her cheek against his shirt. In a raw voice, she said, "But I can't make love to you again."

He exhaled slowly. "As I recall, it wasn't exactly 'making love' the first time. We never got that far."

Before she had a chance to protest, his mouth covered hers in a deep, shattering kiss. Her knees trembled and she stifled a moan. His arms tightened around her, imprisoning her against his chest, while his mouth opened hungrily, his tongue plunging between her lips.

When Hope dragged her mouth from his, she was breathing heavily. "As I remember, we got far enough—"

"Oh, Hope." She felt his silent laughter as he drew a steadying breath. "I meant we got interrupted. By your virginity," he added dryly.

She could feel his heart beating hard and fast. "I've always sort of wished that it hadn't ended so abruptly," she admitted, wrinkling her nose in the way Jake found so entrancing. "But it's just as well, I suppose. As you said, we weren't in love with each other. And for me, sex and love go together." She gazed up at him through soft green eyes. "I guess I'll just keep waiting," she added lightly.

"What do you mean?" Jake stiffened as her words hit home. "You mean there hasn't been anyone else?"

"No. . . ."

He jerked her away from him, holding her at arm's length, staring down at her incredulously. "Not one man in *six years*!"

"No."

How had he ever compared her with Regina? Jake was astounded, and ridiculously pleased, and afraid. . . .

"Never let it be said I don't learn from my mistakes," he murmured more to himself than to her. "Come on, I'll walk you to your car."

"No, I'm okay alone." Hope turned him down. She was surprised and a bit disappointed by his change of heart. Though she knew it was better to stay uninvolved, she hadn't expected him to react *that* way when he learned he was her one-and-only lover.

"Are you sure?"

She risked a glance into his cool blue eyes, expecting to see the rejection she'd heard in his voice. But his eyes were anything but cool. They smoldered with desire and something else she couldn't quite identify.

She left his apartment before those burning blue eyes changed her mind. She hadn't lied when she'd said sex for sex's sake wasn't for her. And Jake wasn't able to love her the way she wanted—needed—a man to love her. No, she would take a page from his own book; she would never open herself up to that kind of pain and misery again. She'd told herself so time and again, and just because he wanted to pick up where they'd left off didn't mean his feelings had changed.

Unlocking her car, Hope was immersed in her thoughts until she caught a flash of movement from the corner of her eye. She glanced up just in time to see a shadowy figure disappear behind a huge circular concrete pillar. Her heart leaped in terror, but the footsteps she heard receding toward the car ramp were unhurried. Just someone walking away, she calmed her heightened senses. Nothing to worry about.

"Holy Mother Mary," Bill Farrell shouted for the fifth time and with the same degree of irreverence. "You're not paying much attention, son," he added, poking Jake's arm with one hard finger. "I'm giving you a five-star piece of information and you act bored!"

Key Largo's music was more hard rock than soft reggae, and at two o'clock in the morning it was loud enough to cause permanent auditory damage. It didn't help that everyone yelled at the top of their lungs in the vain attempt to be heard over the music. Jake, his eyes scratchy and his brain numb, wondered how he'd let Farrell talk him into this meeting. One trip to Key Largo had been enough.

But it was Farrell's ballgame.

"Five-star piece of information?" Jake hollered above the noise. "You haven't told me anything."

Farrell, who was heavyset and sloppy and radiated false bonhomie, slid Jake a sly grin. "You just haven't been listening." He leaned forward, his beer-breath nearly smothering Jake. "It's Friday, son. This Friday."

Jake kept his face carefully expressionless. "What's this Friday?"

"Damn, son! You should be taking this down!"

Jake slowly pulled out a pen and slid a cocktail napkin over to write on. Farrell had been bobbing and weaving all night, tossing out bits of info that had nothing to do with Raleigh Jarvis, who was the main focus of Jake's interest. But now, as the evening wore on, Farrell either felt he'd been unfair to the newsman who'd taken a bullet for him, or he'd just gotten drunk enough to spill some information.

Farrell named a time and place—another warehouse far removed from Seattle's hub. "I'm meeting one of Jarvis's shipments," Farrell added in Jake's ear, his voice sounding remarkably sober. "It's been freighted up I-5 by truck and'll be arriving around midnight Friday night."

"I'll be there," Jake said.

"Nope. DEA wants this tight as a drum. I'm going it alone. I'll call you first, as soon as it's over. You can get it in Saturday's edition."

"Bill, you know I won't get in your way."

"Holy Mother Mary, Dance! *Get* in my way, already! You saved me once, don't stop now!" He roared at his own joke, then added with quiet emphasis, "OK, OK. Show up after ten o'clock—the deal should be done by then. But no sooner, understand?"

"I understand."

And he did. The DEA wouldn't appreciate the press around to foul up the works. But Jake, by right of the painful twinges in his thigh, had earned the privilege of being at the scene of the crime firsthand. He would be there at ten sharp.

The next morning his alarm had barely started to buzz when he leaped out of bed, anxious to talk to Forrester. He considered calling the managing editor at home, then decided he didn't want to start off on the wrong foot. Instead he showered and changed and gulped down coffee and burned toast, then drove hastily to the Tarkette Building.

He was at his work space, lounging in the chair, his ankles propped on the pencil-strewn desktop next to his computer terminal, when Regina Sutton said in her most amused voice,

"Well, well, well. I've been doing a little research on you."

Jake hid his annoyance. "You found out about my illegitimate half brother who's been locked in my grandmother's attic ever since he was kidnapped from the mental institution? Okay. Remove my name from Seattle's Who's Who. I'll recover."

"I found out about you and Diana Mathers," Regina clarified. "I'm still working on Hope Townsend."

The steely look he sent her should have warned her, but Regina's skin was thicker than rhinoceros hide, and after years of sunbathing, nearly as tough and leathery. Jake had never really noticed before, but in comparison to the soft candescence of Hope's skin, he now saw through the scrupulous makeup job Regina used to hide the flaws.

"My relationship with Diana is hardly a secret. But it's not open to discussion." Jake was point-blank.

"You were living together before she died. I didn't know that, Dance," she chided. "You said you were just friends."

"We weren't living together."

"I have a friend of a friend who says differently."

"I don't give a damn what your friend of a friend says. I'm telling you to stay out of this, Regina, if you value *our* friendship."

She lifted her brows at his use of her first name. "I didn't know we were friends anymore, since you failed to honor our date."

"I didn't plan on getting shot," he pointed out flatly.

"Nor did you plan on meeting up with Hope again, I'll wager," she murmured provocatively.

"What do you want?" Jake cut through her efforts to incite him.

"Take me out for a drink and tell me about Diana and/or Hope."

"No." He was positive.

"Diana was killed in your office," Regina said in a more serious and empathetic tone—one that usually invited confidences. "She was estranged from her husband and deeply in love with you. You worked on quite a few stories together."

Jake met her searching gaze deliberately. "I really don't want to talk about Diana," he said quietly.

"Because you were in love with her?"

"Because she's gone. What are you trying to do? Scratch up a juicy story here in the newsroom?" Jake drawled, keenly aware of the gnawing guilt just the mention of Diana's name elicited.

"This isn't for a story. It's hardly society news. This is for me," Regina said with surprising candor. "Just when you started to open up, you've closed me out again. I can't decide if it was the bullet, or your association with Hope, or something left over from Diana's death.

"After all," she went on, watching Jake's expression harden. "There hasn't been one single woman in your life since Diana. If you even *date*, it's the best kept secret in town! I just want to know why!"

"I applaud your honesty. But you're wrong. There have been women since Diana," Jake responded dryly.

"No one special, though." She regarded him through narrowed eyes. "I don't suppose Hope was one of those women."

"As a matter of fact, she was...."

Regina looked speechless at his admission. Eyes brighter, she made excuses to leave. Jake's expression was wry as she hurried away. He'd told her about Hope on purpose, to keep her from scratching away at the still-tender scar over the wound created by Diana's death.

Diana. He shook his head. No one understood about Diana.

Hope rewound her last roll of microfilm and handed it back to the attendant who'd checked it out to her, her expression thoughtful. The Plegman story was similar to Barbara Thomas's—a long spiral into drugs.

The Plegman story had been written by Diana Mathers and Jake Danziger.

"Wait a minute," Hope said to the attendant who was just turning away. "I'd like to see some more *Observer* microfilm...."

Chapter Ten

Through the glass walls of Forrester's office, Hope could see Jake sitting relaxed and indolent in one of the leather chairs, a smile hovering around his lips over something Forrester had apparently said. Forrester looked up, spied Hope heading toward her desk, and motioned her inside. She nearly stumbled as she stopped short in midstride. Jake's dark head swung from Forrester to Hope. He, too, looked surprised.

"Hi," Hope greeted the managing editor as she crossed the threshold. She shot a look toward Jake but his expression was inscrutable.

"I've got something I'd like you to work on," Forrester said without preamble. "Berger tells me you've wrapped up the school-board story. Are you working on anything else?"

"Nothing specific," Hope answered. Kevin Berger had been pleased with her work and had waved away her apologies over missing dinner. He hadn't asked for a rain check, however, and she couldn't help thinking she'd blown it.

"Then I want you to work with Dance. He needs someone to help him."

Jake didn't move a muscle. Hope's uncertain gaze slid from his granite face back to Forrester's. "I already said I'd help with the series. Is that the story you mean?"

"No." Forrester kept his gaze trained on Jake, who stared right back. "I mean the one he's working on now."

"You're out of line, John," Jake said quietly.

"You need someone more responsible than Hughes. Someone who'll be there when you need them. Townsend, you're on the story," he announced dismissively.

Jake looked about to erupt.

Certain she didn't want to get in the middle of this, Hope murmured, "Why don't you two work it out? I'll be at my desk."

With what she'd learned about Diana Mathers's death weighing heavily on her mind, she didn't give the matter of Jake's refusal to work with her again much more thought. It wasn't exactly a news bulletin anyway. Instead, she couldn't help thinking about how Diana had died in Jake's office, in Jake's *arms*. Jake had carried her to the ambulance. And Diana's estranged husband had been quoted, his phraseology clearly showing that he and Diana hadn't been together for a long time.

Hope gazed unseeingly through the window to the Seattle streets three stories below. She suspected Jake's desolation six years ago had been because he'd been in love with the woman who'd died. He'd been grieving deeply, and then she'd stepped in, all innocence and naiveté and foolish desire, and he'd used her to get over the worst of that grief.

"I miscalculated," John Forrester's voice said from behind her. Hope jerked back to the present. "I thought he'd go for it. But he doesn't want to put you in the line of fire."

Hope inclined her head. "I'm not surprised."

"He's barely off crutches. If he's not careful, he'll kill himself getting this story," Forrester stated grimly. "He needs someone, and he and Hughes are too diametrically opposed to mesh. But he could work with you if he'd let himself."

Hope smiled faintly. "Jake never lets himself do anything. He makes a decision and sticks with it, come hell or high water. He's only allowed me on the series because he made a bargain with you." Remembering that he'd also tried to add the condition that she make love to him as part of that bargain, Hope added somewhat bitterly, "He really doesn't like me very much."

"Now, that's the first wrong conclusion you've drawn," Forrester said with a trace of indulgence.

"I *know* Jake," Hope insisted, turning back to her monitor. "He thinks I'm a kid who can't cut it as an investigative journalist. He doesn't want me on his story because he's afraid I'll bumble around and ruin all his hard work."

"He's afraid you'll get hurt," Forrester corrected calmly. "Maybe even killed."

Hope stared at the glowing amber letters on her screen. He was referring to what had happened to Diana. Realizing she could get a different perspective on Jake's emotions, she swung around full of questions.

But Forrester was already halfway down the aisle to his office.

Friday evening she left work late, a sense of uneasiness hovering over her like a dark cloud. She hadn't seen Jake since the scene in Forrester's office. One moment she thought she was making progress; the next he was back to his old obsessively private self.

At her apartment she saw the message light from her answering machine blinking and learned there were two messages, one from Katy, and one from her parents. She called her parents, who just wanted to chat, then she phoned Katy, who was on her way out.

"How're things going at the paper?" Katy asked. "I've been thinking about you, wondering if Dance's forced you to turn tail and run yet."

"You should know me better than that," Hope said with a wry smile, as she pulled a bottle of chilled wine from the refrigerator.

"How is he?"

"Miserable. Exasperating. Intense. Unpredictable." Hope gazed around her tiny kitchen, wishing she were anywhere but in her apartment on a lonely Friday night.

"Is that affection I hear in your voice?" Katy asked, amused. "At Christmas, you didn't even want to speak his name!"

"I've gotten over a lot of my anger," Hope admitted, realizing how true it was. "But it isn't easy working with him."

"Would it be?" she questioned sardonically. "Listen, I've got to run. Don't let Dance get you down, and hang in there." Just before she clicked off, she advised, "If anyone can beat him at his own game, it's you, Hope."

Hope was still thinking that over when her phone rang again. She was amazed this time to hear Elise Danziger's voice on the other end.

"I'm sorry to bother you, Hope," she apologized, "but I've been trying to get in touch with Jake for days and all I ever get is that infernal answering machine. He hasn't returned my calls. Is he—do you think he's all right?"

"He's fine," Hope assured her, annoyed with Jake for letting his mother worry.

"When he's wrapped up in a story, he never calls," Elise put in hurriedly, as if anxious for Hope not to condemn him. "He always waits until the pressure's off first. But with his leg, I was kind of worried something might have happened."

"No, he's doing great. He doesn't even use the cane much anymore," Hope assured her.

"He isn't taxing himself too much, do you think?" Her voice was threaded with worry.

"As we both well know, Jake is made of tough stuff," Hope commented, her voice dry. "Relax. He's well on the road to recovery. I guarantee it."

Elise sighed deeply. "Thank you. You've really eased my mind. And I never got a chance to properly thank you for taking care of him here in Roche Harbor."

Jake apparently had never mentioned the fall down the stairs. Hope opened her mouth to set the record straight when Elise's next words made her mind go blank.

"He doesn't show it much, I know. But he cares about you, Hope. He's never really gotten over what happened between you, you know, and its just his way to pretend it doesn't affect him, but it does."

"Jake and I are past all that now," Hope inserted quickly. After what she'd learned about Diana Mathers, Hope couldn't stand to hear how much he cared for *her*. Elise just didn't understand.

"You mean you're friends now?" asked Elise uncertainly.

"Something like that."

"I'm so glad. I've always sort of hoped, well, you know—" she laughed gently "—that you and Jake might find your way back to each other."

On some level Hope had always known Elise was subtly matchmaking. Her heart twisted, and she suddenly wished Jake did love her. Because she knew now that she was desperately in love with him.

Sounding flustered, Elise said, "Anyway, I'll keep trying to reach him. If you talk to him, tell him to be careful, okay?"

"I'll tell him."

She cradled the receiver carefully, her hand resting on it for several moments. She loved Jake. And she'd probably always loved him, even when she thought she'd hated him. It wasn't just a sexual attraction; she'd known that all along deep inside. She'd just been too frightened to admit how she felt, knowing that it could only bring her heartbreak.

The hours slipped by and as she thought of Jake and the dangerous assignment he was working on, her earlier uneasiness returned. It was ten o'clock, too late to call. Muttering to herself, Hope reached for the phone anyway. Before she could think of the dozen or more reasons she should leave him alone, she dialed his number, connecting with his answering machine. She left a message, asking him to call, then settled down at the table with a cup of instant soup, a piece of buttered bread, and her wine.

Thirty minutes later, she called again, slamming down the receiver in frustration at the sound of his sexy drawl on his answering machine. Knowing she was leading with her chin, she climbed into her car and drove to his apartment complex, parking in the same spot she'd chosen a week earlier.

She pressed on his door buzzer again and again, but he didn't answer. With a weary sigh, Hope concluded that he wasn't purposely neglecting to return her calls; he simply wasn't home.

Brilliant deduction, she told herself scornfully.

Back in her car, she sat beneath the shadowy lighting of the parking structure and wondered what he might be doing and with whom. Was he working, or did he have a date? If he came home with a woman, she didn't know what she would do. Hide? Pray to God he didn't notice that she'd been waiting for him? Smile and wave and ask how things were going?

For reasons she couldn't quite explain, she didn't think he was with a woman. He was with Bill Farrell, or someone else tied in to the reasons behind the shooting. As Elise had said, when Jake was on a case he really didn't think of anything else.

She drew her coat more closely around her shoulders. He wouldn't have a weapon to defend himself if something should happen, because that wasn't how Jake operated. And he didn't have a strong pair of legs to run, Hope reminded herself, her heart jolting with sudden fear. Why wouldn't he let someone help him? Was he trying to kill himself?

The minutes stretched by endlessly. Hope was too keyed up to doze off. Maybe he *was* spending the night at some other woman's place, she warned herself. He wasn't immune to the opposite sex; she knew that firsthand. And he certainly set other feminine hearts quivering, if the longing looks around the office were any indication.

So why do you find it so impossible to believe he might be with a woman?

"Because I don't want him to be," she said on a sigh.

Headlights illuminated the concrete wall at the end of the car ramp. Hope saw the approaching car, a black Porsche. Jake's car.

He came to a sharp halt in his parking space about fifty feet from her car. She was out of her car before she thought, so glad to see him she could scarcely think straight. Jake didn't see her. He climbed from the Porsche with an effort and walked slowly toward the elevator, favoring his injured leg.

"Jake?" Hope asked, her footsteps echoing.

Jake, who'd been contemplating the floor, glanced up sharply. His mouth was grim. "Go away, Hope," he said in a tired voice.

"What's wrong? Something happened, didn't it? No, don't push me away, Jake. I *want* to help you." She drew a sharp breath. "Are you hurt? Oh, God! You met Farrell, didn't you, and something went wrong!"

He grabbed her arm so tightly she gasped, but he didn't say anything. In fact, he was struggling with himself, she could tell, and that worried her even more.

"Jake, tell me. I won't do or say anything to jeopardize anyone's safety, especially yours. Just let me help."

He shook his head as the elevator doors opened, but before Hope could launch another verbal attack, he rasped, "Get in."

The doors whispered closed behind them, and the elevator began smoothly sliding upward. Jake was leaning against the back wall of the cubicle. Hope wisely kept silent, but her insides twisted with fear as she saw him pass his hand across his forehead. His fingers were trembling.

At his apartment, Jake unlocked the door and headed straight for the kitchen cabinet. He yanked out the Scotch and poured two glasses.

"Farrell's dead," he said flatly, handing her a drink. He stared down at his own glass for several seconds before tossing back a hefty swallow.

"Dead," Hope repeated softly, her voice sounding strange to her own ears.

He sighed, sinking into one of the kitchen chairs, his elbows on the table, his forearms stretched in front of him as if he needed support. "Jarvis had him killed."

"Raleigh Jarvis?" Hope asked in a voice that was losing strength by degrees. Her eyes were wide with sudden understanding, and the chill that slid down her spine caused her to shudder.

"Jarvis had Farrell gunned down," Jake told her in that same flat tone. "I was supposed to meet Farrell at ten. I was late. I heard the shots and saw the men take off down an alley. I went to Farrell, but I couldn't help him. I tried to follow the killers but my damn leg—" he broke off suddenly. Hope moved closer to him, wanting to touch him. "Farrell was DOA at the hospital. I gave a statement to the police and came here."

She swallowed. "How do you know Jarvis is behind it?"

"Farrell told me he was. Last week."

"And you were meeting Farrell to find out more information on Jarvis?"

"I was meeting Farrell who was supposedly meeting a shipment of drugs ordered by Jarvis. The DEA was laying low and Farrell was on his own. But it was a setup." He looked at her, his blue eyes dull. "Do you know," he added conversationally, "that if I hadn't gotten your phone message, and then spent about twenty minutes wondering whether to call you back and find out *why* you sounded so worried, that I would have been on time." His lips twisted. "On time for my own funeral."

"Jake." Hope couldn't stop herself from touching his arm. His muscles were taut as a bowstring. "It's not your fault that Farrell's dead."

"I know that." He was terse. Deliberately, he moved out of her grasp. "It's just such a waste. That's all."

Hope couldn't find words to answer so she stayed silent for several moments, wanting to wrap her arms around him so badly it took all her concentration not to.

"What did you want, Hope?" he asked, shaking his head as if rousing himself from a deep sleep.

"Want?"

"Why did you call?" he asked patiently.

"Oh." She licked her lips. "I don't remember," she murmured, half truthfully. "Your mother called and wanted to make sure you were all right. I told her you were."

"She's left me messages," he said distractedly.

"She wanted me to remind you to be careful."

He closed his eyes and drew a deep, shaking breath, and Hope couldn't stand it any longer. She circled his neck with her arms, pressing her cheek against his.

"Hope," he murmured achingly, resisting for only a moment before pressing his face into the richness of her blond hair, his hand winding around her nape, pulling her down to him until she was forced to straddle his lap. She was aware how dangerous the situation was, how Jake's vulnerability would crumble her attempts to keep him at arm's length. And she didn't care. She, who had carefully kept her heart free of entanglements, was willing to take a chance with the man she loved.

Jake didn't say a word. The only sounds Hope heard were the hard beats of his heart beneath her ear as she rested her cheek against his gray cotton shirt.

His mouth brushed against her temple, searching softly, sending shivers down her back. She responded by lifting her chin and gazing deeply into his shadowed eyes. His mouth descended on hers, devouring her lips in a shattering kiss that brought back vivid, sparkling memories of their lovemaking. Hope accepted his kisses but fought the desire to respond with the same tormented fervor. Dimly she realized she needed this eleventh-hour resistance to prove to herself that she was older, wiser, more sophisticated; that she could accept Jake into her life without also risking the same violent heartbreak. More clearly, she realized it was a losing battle. Jake's passion was stoking her own until she was trembling with need, filled with a gigantic ache that seemed to widen within her at each moment of delay.

Her heart was slamming against her ribs when he slowly ended the kiss to stare down at her, his breath rasping harshly. "If you don't want to make love, you'd better leave now," he said. "I'm exhausted, and I'm not...thinking clearly. But I want you."

For an answer she boldly captured his lips with her own. Jake swooped her close with devastating mastery. His tongue plundered her mouth. His hand roved restlessly up and down the back of her cotton jacket, then delved beneath to press warmly through the thin blouse she wore, molding her breasts. Jake shifted in the chair and, worried she might be inadvertently putting too much pressure on his wounded thigh, Hope moved, only to have his hands clasp her hips, pulling her down until the hard length of him was directly against her most feminine area.

"Don't move," he ordered in a soft voice.

She couldn't. She didn't dare. He kept kissing her, soul-burning kisses that made a moan of longing squeeze past her lips. His tongue plunged in and out of her mouth. Her hands were wound around his neck, gripping him in fevered excitement.

Very gently, he moved against her in the time-honored way. It wasn't enough pressure and Hope, unable to keep still, squirmed to heighten the feeling of him stroking against her. Jake groaned, his mouth pressed against her neck, a shudder rocking his hard frame.

Dazed with desire and the ironic realization that she hadn't been wrong at the tender age of nineteen when she'd believed she loved him, Hope slowly broke contact and stood up, managing to get her trembling legs to support her. Her silence was an invitation—one Jake didn't miss. She loved him more now, she decided with aching honesty. But she'd learned from hard experience that she couldn't let him know.

Jake was watching her. Unsteadily he climbed to his feet also, looking at her for a long moment before sliding his hands into the hair on both sides of her head to tip her face up for another kiss.

There was no resistance after that. She followed him to the bedroom. Or he half carried her. The next day, she couldn't remember.

She *did* remember the feel of him inside her, however; the sensual excitement of his hair-roughened legs entwining with hers, the soft glow of light from the living room seeping into the bedroom and illuminating his bronze shoulders, the touch of his lips against her ear, the pull of desire that made her stretch out her legs beneath him. She remembered the enveloping feel of his smooth sheets and the anxious torment in his exploring hands. She remembered her own uncontrollable desire....

"Kiss me harder," he whispered harshly, and Hope tangled her fingers in the thick hair at his nape and brought his mouth down hungrily to hers. She moaned and twisted, wanting all of him, but Jake wouldn't give her what she wanted until his mouth explored her breasts, tugging at her nipples, wringing a moan of pure pleasure from her lips.

Her own hands began a tentative exploration of their own, and she delighted in the sense of power she felt when he shuddered and groaned at the effect of her innocent touches. When she encountered the jagged scars on his right thigh, he responded by caressing her satiny abdomen; when she brushed her fingertips across his nipples, he answered by sliding his hands along her inner thigh; and when she jerked in surprise and fear at the feel of his hard fingers seeking her innermost warmth, he muffled a groan and pulled her trembling knees apart, his hips pressing into her thighs, his control shattered.

"Hope," he murmured brokenly, and she wound her arms around his broad shoulders, her own hips lifting to meet his. Jake plunged into her, burying himself in her welcoming softness. This time there was no pain and no remorse. As Hope dazedly marveled at the silky feel of him moving within her, an irresistible sensation grew inside her—a sensation she'd only guessed about, dreamed about. Feverishly she arched into him, her hands raking down his back. Jake increased his tempo, his breath as ragged and tortured as her own.

Hope's head tossed on the pillow and just when she wanted to cry out from frustration, the world exploded around her. Her cries were moans of ecstasy and she barely registered Jake's shuddering climax seconds after her own. But the way he gathered her to him, as if he would never let her go, and the strong, fast beat of his heart against hers was very real.

He might not love her, but he needed her. And that was enough for now.

Chapter Eleven

Jake jolted awake, a cry on his lips, never uttered. His heart was pounding, his arms clamped tightly around a woman's soft, yielding body. Hope's body. She flinched in her sleep at his hard grip.

Slowly his pulse returned to normal and he loosened his arms. Hope sighed gently and Jake, in the throes of fear and need, pressed his face to her neck, inhaling her sweet scent. He wanted to ease inside her again, squeeze his eyes closed, and hope morning wouldn't come.

But the distant sound of traffic, ten stories below, could already be heard.

A remote sense of déjà vu swept over him. He'd used Hope again, he realized with self-loathing. Used her because he was half in love with her, used her because he needed her.

And he'd dreamed she died in his arms.

Reluctantly, he slowly pulled away from her. She moaned softly and turned into his arms and desire shot through him. Tightening his jaw, Jake stared through the darkness, thinking of what he must do, anger and despair sweeping over him in equal measure. He'd wanted to make love to her, and he had, and the pleasure and joy of it had left him dumbstruck.

But he couldn't make love to her again. He couldn't entangle her in his life, and he couldn't bear hurting her again.

The thought of losing her froze his blood.

His bedside phone purred softly and Jake groped through the darkness for it. Hope's hand innocently touched his hip and he sucked in a sharp breath. He was torn by the desire to make love to her until they were both mindless, and the equally compelling need to stop now, while he had the strength.

"Jake Danziger," he answered in a low, taut voice, gently removing Hope's fingers from his hip. He listened intently for several moments. "I'll be there," he said, and hung up.

He had a sudden image of Diana, and with a groan he pulled Hope into his arms, running his hands over her satin skin, covering her beautiful body with his own.

Once more. He'd make love to her just once more. Then he would quit.

The aroma of coffee seeped into the corners of Hope's brain and she fought her way up from the depths of sleep. Her eyelids felt weighted down, and no wonder. Though Jake had fallen into exhausted slumber soon after making love, his sleep had been restless and punctuated by powerful dreams, keeping Hope awake with his muttering and thrashing.

It hadn't helped that she was in a state of nervous excitement herself. She hadn't meant to sleep with him, and now that she had, she wasn't certain what to do about it. She loved him and she wanted him; but more important, she wanted him to love *her*. Succumbing to his blatant sexual attraction and vulnerability might have been a mistake, and she'd lain awake for hours worrying about where they would go from here and also about the nightmares that obviously still plagued him.

She must have fallen asleep just before dawn, but then Jake had awakened her again, making love to her with a slow languor that brought pleasure to her in intense waves. When she drifted away the second time, it was in the shelter of his strong arms; but now, lifting her heavy eyelids, she was slightly alarmed to see Jake was no longer in bed. He was standing in the doorway, one shoulder propped against the jamb, looking down at her with an unreadable expression. He was already showered, shaved and dressed, and he'd set a cup of coffee on the night table beside her.

"What time is it?" she asked.

"About six. I'm sorry about this, but I've got to get going this morning."

"To work?" She struggled up against the pillows, clutching the sheets to her breasts to cover her nakedness. It was embarrassing and intimidating to be in *his* bed without any clothes while he stood there completely dressed.

"I'm going after Jarvis. I've got a story to write and it can't wait."

Not a word was uttered about what had happened between them. Pushing the tumble of her blond hair out of her face, Hope fought back a sense of panic. "I'd like to help you."

"No."

"You're not a one-man army, Jake," Hope pointed out with a smile. "You're personally involved and that's okay, but the authorities will get Jarvis. You need someone to help you put this story together."

"I don't need anyone, Hope," he answered mildly and implacably. "And the authorities have hardly done a bang-up job so far, have they? I'm putting the pressure on, starting today."

"Don't be a fool, Jake. You need someone to help, whether you like it or not," Hope answered just as implacably, fighting back the hurt his cold words inspired. She had to take her own feelings out of this, she told herself fiercely. This was not the time to worry over a broken heart.

"I'm heading downtown now," he said.

"I'm coming with you."

"Just because we spent the night together does not mean you're invited," he snapped with deliberately cruelty. "Don't complicate things."

Complicate things! Hope nearly gasped from the blow of that remark. With all the strength she could muster, she pulled a mask over her feelings. "Jarvis is not the kind of man to give up. We both know that. By the sheer luck of your nine lives, you've escaped so far. But as soon as you start attacking him directly, your luck might just run out!"

"And what about you?" Jake demanded fiercely, showing his first sign of real emotion. "What do you think he'll do to you, if you're on the case?"

Hope tugged the covers closer and shivered.

"Last night Bill Farrell found out what Jarvis can do," Jake told her flatly. "I'm not going to let it happen to you."

He strode over to the bed, sinking down beside Hope, his expression completely serious. "I've got to ask you something," he said solemnly.

It was impossible to keep up with his swiftly changing moods. "Go ahead," Hope said, her heart beating fast as she rightly guessed he was about to discuss their night together.

"You said there's been no one but me. In that case, I assume you don't use any form of birth control."

"You assume correctly," Hope answered flatly. These were *not* the words of love and commitment she wanted to hear from him. "But don't worry. I'm sure there's little chance I'm pregnant."

"Little chance?"

"None whatsoever," she reassured him, knowing her cycle intimately, but nevertheless growing annoyed at his line of questioning.

He lifted his hand and she thought for a moment that he was going to brush back her hair, but then he abruptly got to his feet and said, "I'll—be in the kitchen when you're ready to leave."

The bedroom door closed behind him and she heard his footsteps fade across that beautiful carpet. Hope flopped back against the pillows for a moment, feeling ridiculously near tears. She was stunned. This was even worse than the first time they'd made love. Then he'd at least felt some remorse for his casual treatment of her. He'd even attempted an apology. But now he acted as if making love to her were some unmentionable act he couldn't even talk about!

With a heavy heart she reached for her clothes. Maybe he had some hang-up about sex and this was how he treated any woman he had a physical relationship with. If so, she wanted nothing more to do with him, regardless of her deep feelings for him.

Hope entertained that thought for about twenty seconds before rejecting it. He only treated *her* this way. And it all stemmed from the fact that he either cared too much and was afraid of losing her, or he didn't really care at all.

On Monday, after two days of soul-searching and not a word from Jake, Hope reported for work early, keeping an eagle eye out for John Forrester. As soon as the managing editor walked through the front doors, she materialized at his office door. His bushy gray brows lifting, he invited her inside, closing the door behind her as she sat down stiffly in one of the chairs.

"Is there something specific on your mind?" he asked by way of a greeting.

"I want to work on the Farrell case," Hope stated evenly. "I don't want to be put off by Dance, or anyone else. You yourself said you thought he needed someone to help him."

Forrester eyed her thoughtfully, rubbing his chin. "He doesn't want you on the case and I got the impression you didn't really care one way or the other."

"I want this story. I only gave you that impression because I knew how Ja—Dance would react."

He inclined his head. "What's changed your mind?"

She hesitated. She didn't want to betray Jake's trust, but damn it, he needed help. "I think he's in danger," she said softly. "I even think *he* thinks he's in danger, but he doesn't care. And now it's a personal vendetta. He almost needs a bodyguard, but failing that, he should at the very least have someone he can contact who knows the case as thoroughly as he does."

"I agree," Forrester said. "But how are you going to convince him?"

"I don't have to," Hope answered with a humorless smile. "I'll work my own angles. I've got some ideas. If he doesn't like it, too bad. He can come in here and try to get me fired."

Forrester stared at her with a mixture of admiration and amazement. "That's exactly what he'll do."

Hope got to her feet, regarding him with regal surety. "Then it's your problem."

"Yes," he answered dryly, noticing the way the edge of her skirt trembled, revealing that she wasn't as cool and aloof as she would have him believe. Knowing he would have a very irate Jake Danziger wearing a path in his carpet before the week was out, he said, "Good luck, Townsend. You'll need it...."

When Jake said he was going after Jarvis, he meant it to the letter of the word, Hope learned over the next week. Every day he wrote a column so pointedly antagonistic that he had the local police, FBI and DEA calling, warning him to back off. Jake's response was typically Jake. He gave them all a curt "No," and kept sailing right on, as if he were on some suicide mission.

Hope took a different tack. She investigated quietly, behind the scenes and away from the front lines.

She concentrated not on Jarvis, but on Bill Farrell, who had somehow—and Hope was determined to find out *exactly* how—placed himself on Jarvis's hit list. She began by interviewing several of Farrell's friends and co-workers. They regarded her with unconcealed suspicion and only by totally dissociating herself with Jake Danziger did any of them open up.

What she discovered was a disjointed picture of a complex, secretive man. Farrell was considered excellent at his job, but no one, including his ex-wife, had ever felt really close to him. Either by the nature of his profession, or by the nature of the man himself, Bill Farrell didn't promote close friendships. Mimi, his ex-wife, summed it up by saying, ''Bill would talk to you like you were his best buddy, but he'd keep a teensy-weensy bit back, just in case he couldn't trust you.''

On Thursday, Hope was near total exhaustion from her own investigative efforts. She'd carefully kept thoughts of Jake at bay, forcing them to a closed part of her mind. Why he'd treated her with such casual contempt, she wasn't sure. But he'd apparently been totally serious about not getting involved with her. If she'd hoped she would see him around the office, that hope was in vain. He'd been nearly invisible. The few times she'd actually spied him at his desk, he'd nodded to her without interest, convincing her he didn't care about her feelings at all.

The way he ignored her was blatant enough to draw comment from Tammy.

''The cold war just got colder,'' she observed from behind Hope's shoulder on the Thursday night following Farrell's death.

''Hmm?'' Hope fought back the stab of pain in her heart, pretending to be absorbed in the words on her computer monitor. Her first piece would be printed tomorrow, as a companion story to Jake's. She'd just turned it in to Berger.

Jake didn't know about it yet.

"You and Dance aren't speaking. Even Regina commented on it."

Hope's mind's eye pictured Regina leaning over Jake's shoulder while he worked, Jake's lazy, indulgent smile stealing across his face at something she whispered in his ear. Not only had Jake refused to talk to Hope, but he'd made a point of cozying up to Regina. Though a part of Hope suspected he was doing it on purpose, that he wasn't really interested in Regina, another part desolately realized the result was the same, regardless: Jake didn't want anything to do with one Hope Townsend.

"We never have spoken much," Hope pointed out, managing a faint, slightly amused smile. It was a facade, but one she would maintain or die trying.

"But aren't you working on the same story?" Tammy asked, her gaze moving pointedly to the computer screen where Bill Farrell's name appeared at least three times.

"Dance doesn't know it yet," Hope said shortly. "Nor do I want him to," she added meaningfully.

"Well, he'll find out tomorrow," Tammy said in a singsong voice as she stuck her pencil back between her teeth and sauntered away.

Friday morning dawned sunny and bright with air so fresh that Hope filled her lungs in deep gulps as she stepped through the revolving doors of the Tarkette Building, her spirits lifting with the weather. She'd read her article this morning, her nerves tingling with anticipation despite the dark cloud of misery that hung over her. It was the first solid piece of writing she'd done for the *Observer*, the kind from which she got an extra zing of pride at seeing it beneath her byline.

As she burst through the doors on the third floor, her good mood was replaced by uneasiness. Everyone seemed to be looking at her out of the corners of their eyes.

She understood when she heard the muffled shouting coming from behind Forrester's closed door.

Jake was on the warpath.

Hope, whose feelings about Jake Danziger had been bordering on despair, suffered an abrupt change of heart. She felt positively murderous! Steeling herself for the inevitable confrontation, she sketched a wave to all and sundry in the newsroom who were watching, then strode toward Forrester's office, her chin held high as she formulated just exactly what she planned to say.

She didn't get the chance.

The door burst open, nearly taking off her nose in the process, and Jake strode into the hallway, not even bothering to look at her though she knew he'd seen her. Hope's gaze clung to his retreating back for a moment, then she stuck her head inside the door.

"Everything A-OK in here?" she asked brightly.

John Forrester emitted a strangled sound. "Couldn't be better."

"Then I'm still on the Farrell story and/or still employed?"

Forrester nodded jerkily. Hope had the distinct feeling that if he were the type of man to keep a bottle of liquor available in a bottom drawer he would have no qualms about pulling it out and treating himself to a nerve-soothing shot or two.

Buoyed by this feeling of success against Jake's stubbornness, Hope headed for her own workstation, keeping a watchful eye turned in the direction of Jake's desk.

She needn't have worried. Twenty minutes later Jake and Regina Sutton strolled past, Jake's head bent as he listened avidly to Regina's clever and caustic running monologue about somebody-or-other who was a social misfit and somebody-else-or-other's black-tie dinner the previous Saturday night. It was the kind of conversation Jake loathed, Hope knew; but she was forced to question whether he'd changed his opinion later that day when she learned from Tammy that Jake had accepted a last-minute invitation to escort Regina to a charity function hosted by Wynona Butterworth, one of Seattle's wealthiest women and a major contributor to the arts.

Hope was so depressed that when she got to her car that night, she closed her eyes and suddenly found them awash in tears. She'd tried so hard all week to ignore Jake's pointed cruelty. She'd tried to be tough and sophisticated and able to take her place in the major leagues both professionally and personally.

But now, with her bottom lip trembling and her heart breaking in two, it was all she could do to keep from wrapping her arms around the steering wheel and sobbing her heart out.

Listlessly, she drove toward her apartment. There was nothing to eat at home so she stopped at a deli and picked up a sandwich. But as soon as she sat down at her table she lost her appetite. She didn't want this cold war to continue. She wanted to work with Jake, to clear the air. And she wanted to do it tonight when the rest of the newsroom wouldn't be able to overhear her.

Knowing he was due to go out with Regina, Hope hesitated before calling him. It was a bad time. He would be in a hurry. Best to wait until tomorrow, or the next day....

She stared at the receiver for long moments before turning on her heel and marching toward the door. She took a chance that he wouldn't have left to pick up Regina yet. She'd have more than enough time to run him down and tell him what she thought of him face-to-face, where he couldn't hang up on her.

What had seemed like a good idea in the security of her own home, however, seemed like a terrible idea in the cold confines of Jake's underground parking lot. Bolstering her courage, she slammed her car door, hearing it echo hollowly throughout the concrete area. She also heard the scrape of a shoe and whirled around to see a man standing beside a dark green car, his shoulders hunched inside a thick overcoat.

When Hope looked at him, he casually searched through a pocket for a stick of gum. It was so quiet in the lot she could hear him unwrap it, and her nerves tingled as she walked rapidly toward the elevator, her low-heeled pumps tapping rhythmically.

At Jake's door she swallowed hard, her stomach in tight knots. Ringing the bell, she stepped back and waited, willing her face to remain expressionless even while her pulse surged wildly through her veins.

The door opened and Jake stood before her, glowering. In a raven-black tuxedo, the tie undone at his throat and the collar of his ruffled white shirt thrown open, contrasting sharply with his bronzed skin, he looked sleek and magnificent and terribly, terribly handsome. Her mouth went dry. He'd never seemed so distant and unapproachable. Only her innate courage kept her from freezing up completely.

"You look wonderful," she said, saying the first thing that came into her head.

Something changed in his expression, and his gaze, which had been centered on her eyes, moved lower, to her mouth, before he looked away.

"I'm on my way out," he said unnecessarily.

"I know. I just wanted a few moments to talk to you."

"No, Hope," he muttered in a weary tone.

"You've made it patently clear how you feel about me," she went on, "and I've gotten the message. I truly have. But I need to say some things to make myself feel better, and I—" She broke off, her heart pounding like a wild thing, panicked because she was suddenly on the verge of breaking down. "And I know that—that I have to speak up now or I'll hate myself for being a coward and not—being honest."

"You've always been honest," Jake answered with surprising understanding.

"Not really. I've had to hide a lot of things because I was afraid to say them. I'm still afraid," she admitted in a small voice, "but I'd like you to hear me out all the same."

Jake looked into her green eyes and saw such pain and love in their emerald depths that something long dead twisted inside him. Wordlessly he opened his door wide and Hope walked past him, her shoulder brushing the front of his suit, her blond hair trailing down her back in a riotous bouncing wake. He dragged his gaze away, wondering what it would take to dull his senses where she was concerned.

He'd done his damnedest to kill what was between them. He'd done it for her. And every time he remembered waking up, his body wrapped protectively around her, his heart thudding with sick fear, his skin damp with perspiration over the nightmare of Hope's limp body lying broken in his arms, her beautiful eyes closed forever, he told himself he'd done the right thing.

He couldn't explain it to her. She wouldn't listen. She thought herself invulnerable.

Diana had thought herself invulnerable, too.

He'd turned to Regina, lavishing attention on her anytime Hope was near. Regina was too smart not to suspect an ulterior motive on his part, but too thick-skinned to worry unduly whether Jake's feelings were honest or not.

When he had to cancel on her tonight because of business, he'd been a victim of the screaming temper he'd always suspected complemented her red hair, and now her tolerance of his motives had changed. She'd colorfully told him where he could go just moments before Hope had rung his doorbell.

But he'd traded one irritatingly boring evening for a devastatingly dangerous one. Hope, whose bland reaction to his ruthless tactics had both wounded his ego and puzzled him, was about to bare her soul unless he missed his guess. And Jake didn't think he was strong enough to hurt her that way—*that much!*—again.

Drawing a long breath, he closed the door and followed Hope into the living room, certain he was making the biggest mistake of his life. "Okay," he invited in a discouraging voice. "But make it quick. I've got somewhere I've got to be."

Chapter Twelve

Hope stopped in the center of his luxurious room. Her luminous green eyes stared solemnly at him. She looked utterly defenseless, somehow, and Jake shoved his hands in his pockets to keep from reaching out for her.

"I know you're meeting Regina. And I know you're furious that I'm working on the Farrell case."

"I'm more furious with Forrester than I am with you," he said mildly.

"Well..." Her mouth twitched in a beguiling way that made his heart ache. "I don't suppose it's a contest of who's most furious with whom. But I'm not giving up and I'd really like to share with you what I've learned. I know the reason you don't want me on the case is that you don't think I'm good enough," she continued doggedly. "Or seasoned enough. But I can help you. I've interviewed almost a dozen people who knew Bill Farrell, including his ex-wife. I'd like to exchange notes, or at the very least *give* you my notes. But first I need to say something." She inhaled deeply, collecting herself. "The other night, when Farrell was shot and I stayed here with you—"

"I'd rather discuss something else," Jake interrupted softly.

Hope nodded. "You've made *that* clear," she said with heart-wrenching honesty. "But I have to talk about it. I can't leave things as they are. I've tried to be like you, but it hasn't worked."

Jake lifted one brow. "Like me?" he asked in spite of himself.

"Tough on the outside. Shutting people out. Keeping all the terrible stuff like *real feelings* locked away where no one can see." She sighed, her lips curving into a faint smile. "I know you better than you think I do."

Jake hardly knew what to say. He didn't want this talk because he was deathly afraid he was going to give in and pull her into his arms, forgetting all the reasons he shouldn't.

Hope took a deep breath and forged on. "I'm not blind, Jake. You act like you're impenetrable, but you carry all sorts of guilt inside you. Your dreams are filled with pain, but anytime I get close—probably anytime *anyone* gets close—you push them away. Six years ago you convinced me you were a total bastard, but I'm not so naive anymore. You're only partially a bastard," she said with a glint of humor.

Jake dragged his gaze away from her lovely face. "Nobody can be partially a bastard. You either are, or you aren't," he pointed out.

"Well, you aren't. Sorry to break it to you like this, but you're one of the good guys. You're after Jarvis because he killed Farrell."

"Want a drink?" Jake asked abruptly, moving toward the bar. He tugged on his bow tie, pulling it from his neck and dropping it across the back of a chair.

She shook her head. "Jake, I don't want you to kill yourself on this assignment because of some need to avenge Bill Farrell's death." She hesitated a moment. "Or Diana's."

Jake's head swung around in shock. *"Diana!"*

Hope inched her chin up, refusing to back down. "I looked through the *Observer*'s microfilm to find out what happened when that bomb exploded six years ago. You and Diana had worked together on several assignments." Swallowing, Hope said aloud for the first time something she hadn't wanted to admit even to herself. "You were in love with her and she died and you still feel responsible for her death."

"I wasn't in love with her."

Hope searched his closed expression, surprised. "You weren't?"

"No." Jake tossed back the Scotch he'd poured himself, grimacing at the burn of the liquor on his throat. Impatiently he added, "Diana's death has nothing to do with the present. You said you wanted to talk about the Farrell case. Let's stick to that."

Hope gazed at him helplessly. She should feel glad that he'd decided to listen to her about Farrell, but she knew he was just exchanging one dangerous topic for another. "All right," she said determinedly. "The point is, while you go around protecting everyone else, you aren't paying attention to the danger to yourself. I want to help you, Jake. You need me. You're just too stubborn and arrogant to admit it. And I can't let you get away with it any longer. I was home tonight worrying about you. I had this terrible feeling something had happened to you, and I—'' she drew a trembling breath ''I *care*, Jake!'' she declared angrily.

He almost smiled at her tone.

''Tell me about Farrell and Jarvis,'' she demanded. ''I'll stay behind the scenes and you can rewrite anything I've written. Just don't push me away.'' At his somber, pensive look, hope flared inside her. Maybe he was finally listening! ''Fair enough?''

''More than fair.''

''Then . . . ?''

''Sit down,'' Jake invited, gesturing to the couch. Hope obediently sank into the luxurious cushions, clasping her hands together. Jake's lashes lowered and he said in his deep voice, ''Tell me what you've found out that didn't go in the paper.''

Encouraged, Hope leaned forward eagerly, then her gaze swept his elegant clothes. ''What about your date?''

''It was called off.''

''Called off?''

''I canceled.'' As Hope assimilated that, he added sardonically, ''Can you really see me at Wynona Butterworth's fund-raiser?''

''No.'' Hope laughed, the joyous sound of it ringing through the quiet room. And Jake realized how little laughter there had been in his home—even when Diana had been alive.

Hope began describing the series of events and investigative techniques she'd employed in her quest to learn more about Bill Farrell, but Jake listened with only half an ear. It wasn't that what she told him wasn't fascinating. And it wasn't that he didn't recognize her skill and admire her for it. He did. It was that her blouse lay loose and soft against her breasts, and her hair fell in luxurious waves, and her mouth curved in the most intriguing way when she spoke.

But then she said something that brought him up short. "Mimi Farrell actually said Farrell *respected* Jarvis?" he demanded intently.

Hope flushed, looking away. She hadn't wanted to tell him a remark she'd found puzzling herself—especially since Jake obviously felt some guilt over Bill Farrell's death. Glancing back, she gazed at him through the screen of her lashes, trying to judge his mood. He was sitting perfectly still, frozen in rapt attention. His right ankle rested upon the opposite knee, his right hand absently rubbed his injured thigh from time to time, and the look in his eyes was fierce.

"She told me Bill kept things back, that in some ways she never really knew him." When Jake's searing gaze never left her face, she added unhappily, "And yes, that's what she said."

Mimi had been chattering on like a magpie, so Hope had written down everything the woman had said verbatim, using her own particular brand of shorthand to keep up. She hadn't used Mimi's comment in her first article since that story had focused on Farrell's personal life: how he'd juggled a dangerous career with the trials of married life and family, and the subsequent breakup of that marriage.

"Do you think it's significant?" Hope asked.

"Damn right, it's significant." Jake lapsed into thoughtful silence, rolling his empty glass between his palms.

"What do you think really happened between Jarvis and Farrell?"

"I don't know." Jake was reflective, his expression tense. "There was one guy I talked to, an ex-DEA friend of Farrell's. He said something that made me think Farrell knew Jarvis on a personal basis. I practically had to bribe the man to get him to talk. Unfortunately, he won't come forward officially. He won't talk to the authorities at all."

Hope's green eyes grew brilliant with excitement. "And?"

The eager expectancy in her voice stopped Jake cold. This was too much like the past. Mentally shaking himself, he forced himself to continue. "He maintains that Farrell knew a lot about Jarvis's operations that hasn't been made public. The kind of information you can only get from the inside. My source suggested Farrell and Jarvis were friendly adversaries, not enemies. And Mimi's remark on top of it . . ." His voice drifted off and his mouth turned down at the corners.

"What are you saying, Jake?" Hope probed gently.

He sighed. "It's possible that Farrell was working both ends against the middle. I know for a fact that he did excellent work for the DEA, but where Jarvis is concerned not a lot was accomplished—by anyone. There's a reason Jarvis is still free, and Farrell could be that reason."

Hope surged to her feet and paced the room. "A week ago you were certain Jarvis was behind Farrell's death."

"I still believe that," Jake retorted flatly. "I think Jarvis and Farrell had a falling-out. I'm still going to nail Jarvis, no matter what it takes. Even if it means exposing Farrell's involvement. Jarvis must have paid Farrell to turn a blind eye to the really big issues, and Farrell did as he was told." Jake's lips twisted. "Dirty business, isn't it?"

Hope hovered by his chair, needing to be near him whether he wanted her to be or not. Jake stiffened at her closeness. "Do you know what their falling-out was over?" she asked.

"I suppose Jarvis didn't like Farrell cozying up to a reporter." Jake shrugged. "My source was on the verge of telling me, but then he stopped himself. I don't know. But it must have been a hell of an issue, considering Jarvis had him killed."

Silence filled the room and Hope walked over to the window. Rain was streaking in uneven rivulets down the wide panes. "Was Jarvis trying to kill Farrell the night you were shot? Or was he after you?"

"I don't know," he admitted, his deep voice serious.

A shiver went down Hope's spine. "He might still be after you."

"I know."

Hope had to close her mind to that idea for a moment. Her chest tightened at the thought of losing Jake. With an effort, she kept up her inquiry. "If it was Farrell they were after, why would Jarvis's man aim for you?"

"That's the million-dollar question, Hope. Why me?"

She glanced back and saw the frustration and guilt written across his handsome face. With unhurried steps she crossed to where he sat, kneeling down beside him. "Because you're good at what you do?" she suggested. "Because Farrell confided in you and that made you dangerous and Farrell untrustworthy."

"I doubt it's that simple," Jake argued stubbornly.

"Think about it, Jake. If what you suspect is true, it's the only logical conclusion. Jarvis and Farrell were working together. Maybe not all the time—after all, some of the time Farrell was Mr. Perfect DEA Man. But the rest of the time they were, well . . . drug smugglers. Then Jake Danziger, the best investigative reporter in all of Seattle—" he started to protest and she grabbed his arm "—the *best* investigative reporter in Seattle," she stressed, "starts doing a few stories on the drug scene. Jake contacts Farrell. Farrell and Jake have a working relationship. Jarvis gets very nervous, but he doesn't want to lose Farrell as a connection. So who has to go?"

Jake's penetrating blue gaze was focused on Hope. She saw she wasn't telling him anything he didn't know. He just hadn't faced it yet.

"It doesn't matter that Jarvis wasn't the focus of your investigative series," Hope went on gently. "He decided to take you out as a warning to Farrell to keep his mouth shut. And to solve future problems."

To solve future problems.

Abruptly Jake was yanked back in time, to that terrible day when the mail boy told him the mail had been delivered to his office. "There's a package for you, Dance. I left it on your desk."

"What kind of package?" Jake had asked disinterestedly.

"Brown paper package. They spelled your name wrong. Put an *S* where the *Z* should be. . . ."

And then he'd known. The threatening note he'd received three weeks earlier had been spelled wrong also. In one motion he'd turned and started running toward his office.

The glass wall exploded with a deafening boom before he'd taken two steps.

And Diana, who'd been waiting for him in his office, had died.

Brandt, the wretched penny-ante criminal who'd sent the package to Jake, had explained that the *Observer* reporters were bothering him. So he'd contacted a buddy of his who was "good with bombs" and had one fashioned for Jake.

To solve future problems.

Now Jake shuddered, knowing Diana's death could have been avoided if he'd taken that threatening note seriously.

"Jake?" Hope asked, alarmed at his pale, set face.

"If Jarvis wants me dead, the fact that you're on this assignment with me puts you in danger."

"What are you doing?" she demanded when he suddenly bounded to his feet and headed for his bedroom.

"I've got to call someone."

"Who?"

He didn't answer, just closed the door behind him, his low voice sounding through the panels a few moments later. Hope couldn't make out the words and she didn't try to eavesdrop. Jake would tell her what was going on; she would make him.

It took him fifteen minutes to emerge, and in those same fifteen minutes Hope's jumbled thoughts fell into place. Her whole body started trembling as she realized the magnitude of what she and Jake had unearthed. And then she remembered the man in the parking lot.

"Jake, there's something else," she said anxiously as soon as he crossed the room toward her. "There was a man in the parking lot tonight, just waiting around. It might not be anything, but could it be—one of Jarvis's men?"

"Which parking lot? My parking lot?" he demanded sharply.

She nodded jerkily. "And there was another man when I was here last week, but he was walking away."

Jake considered for several moments. "I don't think it's anything to worry about."

"You *don't*?"

"Ever since Farrell's death—and my subsequent news stories," he added with a sardonic twist of his lips, "I've been dogged by a couple of federal investigators, Enright and Corelli. They seem to think my life's in danger."

Real fear swept through Hope's veins. "When did you learn you had—bodyguards?"

"Saturday morning."

Hope stared at him in frustration. "So you've known all week. Then, why did you overreact when my story came out?"

"I overreacted because you threw yourself into the path of an oncoming freight train," he pointed out as if she were very, very dense. "Now you're in danger by default, and my heart can't take it."

Under other circumstances Hope would have been overjoyed by his admission that he cared. Now, it only made her certain she wasn't going to like what he said next. A moment later she was proved right.

"You're off the story," Jake told her, mildly but implacably. "Thanks for your help. I appreciate it, but this situation's too damn hot. I just called the feds and spoke with Corelli. He wants you out of it, too. I'll walk you to your car.''

Frustration burned through Hope. ''I have no more desire to throw myself 'in front of a freight train' than the next person, but I'm not leaving you!''

''You don't have a choice. Enright's somewhere outside, watching over me apparently. I'm going to introduce you to him, so he'll know to keep you away from me, and out of harm's way. Then I'm meeting with both Enright and Corelli to see if we can set a trap for Jarvis.''

''I'm going with you,'' Hope said stonily.

''Over my dead body, which it just might be if you insist on getting in the way.'' He held the door for her and Hope strode through in a fine fury.

''Your sudden interest in letting me think I was working with you was just a means to get rid of me, wasn't it?'' she demanded as they headed down in the elevator together.

''I hadn't thought of it that way, but yes. I suppose so.''

His utter lack of guilt infuriated Hope. ''You couldn't be honest if your life depended on it!'' she declared heatedly. ''Well, I'm sick and tired of being treated as if I don't have a brain. You told me more than you should have tonight. Now it's my story, too!''

''Would you get off this 'your story/my story' fixation?'' Jake snarled. ''Jarvis doesn't give a damn who's writing copy about him! Me, you, or even Regina Sutton, for Chrissakes! If he thinks you're a threat, he'll simply eliminate you. Now get out of here, and let me take care of this before one of us gets hurt!''

Hope was too wounded and angry to argue with him. She turned her head away, watching the elevator lights flicker on and off, marking their progress.

"I'll go to the DEA, too," Jake added as the elevator doors whispered open on the basement level. "I've got a call in, and I'm hoping my source will open up when I show him what I've got. All you have to do is sit tight and wait. If you want a story, I'll give you a story, but don't fight me on this."

"I don't care about the damn story!" Hope said in a low, taut voice as she strode through the parking lot ahead of him. "Surely you know that."

Jake stopped beside her car, his expression unreadable in the dim overhead light. "Then what are we arguing about?"

"*You!* You and me. Your obsessive need to protect me even though I'm perfectly capable of taking care of myself."

He seemed slightly disappointed by her answer, but his lips twisted self-deprecatingly. "I'm beginning to believe you," he said dryly.

"Jake..." she murmured as he reached for the car keys she held. "When we spent the night together, was it just like before? Like the last time?"

"The last time...?" He paused, the door swinging open.

"Six years ago you didn't really want to make love to me. It just kind of happened. And last Friday I thought it was different until I woke up and you were so cold and collected, and then you wouldn't talk to me all week." Her words tumbled over one another when she saw the forbidding mask come over his face. "Please don't shut me out now," she begged wearily. "If you want me, take me. I'm *here*. I'm willing to risk it. But if you don't, tell me now so I can start forgetting about you."

Jake looked down at the alluring beauty whose eyes warned him to play fair at the same time they beseeched him to admit he cared for her. He'd told himself for years that he would never, *never* get involved with another woman—not to the extent he had with Diana, not to the extent he had with Hope. His job was too dangerous, his life too one-track.

Yet, that part of him encased in ice had started melting from the first moment she'd reentered his life. He was fast losing his heart to her. "Hope," he whispered, reaching for her. At the same moment he caught movement in his peripheral vision. Half turning, he saw the barrel of the gun the same moment he instinctively blocked Hope's body from danger. A single thought hammered through his mind: *This can't be happening again! Not to Hope!*

"Jake?" Hope cried.

A bullet whined past his ear and exploded into the side of Hope's car. Jake's body slammed into Hope's, sending them both to the concrete. Her scream was a muffled gasp against his ruffled shirt. His right thigh connected with something hard, the sharp edge of the door, and he heard the rip of fabric and felt a shooting jab of pain.

But all he could think about was Hope, and he covered her body with his own as bullets shrieked and scattered around them, pummeling the car, the pavement, and blasting out the lights. He heard shouts and running footsteps. A deafening cacophony of explosions and ricochets ensued and with superhuman effort Jake shoved Hope beneath the car.

Hope's hands were clutching him. She was shaking violently. He wrapped himself around her. "Are you all right?" he rasped.

Her answer was a moan, and his heart nearly stopped. His anxious gaze raked the pale outline of her face. She was hurt. She'd been shot. "Hope, oh, Hope," he murmured brokenly.

"Danziger!" a voice called authoritatively in the sudden silence that enveloped the lot. "Danziger! It's Enright. You okay?"

Enright. "Yeah," Jake muttered, then added unsteadily, "But call an ambulance for my friend. She's been hurt...."

Chapter Thirteen

From the far reaches of her mind, Hope heard Jake's deep baritone softly soothing her, repeating the same words over and over again. She felt his hands brush her hair from her face and she tried to speak, but the only sound that escaped her was a low moan.

"Don't worry, Hope, darling," Jake's voice cracked. "You'll be all right soon."

She could scarcely hear above the shrieking noise penetrating her senses. An ambulance siren. She and Jake were being taken to a hospital.

Comforted that he was near, she slipped deeper into unconsciousness.

"Relax, Miss Townsend. Just relax...."

Hope didn't know which aggravated her more: the doctor's supercilious voice or the penlight currently blinding her. Her eyes watered from the effort of holding them open. Somewhere beyond the emergency-room curtain, she could hear the sound of rapid footsteps and the thrum of conversation. Jake was out there. She'd heard his anxious voice more than once. But until she could convince this doctor that she was all right, she was trapped.

He stepped back and snapped off the light. In a severe tone, he said, "Well, you aren't concussed. How do you feel?"

"Fine. Great. Really." She waited anxiously for his professional verdict, needing to find Jake as soon as possible. The doctor's scowl wasn't encouraging and, exasperated, Hope said, "I'd like to see Jake Danziger. He was with me in the ambulance, I think."

"Jake Danziger. The newspaper reporter?" another male voice piped up.

Hope turned her head slowly, spying a white-suited orderly near the end wall. "Yes!" she answered eagerly, wincing as a shooting pain ran through her temple to the back of her brain. With her fingertips, she gingerly examined the doozy of a knot that had developed above her ear. It was somewhat mortifying that she'd cracked her head hard enough against the concrete to knock herself out and consequently knew nothing of what had happened since. "The newspaper reporter," she agreed.

"He's in the waiting room," the orderly replied. "He's been asking about you, too. Not to mention the rest of your waiting entourage, miss."

"Entourage?" Hope asked blankly.

"A veritable army of men in suits."

The feds. The police. The *paper*! She could well imagine the scene taking place outside. "Jake's okay, isn't he?" she asked in concern.

"Looks good to me," a nurse answered from the corner of the room, drawing a scowl from the officious doctor beside Hope's examining table.

"Can I sit up?" Hope asked, struggling to do so before she was given permission.

"If you feel like it." The doctor eyed her thoughtfully.

Hope managed to swing her legs over the side of the table. She was still dressed in her own clothes, thank God. Feeling a little woozy, she waited several moments for her head and her stomach to settle down.

"Your X rays are fine, and you look well enough," the doctor told her, sounding slightly annoyed that she was so disgustingly healthy. "But you'd best take it easy the next few days."

"I'll bear that in mind." Hope gave him a jaunty smile and slid off the table, glad her legs were steady enough to support her weight. She felt his sharp eyes watching her every move as she stepped into the hallway outside her partitioned cubicle.

She could hear the noise of the waiting crowd. Hurrying, she pushed against the door at the end of the hall, her gaze anxiously scanning the groups of people that seemed to fill the spacious room.

Jake was leaning against the post right in front of her, his head bent, listening to a man who was talking to him in a low, steady drone. Another man glanced her way and straightened.

Jake's eyes clashed with Hope's. For a moment his expression was naked and filled with fear; then relief lightened his tight, drawn features.

"Hope," he said in a voice she could scarcely recognize. "Are you all right? God, I've been so worried! I thought you were shot."

"No, I—it's just my head." She touched the lump. She, too, was relieved that he seemed to have escaped serious injury.

Jake made a move toward Hope, but the man who'd been talking to him laid a detaining hand on his arm. "Mr. Danziger," he began, only to be cut off by a woman's ringing voice.

"The doctor will see you now, Mr. Danziger!"

Jake looked impatiently at the square-faced matron who'd entered the room. She was built like a supertanker and appeared as if nothing would stop her from getting what she aimed for.

"I don't have time to see the doctor," he informed her coldly.

"Mr. Danziger," the man said again, more urgently.

"Your wound needs to be examined," the woman warned in a dire voice, impervious to Jake's sharp tone.

"Jake," Hope murmured unsteadily as her eyes belatedly focused on his ripped pant leg and the dark, spreading patch of blood on his right thigh. At first she hadn't noticed the blood because of the tuxedo's black fabric, but now her heart twisted. He'd reinjured his wound, she realized with a sickening jolt of her stomach.

"*Mister* Danziger," the man said again.

Swearing under his breath, Jake told Hope. "It looks like I'm a little busy. Enright—" he jerked his head in the direction of the man who hadn't spoken yet "—will take you back to your apartment. I'll meet you there later."

"Jake, I—"

A flashbulb popped.

Jake skewered the offender, one of the *Observer*'s top photographers, with a murderous look. Beyond him, Hope saw Martin Hughes lounging in one of the narrow chairs, his bulky body relaxed. He waved at Hope, waiting his turn to help the *Observer* get the story first.

"Go," Jake told her.

"I'd like to stay until I'm sure you're okay."

"I'm okay." He was terse. Then his gaze swept her face and the warmth in his eyes convinced her not to argue the point further. That, and his softly spoken parting words, "I'll be there soon. I promise."

Turning over, Hope's cheek grazed a scratchy, textured surface, bringing her up from the fogs of sleep. Dimly she realized she was sleeping on her couch, and the rough texture was from one of her woven throw pillows.

Blinking, she sat up, pushing her hair off her forehead. Immediately, she bit back a cry of pain as her hand touched the tender lump above her temple.

The previous night came back in a flood. Jake! He'd promised to come to her apartment, but now it was—she glanced at her watch—eleven o'clock in the morning!

Tossing off the blanket she'd thrown over herself, Hope stripped off her clothes, raced through a shower, then yanked on a fresh outfit. Brushing her hair, she dialed Jake's number, then slammed the receiver down when his machine answered and she heard his drawling voice ask her to leave a message.

Where was he?

The answer was blinding: the *Observer*.

It was just after twelve-thirty when Hope strode through the doors of the *Observer*, her color high. She could hardly blame him, she supposed. The story came first. She should be mad at herself for the delicious feeling of contentment and anticipation his soft promise had wrapped her in.

When would she ever learn?

She was halfway across the floor when the sound of Regina's distinctive laughter stopped her short. Jake's lazy response, which she couldn't quite make out, propelled her forward again.

She found them standing near John Forrester's office: Jake, Regina, John, Tammy, and Kevin Berger. Jake was leaning heavily on a single crutch.

"Read about it tomorrow," he was saying to Regina, who looked torn between the desire to wring his neck—apparently she hadn't quite forgiven him for canceling on her—or the equally strong desire to take him home and coddle him.

Everyone turned at the sound of Hope's approaching footsteps.

John Forrester's face brightened. "I'm glad to see you're as fit as Jake and Martin said you were. I was going to call you, but Dance thought you should take it easy today."

"Is that right?" Hope's green eyes turned accusingly to Jake, whose own expression changed from lazy amusement to careful neutrality.

"I hear you took a whopping head-banger," Tammy said, grimacing sympathetically.

"My fault," Jake explained, grimacing. "I threw her down."

"In the name of survival?" Regina questioned, lifting her winged brows.

"Could I talk to you in private?" Hope asked Jake in a decidedly icy tone.

Her dangerous mood penetrated the atmosphere, and with varying excuses everyone left except Regina and Jake.

"Excuse us a moment, would you, Regina?" Jake asked casually.

Reluctantly, the society-page columnist moved off.

"Well?" Jake asked.

"You lied to me, and you pushed me out of this story. You did it on purpose."

Jake frowned, but he didn't argue with her. "I put your name on the story."

"You've already *written* it? All of it?"

He nodded. "I intended to come by your apartment last night, but the feds were all over me. As soon as I got away I called my source and told him that one of Jarvis's men had been caught after he'd tried to kill you and me. He started panicking, so I went to see him and try to convince him to tell me all he knew. It took most of the night, but he came through."

"And?" Hope's voice was brittle.

Jake looked at her strangely. "And we were right. Farrell was Jarvis's occasional partner. They did some deals together. But then Farrell decided he didn't want to work both sides of the law any longer, so he planned to nail Jarvis and put the man out of business."

Jake shifted his weight and Hope felt a pang of worry. She still didn't know the extent of his injuries. Beneath his jeans, she could once again see the outline of his bandage.

"Are you okay?" she couldn't help herself from asking.

"A minor setback."

He sounded grateful that she'd asked about him, but Hope wasn't ready to forgive him for lying to her, even if it had been inadvertently. "What made Farrell decide to go after Jarvis?" she asked, dragging her gaze away from his lean, attractive features.

"Apparently Bill didn't like Jarvis coming after me," Jake drawled. When Hope gasped involuntarily, her eyes full of questions, Jake nodded and explained, "Jarvis was suspicious of my friendship with Farrell so he warned him to cut off the contact, then he tried to remove me. However, all he accomplished was to make an enemy out of Bill Farrell and, well—" he shrugged "—you know the rest."

"Is there enough evidence to indict Jarvis?"

"Hopefully there's enough to convict him. My source has opened up and is talking to the feds and DEA right now."

Hope absorbed that bit of good news in silence. She was glad Raleigh Jarvis would likely see the end of his criminal career, and she was proud of her small part in helping bring him down, but she wasn't happy with Jake's tactics. Even now, she sensed he wasn't willing to include her. "Don't put my name on that story. I didn't write it."

"I put both our names on it. You were as instrumental in bringing this case to a close as I was."

That was the first encouraging remark he'd made. She shot him a speculative look from beneath her lashes, then asked, "Does that mean you've changed your mind about working with me in the future?"

Jake struggled with the answer; she could see how difficult it was by the swift progression of feelings that crossed his face. Jaw hard, he finally bit out, "No."

"No?" She blinked disbelievingly.

"I won't be happy until you quit investigative journalism entirely," he admitted in a completely serious tone. "Maybe it's not fair, but it's how I feel."

Hope's lips parted in shock. After everything they'd been through, she'd at least expected some modicum of understanding and respect. "It's *not* fair."

Emotion darkened his eyes and he glanced away from her. "I can't go through it again," he muttered, as if arguing with himself. "The worst moment of my life was when you were unconscious. I thought you'd been shot. I thought you were..." He drew a ragged breath, cutting himself off.

The surge of joy that swept through her at this sign of caring was swiftly extinguished, however, when he added flatly, "I'm afraid it's going to come down to a choice. The job or me. And I already know which you'll pick."

Her hopes were dashed. Then she felt herself consumed with sudden anger at his outrageous ultimatum. "*Do you?* Do you really? I've spent years loving you and paying for it," she choked out, her words tumbling over themselves in a torrent of emotion. "*You* can't go through it again? Well *I* can't live this way a second longer! I'm not going to quit my job for you, or anybody. If that's the condition, then it's—it's over."

For the first time since their ill-fated love affair had begun she saw real regret in his eyes. Regret that he was losing her. Regret that he'd thrown away her love. She held her breath, hoping against hope that he would change his mind, give a little bit, but with a slumping of his shoulders he began to turn away. Her heart cried out, pain tightening her chest. She couldn't believe he could turn off his feelings so completely, but he did. *He did!*

Hearing his dispassionate tone convinced her.

"Good luck, Hope."

The crash of the breakers was a dull, comforting roar as sea gulls swooped over the headland toward the endless sun-sparkled waves. Hope inhaled deeply, dragging salt-tinged air into her lungs, turning her face up to the hot summer sun.

It was June. A warm June by San Juan Island standards. Yesterday, walking through Roche Harbor with her mother, she'd started perspiring in her cotton shirt when it was barely ten o'clock in the morning. If the weather was any indication of the future, the rest of the summer would be beastly.

She was on a minivacation; she'd taken Friday off and didn't have to be back at work until Monday. John Forrester had actually suggested she take the extra day, telling her she'd been working much too hard and that he wanted her fresh for a new assignment the following week.

Hope had at first reluctantly, and then eagerly, accepted the time off. She was tired. She *had* been working too hard. But work was the panacea to the dull ache in her heart and the misery of her soul. For months she'd kept her nose to the grindstone and her thoughts removed from the dangerous memories of Jake Danziger.

She'd been only partially successful in the latter endeavor, because she ran into Jake at the office at least once a week. Those moments were always difficult. Her heart would leap and her blood would race. Then Jake would offer her a curt hello, and she would answer back in kind, and they would drift away from each other, each refusing to look over their respective shoulders to see if the other might reveal some sign of regret, remorse, or love.

She was lucky, really, that he seemed just as anxious to stay out of her path as she did his. As things were, she could handle the situation; at least she'd coped so far. If and when the day came when she could no longer bear her close proximity to Jake, she would apply for a job with another paper. With the experience at the *Observer* behind her, it was a cinch to get a job of equal importance somewhere else.

Thinking of Jake, her mind touched on the strange conversation she'd had with John Forrester last week. Forrester, who'd been scrupulous about keeping her and Jake off the same stories, had come across an assignment he wished she and Jake could work on together. He'd posed the idea to Hope first, to see her reaction, and when she'd vehemently objected to doing anything with Jake, he'd pulled the shades down on the glass walls of his office and bade her sit for a moment.

"Does the name Diana Mathers mean anything to you, Townsend?" he'd asked her without preamble. When Hope visibly tensed, he'd said, "I see it does. How much do you know?"

She hadn't wanted to answer. She didn't want to think about anything to do with Jake Danziger. But Forrester was waiting, and after drawing an uncomfortable breath, Hope murmured, "You mean about the bombing? Only what I read in the *Observer*'s microfilm."

"Normally, I don't get involved in the personal lives of the *Observer*'s employees, but I'm tired of feeling like lightning will strike if I mention your name in Dance's presence, or his name in yours," Forrester explained. "If you know something about Dance's relationship with Mathers, it might help, and since Dance isn't likely to tell you, I will." He sighed. "At least, as much as I understand."

Hope had bent her head, uncertain she wanted to hear, especially now, with the war between herself and Jake at its coldest. But Forrester was determined.

"Mathers and Dance were friends and co-workers. Mathers was in love with Dance, and he cared about her. They started a relationship at some point, about two or three months before the bombing, I guess, and it got kind of intense. Dance didn't know she was married."

Hope's head snapped up in disbelief, but Forrester nodded. "She didn't tell him. She didn't tell any of us. She always referred to him as her ex-husband, so we naturally assumed it was true. Actually, I think Mathers thought of him as her ex, too. They weren't living together.

"She told Dance the truth the day of the bombing. He was furious with her for duping him. They were in his office, the one Regina Sutton uses now, and you could hear him shouting all across the newsroom. He told her to stay put while he had a word with his editor before the man left for the day. And he wanted to cool down a bit."

Hope's heart had started beating hard and heavy. She'd known what was coming next and her face must have revealed it, because Forrester nodded sympathetically. "She did as he told her. She stayed right there. The short time Dance was gone a brown paper package arrived and exploded. Diana died in Dance's arms that day, and he feels responsible. It's why he can't bear to have you in the front lines, so to speak,'' he added gently.

She'd known it was because of Diana even though Jake had never put it in those terms. But it didn't change anything. His exaggerated fear for her life wasn't reason enough for her to give up everything she'd worked for. She couldn't give Jake that much power, and she didn't want to.

Needing to divert her rampaging emotions from the image of the woman Jake loved dying in his arms, she'd turned automatically to the facts. ''What was the name of the man who sent the bomb, again?''

''Brandt. A low-life, penny-ante criminal with a history of robbery and violence. Dance had done a few stories in which Brandt's name was mentioned, but it was Mathers who decided to focus on Brandt. She wrote some scathing stuff that really showed Brandt for what he was. Brandt apparently didn't appreciate the notoriety, but instead of targeting Mathers, he went after Dance. I don't think he ever paid attention to which reporter was really after him.

''He sent Dance a threatening letter, which neither Dance nor Mather took seriously. Dance didn't tell me about it until after Mathers's death. Anyway, a few weeks after the letter, Brandt sent the bomb to Jake Danziger and the mail boy took it to his office.''

Remembering how grief-stricken and desolate Jake had been that Christmas, Hope suspected he had loved Diana deeply, no matter what he said to the contrary. He'd turned to Hope only as a means of assuaging his guilt and grief, and she'd mistaken his feelings for love. And then she'd walked into his life again and he'd tried to force her out by using every tactic available to him. He cared about her, she recognized, at least in some way, but he couldn't bear to care about anyone who might, in his eyes, meet the same terrible fate as Diana.

"He must have loved her very much," Hope had commented, when it appeared Forrester was waiting for a response.

"I don't think he loved her at all," Forrester had answered. "And that's what's killing him most."

Hope let the sea breezes tangle her hair, enjoying the feel of it against her face and neck. Forrester's revelations explained a lot, but they made little difference. Until Jake got over his paranoia, he and Hope were at a stalemate.

A dazzling flash of light caught her eye. She glanced at her house, to the windows of the den, and realized someone was pointing the telescope either at her or the ocean beyond. Her father, she thought with a slight smile. Waving an acknowledgement, she walked down the path to the back door.

Scraping her feet on the kitchen mat, she went straight to the den. "Is Maxwell still telling fish stories?" she asked lightly as she stepped inside.

"I don't know," an achingly familiar voice answered. "I guess you'll have to ask your father."

The smile faded from Hope's lips. "What are you doing here?" she demanded.

Jake was still standing by the telescope. "Your mother let me in. You can ask her yourself, if you don't believe me. She's upstairs. Your father's at Maxwell's, probably listening to fish stories," he added with a quirk of his lips.

"You're supposed to be in Seattle!"

He lifted a brow at her sharp tone, then said softly, "I decided to come home for a visit—after I learned this is where you'd gone."

Jake's gaze swept the healthy glow of her wind-pinkened cheeks and the tumbled glory of her honey-blond hair. Her short-sleeved top was emerald green, almost the same shade as her eyes, and the way she looked in those snug, worn jeans was enough to bring a dying man back to life. He drew an unsteady breath, anxious to say everything he felt: how the days had seemed endless these last months; how his fear for her safety had kept him awake at night, but not as often as the aching desire to be with her left him counting the minutes until daylight; how he'd treated her unfairly time and again and wanted to make amends; and how he craved the joyous sound of her laughter, the touch of her skin, the sweetness of her smile.

But he never got a chance.

"If you're here for the reason I think you're here, you'd better understand one thing first," she said in a low, shaking voice. "I'm not quitting my job. I'm an investigative journalist and I plan to remain one. You can't change my mind."

"I know that."

Hope eyed him warily. His capitulation had been too quick. "But you're going to try anyway, is that it?"

Jake couldn't stand it one more minute. He crossed the room in two giant strides, and looked down into her beautiful face. "All I want to do is hold you," he said with the devastating frankness that usually shattered her. This time her heart lifted at his tone, and she didn't mistake the warmth and desire in his eyes.

But she couldn't believe him. She couldn't! "You only want to hold me? That's all?" she asked suspiciously.

"And kiss you," he admitted with a trace of amusement. "And, well, maybe a few other things, too."

"I'm not quitting my job, Jake."

"Hope," he murmured softly. "As much as the thought of losing you tears me apart, the thought of never having you hurts infinitely worse. Where you're concerned, I've compounded mistake upon mistake. In my own defense, I couldn't help it. You reminded me too much of Diana, and I've been trying to get over her for years."

He took her into his arms and Hope didn't protest. She couldn't. She wanted him too much; and though her head told her she was a masochistic fool, her heart cried at the thought of resisting the support of his strong arms.

"I need to tell you about Diana," he said, and when Hope tried to tell him it wasn't necessary, he covered her mouth with a searing kiss that melted her strength and effectively cut off any protests.

"I never loved her, not the way she wanted me to. I didn't want to love anyone—even a beautiful nineteen-year-old with blond hair and green eyes," he admitted. "Diana was married, and though you probably won't believe it, I didn't know it at the time."

"I believe you," Hope answered in a voice muffled against his shirt. "Forrester told me."

"Forrester told you?" he repeated in astonishment.

"He wanted me to know about Diana so I could understand why you were so—adamant—that I couldn't work with you."

He cupped her face in his hands, his eyes searching her face. "Do you understand?"

"I think so. But it doesn't change anything," she added quickly.

"I had dreams about Diana's death. Nightmares where she was lying limp and broken in my arms. The last few dreams were about you, Hope. *You* unconscious in my arms. *You.*" He took in a fortifying breath. "The dream you woke me from last Christmas, and the ones I had the night we were together at my place—they were about you, Hope."

"It still doesn't change anything," she said in a less certain voice. "Don't force me to make a choice!"

"I won't," he assured her, and to her amazement, she realized he was telling the truth. "I promise I won't, darling." Hope gazed at him in wonder, and Jake brushed his knuckles gently against her cheek. "I've been doing some soul-searching these last few months. It's been pure hell."

"For me, too," she cautiously admitted.

He smiled. "I want you to know why I've acted the way I have. What exactly did Forrester tell you about Diana?"

Haltingly, Hope explained the entire conversation, half afraid Jake would close up on her again. But he listened in silence, then said softly, "I've been sick with guilt for not loving her. I didn't even realize it— not at first. And I blamed you for making me feel things I shouldn't. I didn't want to love you. And maybe, subconsciously at least, I knew that's where my feelings were heading."

"You weren't in love with me," Hope reminded him, unwilling to believe more than the truth. "You even said so."

"I was falling in love with you," he admitted. "I had a six-year reprieve and then there you were again. I've tried to fight it, but I can't. I love you, and if it means risking losing you, over not having you at all, I'll take the risk. You're a good reporter, Hope. If that's what you want, I'll learn to live with it. *I love you,*" he repeated intensely. "And I can't give you up for any reason."

"Oh, Jake," she cried in a shaking voice. "Do you mean it?"

"Yes, I mean it," he muttered, crushing her to him, his mouth capturing hers with hungry desire.

A long time later, he reluctantly relinquished her lips, but he gathered her to his chest where his heart beat hard and fast. "There's something else," he added hoarsely. "Something Forrester didn't know about. As long as we're clearing the air..."

"Something—about Diana?" A slight shudder swept his tall frame, alarming Hope. "You don't have to tell me if you don't—"

"She was pregnant," he cut her off bluntly. "She told me the same day she was killed."

Hope gasped, her eyes opening wide.

"She wanted me to marry her and said if I didn't, she was going back to her husband. I was angry, as you can probably well imagine. She'd manipulated the whole thing, and I wanted to wring her lovely neck. We were in my office and I had to get out of there for a minute to clear my head. I told her to wait for me. 'Don't leave,' I warned her. *'Don't you dare leave!'*

"Diana wasn't good at listening, but she listened that day," Jake continued in an agonized voice. "She stayed right there. Right where I told her to."

"Jake," Hope murmured painfully.

"I was on my way back when I ran into the mail boy. He told me he'd just delivered a package to my office. I barely heard him, I was in such a daze. And then he said that whoever had sent the package had spelled my name wrong. Danziger was spelled with an *S* instead of a *Z*. Brandt had sent me a threatening note a few weeks before. He'd spelled my name with an *S*."

Jake was squeezing Hope so tightly she could scarcely breathe. His breath was ragged as he relived those moments. Hope shut her eyes against the images of that terrible day, her heart spilling over with pain.

"I started running, running. But I'd barely moved when the bomb blasted the glass wall out. It was— horrific." Jake was trembling beneath her comforting arms and she pressed her cheek against his chest, tears stinging her eyes. His voice changed, becoming low and urgent. "She was still alive when I got there. I picked her up. And then she was dying—dying in my arms, and she whispered how sorry she was. And then she died, and it was my fault. My fault for making her stay there."

He leaned down to brush his cheek against hers and encountered the wetness of her tears. "Don't cry, Hope," he said gently. "It's over. Long over."

She remembered his reaction to the thought that she could be pregnant, and now she understood why he'd been so cold, so harsh. "Diana's death wasn't your fault," she whispered.

"I know that now. I knew it then. But it just—hurt—so badly. God, how can you forgive me for taking it out on you?" he asked in a tortured voice.

"Because I love you," Hope answered honestly, as Jake stared down at her through emotion-glazed eyes, his thumbs gently rubbing away her tears. "And now I know you love me."

"I think," he said on a hard swallow, "that we would work well together. Personally and professionally. What do you think?"

"Forrester would love it," Hope teased gently.

"I want you near me," Jake responded. "Always. And not just because I want to protect you," he added quickly, seeing the look that crossed her face. "But because you're good at what you do."

"Does that mean I've been promoted to the major leagues?" she asked, drawing his mouth back down to hers.

"I love you, Hope."

"I love you . . . Dance," she answered with a heartbreaking smile.

Muffling a half groan, half laugh, he gathered her more tightly in his arms and made it clear that he was never, ever, going to let her go again.

* * * * *

Silhouette Special Edition

proudly presents
the long-awaited "prequel" volume of

★ LOVE AND GLORY ★

by
LINDSAY McKENNA
Dawn of Valor

In the summer of '89, Silhouette Special Edition premiered three novels celebrating America's men and women in uniform: LOVE AND GLORY, by bestselling author Lindsay McKenna. Featured were the proud Trayherns, a military family as bold and patriotic as the American flag—three siblings valiantly battling the threat of dishonor, determined to triumph . . . in love and glory.

Now, discover the roots of the Trayhern brand of courage, as parents Chase and Rachel relive their earliest heartstopping experiences of survival and indomitable love, in

Dawn of Valor, Silhouette Special Edition #649

This month, experience the thrill of LOVE AND GLORY—from the very beginning!

Silhouette Books®

DV-1A

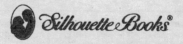

You'll flip . . . your pages won't!
Read paperbacks *hands-free* with

Book Mate • I

The perfect "mate" for all your romance paperbacks

Traveling • Vacationing • At Work • In Bed • Studying • Cooking • Eating

Perfect size for all standard paperbacks, this wonderful invention makes reading a pure pleasure! Ingenious design holds paperback books OPEN and FLAT so even wind can't ruffle pages — leaves your hands free to do other things. Reinforced, wipe-clean vinyl-covered holder flexes to let you turn pages without undoing the strap . . . supports paperbacks so well, they have the strength of hardcovers!

Pages turn WITHOUT opening the strap

SEE-THROUGH STRAP

Reinforced back stays flat

Built in bookmark

BOOK MARK

BACK COVER HOLDING STRIP

10˝ x 7¼˝ . opened
Snaps closed for easy carrying, too

Available now. Send your name, address, and zip code, along with a check or money order for just $5.95 + .75¢ for delivery (for a total of $6.70) payable to Reader Service to:

Reader Service
Bookmate Offer
3010 Walden Avenue
P.O. Box 1396
Buffalo, N.Y. 14269-1396

Offer not available in Canada
*New York residents add appropriate sales tax.

BM-GR

NORA ROBERTS
Night Shadow

People all over the city of Urbana were asking, Who was that masked man?

Assistant district attorney Deborah O'Roarke was the first to learn his secret identity . . . and her life would never be the same.

The stories of the lives and loves of the O'Roarke sisters began in January 1991 with NIGHT SHIFT, Silhouette Intimate Moments #365. And if you want to know more about Deborah and the man behind the mask, look for NIGHT SHADOW, Silhouette Intimate Moments #373, available in March at your favorite retail outlet.

NITE-1

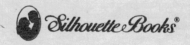

WRITTEN IN THE STARS

MAN FROM THE NORTH COUNTRY
by Laurie Paige

What does Cupid have planned for
the Aquarius man? Find out in February in
MAN FROM THE NORTH COUNTRY by
Laurie Paige—the second book in our
WRITTEN IN THE STARS series!

Brittney Chapel tried explaining the sensible
side of marriage to confirmed bachelor
Daniel Montclair, but the gorgeous grizzly bear
of a man from the north country wouldn't
respond to reason. What was a woman to do
with an unruly Aquarian? Tame him!

Spend the most romantic month of the year with
MAN FROM THE NORTH COUNTRY by
Laurie Paige in February... only from
Silhouette Romance.

MAN FROM THE NORTH COUNTRY by Laurie Paige is available in February at your favorite
retail outlet, or order your copy by sending your name, address, zip or postal code along with
a check or money order for $2.25 (please do not send cash), plus 75¢ postage and handling
($1.00 in Canada), payable to Silhouette Reader Service to:

In the U.S.	In Canada
3010 Walden Ave.	P.O. Box 609
P.O. Box 1396	Fort Erie, Ontario
Buffalo, NY 14269-1325	L2A 5X3

Canadian residents add applicable federal and provincial taxes.

Silhouette Books ™

FEBSTAR

BEGINNING IN FEBRUARY FROM

SILHOUETTE® Desire™

Western Lovers

An exciting new series by Elizabeth Lowell
Three fabulous love stories
Three sexy, tough, tantalizing heroes

In February, *Man of the Month* Tennessee Blackthorne in *OUTLAW*
In March, Cash McQueen in *GRANITE MAN*
In April, Nevada Blackthorne in *WARRIOR*

WESTERN LOVERS—Men as tough and untamed as the land they call home.

Only in *Silhouette Desire!*

DOU-1A